OUT OF CONTROL

Out of Control

Rebecca Ambrose

HEADLINE
Liaison

First published in 1995
by HEADLINE BOOK PUBLISHING

A HEADLINE LIAISON paperback

10 9 8 7 6 5 4 3 2 1

ISBN 0 7472 5168 1

Typeset by Keyboard Services, Luton, Beds

Printed and bound in Great Britain by
Cox & Wyman Ltd, Reading, Berks

HEADLINE BOOK PUBLISHING
A division of Hodder Headline PLC
338 Euston Road
London NW1 3BH

Out of Control

Chapter One

A woman with droopy earrings and rabbity teeth was droning on about multi-media opportunities for those already in the television industry, but Shelley was scarcely listening. She had come on this conference weekend for one reason and one reason only: to get laid by Duncan McFain. Shelley knew all the arguments why she shouldn't. For one thing, she was a married woman. For another, she shouldn't be thinking about mixing work with pleasure. Her job as a director with an independent television company was precious to her, and she'd be a prize idiot to put it in jeopardy.

Yet the sight of that dark, perfectly-sculpted head tilted fractionally to one side as Duncan concentrated on the speaker's words was enough to fill her stomach with wild flutterings that bordered on panic. Shelley had sat behind him on purpose, needing to look at him but not wanting to catch his eye. Most people would find the back of a man's head not in the least erotic but, the way she felt about Duncan, even the sight of his little finger would turn her on. She noticed the way his dark brown curls swirled enticingly around the delicate tips of his ears. She saw a hundred shades within the overall brown of his hair, golds and reds and blacks that filled the luxuriant depths with hidden colour. The layers thinned as they approached his neck, finally giving way to a smattering of golden down that must have been there from childhood when, no doubt, his hair was fair.

Although Shelley had never touched him, she had convinced herself that she knew exactly how it would feel to bury her fingers in that tawny-sable mane. She imagined clutching at it when he brought her, slowly, towards the peak of her pleasure and thrust himself deep into the secret heart of her body, the part that made her a woman. For weeks she had day-dreamed about it, wanted it to happen, and gradually she had noticed a corresponding interest on his part. Perhaps it was impossible to desire a man so much and not have him want her in return. Maybe telepathy had played a part in it, after all.

Because when she'd said she was going to the conference, his face had lit up. 'I'm so glad, Shelley,' he had said. 'I thought it was going to be a really boring weekend, but now I know you're going I shall look forward to it.'

What more direct come-on than that could she want?

Yet so far it had been frustrating. Shelley had been put on the far side of the hotel, in the annexe, while Duncan was in the main building. That was not an insuperable obstacle, of course, but ever since they'd arrived he had been surrounded by other people and she had been unable to get near him. All her hopes were pinned on dinner that evening and the informal chat in the bar afterwards.

The woman stopped speaking and there were a few half-hearted questions from the floor, before the chairman announced the end of the session. Shelley sighed her relief. People began standing, shuffling, pushing back chairs and she watched Duncan anxiously. He rose to his feet, turned round and looked straight at her. His grey eyes moved momentarily heavenward, as if he were as glad as she that the boring woman had finished, and Shelley smiled encouragement. To her delight, he began to move through the ranks of chairs in her direction.

'Can I buy you a drink, Shelley?' he asked, glancing at his Cartier watch. 'I feel in need of one myself.'

'Thanks, I'd love one.' She lowered her voice, turning him into a fellow conspirator. 'Maybe we can manage to avoid the others.'

'There's one way we can make quite sure of it,' he grinned back. Leaning towards her ear he murmured, 'We could nip into town, eat someplace else. Are you game?'

'Absolutely!' she laughed.

'Meet you in the car park in five minutes, then.'

Shelley left the room walking on fluffy clouds but as she freshened up in the Ladies, combed her auburn hair, re-applied her lipstick and perfume, she was dismayed to find herself experiencing a twinge of guilt. What about poor old Ben? Her spirits sank, but she told herself that was exactly the problem. She always got depressed when she thought about her husband. Of course she was sorry about him losing his job. The trouble was, sorry wasn't how she wanted to feel about the man in her life. She wanted him to lift her up, as Duncan undoubtedly did, to feel a rush through her veins when she thought of him, a real sexual buzz.

It was a long time since she'd been that way over Ben, which was why it was all the more irresistible when it had happened with Duncan. She loved being in love, the miracle that turned blood into champagne and made her see everything with new eyes. If she could feel that way about Ben again she wouldn't need Duncan – but she couldn't, so she did. Only that gorgeous hunk of a boss of hers really had the power to do it to her, and he was waiting for her now, in the car park.

Shelley slipped into the front seat of the Mercedes. As Duncan reached over to help fasten her seat belt, his hand brushed against the hard points of her nipples, visible beneath her clothes in her new softline bra. She knew he was doing it deliberately and, furthermore, he knew that she knew. The smile he threw her afterwards was both knowing and satisfied, convincing Shelley – if she needed convincing – that he was as interested in her as she was in him.

'Not a very promising start to the conference was it?' he commented as he drew smoothly away, his hand in firm control of the steering wheel. 'Still, at least it gets us out of London. You're married, aren't you Shelley?'

The question came out of nowhere, stunning her into replying. 'Er . . . yes, I am,' she faltered.

'Happily?'

She hesitated. 'I wouldn't say so. Ben is unemployed, you see. Has been for over a year. And somehow it seems to have affected our relationship.'

'Bound to. What was his job?'

'Computer programmer. Nowadays he spends all his time on the Internet.'

'Hm. I prefer to live in the here and now, not wallowing in some virtual reality with a bunch of nerds who have problems interfacing with the real world.'

Duncan threw her a smile that had her heart racing like the engine. Shelley found his chiselled profile – straight nose, firm chin – even more appealing than full face. When he gave her that sidelong look his grey eyes flickered at her with a cheeky suggestiveness that fuelled her libido and had her longing for the merest touch of him. To satisfy that longing, she pretended to pull down her skirt and her knuckles made contact

4

with the side of his thigh, his trousers drawn taut over the muscled flesh beneath.

Shelley gave an involuntary shiver, then asked huskily, 'How about you, Duncan, are you married?'

'Divorced. Three years ago. No kids. Ah, this looks just the place, don't you think?'

He pulled into the forecourt of a small country hotel. It was quiet, out of season, and the landlord welcomed them genially in the bar. Duncan asked to see the menu as they drank their aperitifs, then they moved into the small dining-room beyond. Away from the tedious media types at the conference, Shelley began to relax and feel more herself. She chatted away about her childhood visits to her loony maiden aunt, Jean McIntyre, who lived in Inverness. Duncan offered tales of his Aberdeen childhood in return.

There was an inevitable closeness developing between them. Shelley knew that, before the night was out, they would become even more intimate. She loved savouring this mixture of desire and elation, the near-certainty that his feelings and intentions mirrored hers, spiced nevertheless with a dab of uncertainty. It was only when Duncan mentioned, casually, that there were rooms available at the hotel that Shelley felt her hopes soar unstoppably.

'What do you say?' he asked, as they sat in the lounge sipping coffee, heads intimately close. 'Shall we give them all the slip for the night and stay here? It would cause a delicious scandal, I'm sure. If they bother to notice we're missing, of course.'

'Oh Duncan, do you think we could?'

Shelley felt her body responding to his like a flower to rain. She was opening up, feeling soft and vulnerable, her tender parts longing for the sweet ministrations of his hands and tongue. He leaned forward and pressed his lips to hers, just for a moment. They felt full and soft, brushing hers with an electric tingling that left her inwardly clamouring for more.

'I'll see to it. You stay here.'

Shelley stretched her legs out languidly before the open fire, enjoying the warmth on her shins. She had lusted for Duncan for months and now, in just a few minutes, they would be alone together in a hotel bedroom. The knowledge that he wanted her as much as she wanted him was a powerful aphrodisiac, turning what had once been a vague desire into a raging need, to kiss and be kissed, touch and be touched. God, how long was it since she had felt this vibrant, this alive?

The thought of her husband intervened briefly, but Shelley reminded herself that she'd been trying to inject life into their failing marriage for the past six months. She couldn't remember how long it had been since she and Ben had made any attempt at love-making. It was amazing that her libido hadn't withered away altogether. For months she'd lived a celibate, frustrated existence – surely she deserved better than that. As a red-blooded female in the prime of life, she considered that sexual satisfaction was her right. And now that the opportunity had at last presented itself, she was going to seize it with both hands, not to mention the rest of her anatomy!

Duncan reappeared, smiling, and Shelley knew it was all arranged. Feeling like a couple of naughty children playing truant, they mounted the red carpeted stairs and found their room. It was large and pleasant, with a double bed and en suite bathroom. No doubt there was also a view, but neither of them paid any attention to it. They were too occupied with the sight of each other, relishing the last few moments of hunger before the feast, letting the idea sink in that they were about to make dreams become reality.

Shelley looked into his eyes, her pulse racing. His gaze was candid, telling her that he wanted her right now, and wanted her a lot. Nothing else mattered. She wasn't going to argue. Whatever romantic notions she might once have had were well and truly shattered by now, and all that mattered was the fact that she needed to make love again, if only to prove to herself that she still could. Slowly they drew together and she focused on the open invitation of his smile, the full, tempting lips and gleaming white of his teeth.

The minute he kissed her, any lingering doubts vanished. It felt so right, so good, to be with a man again. His mouth was soft and relaxed, his tongue in no hurry to penetrate, and Shelley began to do what she'd longed to do earlier. Reaching up she plunged her fingers into the thick softness of his dark hair, loving its silky caress. Duncan responded by stroking her hair too, only his fingers remained on the sleek surface.

Experimentally, Shelley let her tongue slide out and touch the tip of his, protruding between the cushioning lips. For a moment he let her touch him, then withdrew. Seconds later, it was he who was making the move, pressing his tongue slowly against her lips until she yielded and let him enter, playing a combined game of hide and seek and catch with her.

Soon Shelley's mouth was running with juices and she could feel a corresponding fountaining between her lower lips, where she was already well prepared for what was to come. Although the rest of her body was crying out for stimulation, it was clear that Duncan was in no great hurry to provide it. He continued to stand there by the bed, gently stroking her hair while their tongues played with each other. She moved her hands down his powerful shoulders and strong back, feeling the maleness of him beneath his clothes and exulting at the difference between his hard, close-packed flesh and her own softer, more rounded contours.

Then, at long last, she felt his exploratory fingers on the buttons of her blouse at the back of her neck. While he slowly unfastened them she felt inside the waistband of his trousers and drew out his shirt, reaching under it to find the warm, smooth skin of his back. Shelley sighed with the relief of feeling muscles that did not tense against her touch, a body that allowed her free access to stroke and enjoy, flesh that offered no resistance.

'Shelley,' she heard him murmur into her ear. 'I want to see your body.'

For a while they stood apart, but only to allow their eyes to send erotic messages to their already teeming imaginations. They undressed in tandem, slowly revealing themselves to each other. While Shelley slipped off her blouse, Duncan removed his shirt. She examined the broad musculature of his chest, the light smattering of black hairs down the central cleft that ended in a swirl around his navel, aware of his eyes on the curving uplift of her breasts in her bra, their nipples showing as dark shadows within the white lacy cups. She reached behind her back and unclipped the garment, freeing her bosom to the frank delight of his gaze. He groaned softly, and she knew how much he longed to touch her rigid nipples, but instead his hands went to unbuckle the belt at his waist.

Although it was quite warm in the room Shelley felt a light shiver pass through her, making her nipples contract further and her clitoris tingle with anticipation. As Duncan unzipped his fly she did the same to her skirt and soon they were both stepping out of their lower garments until they stood in their underclothes, Duncan in a pair of striped boxer shorts and Shelley in charcoal grey tights that she slowly rolled down, revealing a pair of white lace panties that were already sodden at the crotch.

Shelley stared in fascination at his burgeoning erection, conscious of the fact that her pubic hair was visible around the edges of its lacy covering. The thin material was sticking to the cleft between her labia and, no doubt, gave Duncan a good view of her bulging mound. His eyes were fixed there, bright and lascivious, as his brain worked overtime to probe beneath the flimsy cloth and figure out what she looked like beneath. Her eyes were trying to work out how much of that impressive bulge was solid flesh and how much mere folds in the crisp cotton.

Then, acting in slow synchronicity, the pair of them finally stripped off the last vestiges of modesty and revealed themselves to each other in their full glory. Shelley felt a ripple of excitement as his hungry eyes roved all over her. His penis sprang up in sudden response, pride in her own body mingled with appreciation of his. Duncan's prick was long, thick and pink, his balls hanging full and ripe beneath. Seen in the context of his sturdy and well-maintained frame, his equipment was what she would have expected, perfect tools for the job.

His delight in her body was also evident, along with his increasing desire to touch her again. They walked towards each other, smiling, but instead of falling into each other's arms they still kept their distance, wanting to see as much as to feel. His hands reached out for her breasts and cupped them lightly underneath, his thumbs resting on the pert tips of her nipples. She reached down towards his balls and held them equally lightly, feeling their hot hairy fullness in the palm of her hand. Gently, each began to squeeze and caress, sensually playing with the weight of each other's flesh, and Shelley felt her knees weaken a little.

Their lips met, and the kiss that had been interrupted before resumed then deepened. Their tongues entwined as they tasted each other to the full. Soon he was applying firmer strokes to her breasts, brushing quite roughly against her nipples in a way that sent wild messages up to her brain and down again to the throbbing flesh of her vulva. Shelley couldn't resist the urge to touch his dick, and she sighed her pleasure in the feel of the velvety skin over the steely inner core. Slowly she lifted her fingers up the shaft until she reached the ridge below the glans. She slid her thumb over the ultra-sensitive surface of the tip. It was sticky with a slight leakage of his fluid, ready to slide easily into her own well-lubricated quim. Another sharp shudder of longing passed through her, its intensity bordering on pain and making her gasp.

Suddenly they were lying on the springy expanse of the bed. The hunger that they had been holding in check was containable no longer. With avid speed Duncan was passing his hands all over her body, clutching and stroking beneath and between, while his mouth travelled down first to one yearning nipple then the other. Shelley was feeling equally rapacious. Spurred on by his stimulation of her breasts, she began to fondle his taut buttocks and take soft bites into the tender flesh of his neck, making him squirm with lust.

'God, Shelley, I can't wait to get inside you!' he breathed, as his finger found her wet opening and made an unceremonious entry. She arched her back and ground the fleshy pad that surrounded her clitoris against his hand, gasping at the brief foretaste of the delights to come. She knew he had found her open and ready for him, knew he had no more will to hold out. His prick was rearing like an impatient stallion and she loved the feel of it thrusting against her soft belly.

'Come in, then,' she whispered, knowing that he needed no further invitation than the one her body was already issuing.

That first long, sweet lunge into the centre of her being fulfilled a craving Shelley had been only dimly aware of. As her inner walls embraced the full length of him, her own arousal flipped onto a higher plane, making her whole body an instrument of quivering, subtle sensation. Duncan's hands worked on her breasts, teasing the already fully stretched nipples with his thumbs to attain new dimensions of size and density, brushing the surrounding skin with his nails to perform a twin assault upon those helpless globes. Wildly her awareness sped back and forth between the two pleasure-centres, each intensifying the experience of the other. When he took one roused nipple into his mouth and chewed softly upon it, Shelley tilted and gyrated her pelvis with increased fervour, needing more direct contact between the racing pulse in her clitoris and his strong thrusts.

Sensing her need, Duncan speeded up until he was moving with rapid force, plunging into her again and again with increasing lack of control. She could hear his breath rising and falling in time to his movements until he was gasping out his impending climax and Shelley knew she was about to come too.

The fierce contractions hit her before she knew it, hot waves of unadulterated bliss searing through her like wildfire. Shelley made a noise in the back of her throat that sounded like the guttural cry of some rutting animal. She could feel her breasts and buttocks quivering with the shock of the repeated convulsions and she was caught in the throes of it, experiencing the thrill over and over, unable to believe it could last as long.

Slowly, almost imperceptibly, the intense orgasm waned, delivering a last few tremulous stirrings before she was allowed to sink into utter satiation. Duncan's body felt warm and comforting next to hers, his chest still heaving from his exertions.

'Wow!' he breathed. 'That was fantastic, Shell. You're some woman!'

'Mm!' She snuggled close, pleased that he had not found her wanting. There had been a moment, just before they entered the hotel room, when she had wondered if she was up to it, being out of practice and all, but her enthusiasm had evidently carried her through with flying colours. Just as well, she thought with a smile, she couldn't afford to let her boss down.

Remembering all the times she had secretly lusted after him, Shelley felt a deliciously wicked thrill run through her, like an aftershock from her climax. Not only had they just made love, but they'd done so while the rest of that stuffy crew were talking about the boring old digital broadcasting revolution over their post-prandial brandies. Well, she knew where she would rather be!

Shelley dozed in the dim light of the bedside lamp for over an hour, then found herself suddenly wide awake again. She rose as carefully as she could and made her way into the bathroom, where she rejected the shower in favour of a soak in a warm, scented bath. Lying there contentedly with closed eyes, the sticky residue of their love-making gently dissolving in the water, she was sunk in reverie when a deep voice suddenly enquired, 'May I join you?'

Smiling, Shelley made room for him. Duncan's long, lean legs stepped in behind her and then he invited her to lean back against him. Soon his well-lathered hands were soaping her breasts in lazy, sensual strokes, invoking a deliciously languid mood in her. One hand moved down over her stomach and then proceeded to rub the silky foam into her pubic hair. He lifted her up onto his thighs and his fingers went lower, parting the wet folds of her labia.

Relaxed and content, Shelley let Duncan's hands roam freely all over her, loving the feel of his slippery body under hers. Beneath her buttocks she could feel him growing hard, his penis stretching the length of her crack and beyond, up her back. She wriggled a little and he groaned, 'Do that again!' Her hips moved over his, squashing the root of his prick between her bum cheeks, feeling his balls slap and squidge against the backs of her thighs.

One of Duncan's soapy fingers entered her vagina, feeling its way through the taut opening until she felt loose and soft inside, readying herself. He held her away from his supine body for a few moments, long enough to position himself between her thighs and find the way in again, this time for his tumescent organ. She sighed as the head of it nudged its way past her swollen lips and found the entrance, then Duncan let her down slowly onto him again.

He hitched himself up the bath and pulled her to him so that, in a semi-sitting position, they could both move more freely. The water slopped around their thighs as they moved tentatively up and down, like a pair of boats at their moorings. Duncan let her lie back so that her mound was out of the water and her vulva more accessible to him, then he worked the soap between his hands until he had a rich lather once again. Reaching down he ran his slick fingers along the groove between her outer and inner lips then, at last, found the part she most wanted him to touch. His fingertip pressed on the fleshy pad, making her shudder, and slowly began to circle around it while she rested her arms on the side of the bath, levering herself up and down.

Shelley could have lain there for hours revelling in the slow, delicate stimulation of her pleasure-centres, but after a while she could tell that Duncan was becoming restless. His upward thrusting movements were more vigorous, as if he were straining for release, and the water in the bath was becoming a choppy sea.

'Hey, we're going to flood the place in a minute!' she warned him.

'Then let's get out. I need to screw you more forcefully, Shelley. This gentle stuff is fine for a while, but it won't bring me off.'

'Okay.'

Shelley moved off him and stepped out of the bath. Soon they were lying on a pile of fluffy towels and Duncan was lubricating her body with scented oil, making her skin gleam. Her nipples stood out like polished tawny pebbles and, below the glossy plane of her belly, her bush resembled shiny, tangled wire. The flat of his hand skated smoothly over the surface, her skin offering no resistance to his.

This time his penis slid more easily into her. With the firm surface of the floor beneath them, their movements became swift and sinuous, thighs and stomachs gliding against each other, in every way a well-oiled machine. Shelley could feel the familiar mechanisms of her arousal kick into action too, taking her out of her lazy state of voluptuous sensuality into a more insistent mood where her desire was sharply focused. She would have liked to get on top of him but their momentum was gathering to the point where it would have been disruptive to change position. As Duncan's shaft wove in and out, the friction against her clitoris was increasing, making her gasp with the escalating pleasure that coursed through her like a rich, warm liquid.

Then she felt the first teasing buzz of her orgasm as it was triggered by Duncan's movements, the initial small thrill developing into a series of cumulative peaks, each one more potently pleasurable than the last until she was aware of a fading, a diminution of all that wildly ecstatic energy that left her spent and breathless.

While she came down, Duncan was making his ascent so that she felt him spurt just as she was falling back exhausted. He moaned out his long moment, clutching at her shoulders, until he too was finished. They lay embracing on the floor for quite a while before Shelley decided she was getting cold and stiff and they returned to bed. Cuddling up to him, she sank slowly into oblivion.

The following morning was one long scramble as the pair grabbed coffee in their room and then prepared to race back to the other hotel in time for the first of the Saturday morning sessions. Giggling like naughty school kids, they sneaked in at the back of a meeting already in progress. Shelley saw raised eyebrows as a few of their colleagues spotted their late entry. No doubt they'd been missed at the informal chat in the bar, too. Not that she cared. Playing hooky with Duncan had been worth every minute.

Today, though, she had to take the proceedings seriously. Even so, Shelley found it hard to concentrate on what was being said when her body was still crying out for Duncan's touch. She felt like an addict having her first fix after a long period of abstinence. Every cell in her body was crying out for more of the wonderful stuff, wanting that glorious high, needing it so badly. There had been no time to make plans with Duncan for another secret meeting. All through the day she tried to catch his eye, seeking the reassuring wink or grin that would tell her he was as desperate to repeat their illicit encounter as she.

Yet somehow she couldn't get near him, not even during the breaks. Duncan McFain was always surrounded by a coterie of her superiors and Shelley felt she just couldn't barge in and claim his attention. Instead she was obliged to mix with the other directors and production assistants, enduring their bright discussion and keen attitudes. Not that she wasn't equally interested in the possibilities of digital broadcasting, it was just that she would have preferred to discuss them with those who had a broader view. People like Duncan, for example.

Shelley's hopes were pinned on dinner, but she was bitterly disappointed to find that Duncan was absorbed in the company of Fay Lewis, one of the guest speakers. He seemed to be taking seriously his hint, briefly uttered over coffee that morning, that they would both have to show more of a high profile for the rest of the weekend to make up for their initial absence. While those around her chattered amiably, Shelley's eyes were pinned on the two figures at the long table. Duncan and Fay appeared to be having a very animated conversation, punctuated with laughter, and Shelley was dismayed to find that she was actually feeling jealous.

The female representative of Digicorp was certainly attractive. In her mid-forties, she had the understated style of American women who have long been at the top of their profession without needing any special legislation to smooth their path. Fay Lewis was incredibly bright, charmingly feminine and with all the sex appeal that boundless self-confidence could bring. Dismayed, Shelley told herself that, if Duncan were interested in more than Fay's mind, then she couldn't hope to compete for his bed that night.

Everything seemed to point in that direction. After the meal Shelley saw them in the bar, tête à tête in the corner, and somehow she knew that he was no longer interested in her. Forlornly she rejoined her group of cronies and started on the Southern Comfort. When she saw the pair rise, half an hour later, she tried to catch Duncan's eye, but without success. The woman wafted past on a cloud of Estée Lauder and Shelley finally admitted to herself that she had been a one-night stand.

It hurt. Not for years had she been sexually humiliated in that way, and she cursed her own stupidity in expecting any more from the encounter than Duncan had been prepared to deliver. But she couldn't afford to let her feelings show. Affecting a bright nonchalance, she joined in the discussion with her colleagues and put her bruised emotions on hold.

That night was a cruel contrast with the preceding one as Shelley struggled with her frustrated lust as well as with feelings of mortification. Under the shower she caressed her own needy body, trying in vain to reproduce the sensual excesses of her love-making with Duncan. Although she succeeded in bringing herself to orgasm, it was almost painful, a series of sharp spasms that left her feeling more wounded than cherished.

Lying in bed, her thoughts turned towards Ben, waiting at home immersed in his electronic subculture, and she wondered if she had been too hard on him. It couldn't be easy, losing your job while your wife still had hers. However liberated people's views had become, it was still not acceptable for a man to be a 'house-husband'. Not when there weren't even children involved.

Children. Shelley sighed and turned over into a foetal position, ready for sleep. Once that had been on the cards, put off until that hypothetical time when it would 'seem right', but now it seemed more unlikely than ever. Besides, she wasn't sure she wanted it any more, not with Ben. He just wasn't the sort of guy who should be at home all day looking after kids. Maybe they would drift into divorce, giving each of them a chance to find someone more compatible while they were still young. Quickly Shelley reviewed those of her friends who had married around the same time as she had: already, fifty per cent of those marriages were on the rocks. Yet the thought of playing the field again, of being victimised by the likes of Duncan, was not a pleasant prospect. If only she were the type who could take sex at face value, but she wanted more. Love, commitment, the whole damn thing. Maybe she was just a hopeless romantic, after all.

Chapter Two

Ben was lurking. He'd been lurking for several weeks, surfing the alt.sex news groups and reading other people's fantasies. Right now, while Shelley was away at her conference, he was sharing the dubious delights of making love on a bed of Krispy Snax and then licking off all the crumbs. Not quite his mug of Orange Pekoe.

Maybe it was time, he wondered, to come out of the computer closet and make a contribution of his own. Ben thought about what turned him on but it all seemed too boringly normal for the cybersex freaks who swapped tales of debauchery and delinquency over the Internet. If he started on about girls in tennis shorts and doing it at the kitchen sink they'd have him sussed as a Clueless Newbie and his name ('Bender', short for Ben Derwent) would be a bad joke. Perhaps he should go in for a little Electrotransvestism, as his user name suggested.

He could even pretend to be Shelley. Ben smiled as he imagined putting ideas into his wife's head, ideas he would have liked her to have spontaneously but which she was quite incapable of inventing. While she toiled away in a hot studio all day, he would be creating a wonderful alternative lifestyle for her, full of handsome young Scottish studs with names like Phil McCavity and pricks the size of cabers that got tossed regularly.

Stop it, he told himself. You don't know for sure that she's having an affair with that dork Duncan. You don't know for sure that she's having an affair, full stop. Yet it hardly seemed to matter either way any more. The fact was, since he'd lost his job, Shelley had become progressively less interested in him, both in and out of bed. He saw little hope of any improvement in their five-year-old marriage.

Which was why he'd got into this cybersurfing lark, making the best of a bad job. If he was going to have to stay at home all day he might as well get something out of it. And, right at this moment, what he was getting was a hard-on. Chopper and Lovelips had moved on from the Krispy Snax and were now making whoopee with the contents of the cat litter tray.

'*The scent they put in 'Kittylit' to deodorise it is enough to drive Lovelips wild,*' Chopper reported. '*So we filled a bean-bag with the stuff and we make love on that. Before Tibbles has got to it, of course. Lovelips wears her leopardskin leotard for this particular session.*'

Who are these people? Ben wondered. More to the point, where are they? Any woman who can get turned on by cat litter is welcome in my home. I've got tons of the ruddy stuff out in the garage!

The narrative continued. '*Lovelips parts her thighs and I discover, to my delight, that the catsuit has a strategically-placed catflap. I rip open the velcro and spy her pink pussy lips, all moist and swollen as the wonderful odour works directly on her olfactory nerve to stimulate the sex centre in her brain. Beneath the skin-tight tawny and black leotard I can see her nipples surging like twin rockets about to enter the stratosphere and I almost go off like a rocket myself, but hold back just in time. Not that Lovelips wants me to hit the delay button. No, she is begging for it, staring at me with her tigerish eyes and mewing like a hungry kitten. She is pawing at my stiffy like a cat playing with a mouse, willing me to enter into the game. I growl like a tom on the prowl and open my fly to display my impatiently rearing dick . . .'*

Ben loosened his belt to allow his own expanding organ more room to manoeuvre. Ludicrous as Chopper's prose might be, it was certainly having the desired effect. Ben reflected that once they got computers fitted up with cybersex gear, the age-old problems of relations between men and women would probably disappear overnight. Well, it was a nice thought. For the time being, logging onto to the alt.sex stories saved him the bother of getting a dirty video or under-the-counter mag from the corner shop and was about as arousing. The thought of several thousand users abusing themselves simultaneously over the Internet was quite a turn-on in itself.

'Lovelips spreads them wider and guides me in, grinning like a cat that's got the cream. And she will have, soon. I'm practically creaming myself already. One plunge into that molten pussy and I'm in cock heaven. She likes me to stroke her tits through the stretchy material when I'm inside her, and starts purring like a feline dynamo. Her nipples are huge beneath my fingers, and I can feel her come-button getting bigger and bigger as I stroke it with the base of my thick shaft . . .'

Ben had his own tool out now, and was giving it the kind of firm but gentle stroking that he always wished Shelley had done for him. Why was it that so few women knew how to tackle a man's . . . well, tackle? He recalled the way she'd mouthed it, back in the days when she was still interested in that sort of activity: ramming it halfway down her throat as if she wanted to swallow it whole, then grazing it with her teeth as she yanked it out again. How on earth had she expected him to be aroused by that? Most of the time he'd been in mortal fear of being Bobbitted.

The words on the screen scrolled down further. '*Lovelips is moving a treat now, squirming the way she does when her climax is fast approaching. I can feel my own control slipping away from me. She scrunches her bum into the bag of gritty cat litter, turns her face and rubs her nose in it, and I see that delicious smell turn her from a purring pussy into a ferocious wildcat. Then, just as we are both on the brink the bag bursts, releasing the overpowering scent, and the gritty Kittylit is spilling everywhere. Lovelips moans and giggles, wallowing ecstatically in the avalanche of grey granules. She tears down her leotard and asks me to rub handfuls of the stuff into her great, gorgeous tits. I'm happy to oblige. She loves the way the gravelly particles scour her nipples, masking the musky scent of her quim with its own artificial aroma, and I'm reminded of the way our dog loves to roll in smelly things. I know it won't be long now before she comes and I'm ready for my cue. I love to join her when she starts to thrash and moan and clutch at me with her orgasming wet walls. This time, as always, it starts me off and I thrust hard into her convulsing pussy with the Kittylit crunching beneath her bum cheeks . . .*'

Oh God, Ben gasped, feeling his own inevitable rise towards orgasm begin. He was about to speed up his light friction at the ultra-sensitive point just beneath the glans, when he heard the unmistakable sound of Shelley's key turning in the lock of the front door.

'Oh, bollocks!' he exploded, hastily cramming his erection

back into his trousers and climbing back onto his virtual surfboard until he found a more appropriate net address to visit. When Shelley entered he was staring, red-faced, at his screen, apparently absorbed in a discussion on alternative solutions to the ozone problem.

He heard his wife dump her bag in the corner and enter the kitchen. Ben mumbled a greeting but instead of responding in kind she called out, 'Did you get more coffee?'

'Coffee?'

Shelley came to the door, a look of resigned fury on her face. 'Yes. You know, that brown stuff that gets you up and running in the morning? We'd run out and I asked you to be sure to get some more.'

Reluctantly, Ben dragged his gaze away from the screen and looked at his watch. 'Shit! I forgot. I was going to go after I'd done the washing-up. I had no idea it was so late.'

Shelley gave him The Look. If she hadn't managed to turn his heart to stone ages ago, it would certainly have done the job right then. Her normally pretty blue eyes were now a dull shade of gunmetal grey and her mouth, which had been known to smile in a way that made Ben's heart leap half out of his chest, was now fixed in a kind of frozen insult that plainly said, without needing to utter an actual word, 'You lazy fucking bastard!'

'I'm sorry, love. I really am. I'll go straight out now and get some. The corner shop will still be open.'

She spoke to him in a sentence elongated by ominous pauses: 'They don't have the right kind. I must have Spenders own label, it's the only sort I like.'

'Will they still be open? I think it's half-eight they close, isn't it?'

'You have ten minutes.'

The way she said it sounded like a brief stay of execution ordered by a sceptical and world-weary judge. Ben hurried out of the house and into the car, not even bothering to put on a jacket or take a bag. They always gave you dozens at the checkout anyway, he remembered, flicking them open one after the other like there was no tomorrow when all you were buying was a jar of coffee, making you feel small because you weren't spending loads and getting to be a member of their bloody discount club. He despised it as a transparent ploy to get you to shop there more often.

As Ben drove at speed through the early evening streets and into the vast, half-deserted car park of the supermarket, he was aware of a tide of anger beneath his depression. It was partly due to him being disturbed in mid-wank, of course, which was never a comfortable experience. But it was also the thought that he'd been caught out by his wife and, worse still, allowed her to get at him for it. Okay, he should have done the shopping and the washing-up and had a meal waiting for her on the table when she got home. After all, it was only what a million women did for their menfolk every night. And it wasn't fair to expect her to come home to a pile of dishes in the sink and no coffee. Of course not. But somehow that wasn't the point. He'd felt guilty because he was getting it on through the Internet and, rationally, he didn't see why he should have any such qualms. If she wasn't giving it to him, what did she expect him to do, have an affair?

Unwilling to pursue that line of thought, Ben strode in through the automatic doors, irritated by the fact that there were no baskets, only trollies, and he was going to look a right berk peddling one jar of coffee through the checkout. Once he was strolling down the aisle, however, the usual mix of soothing music, abundant goodies and familiar geography worked its mysterious magic on his soul. He found himself putting more than just the coffee into his trolley. Somehow a bottle of wine and some flowers made their way there, not by any rational choice but through some atavistic urge towards appeasement that welled up from the murky depths of Ben's psyche of its own accord. A large frozen pizza and some curly salad in vivid hues of green and red also ended up in the trolley and only when a double choc gateau almost joined them did Ben awaken from his reverie. Shelley hated him giving her chocolate.

'You know I can't resist it!' she would moan, accusingly. 'You know I absolutely yearn for it, mean pig!'

'A little won't do you any harm, surely?'

'You know that once I start, I'll eat the whole box! You did it on purpose!'

And so the pointless, illogical argument would continue until Ben threatened to eat the lot himself, at which point she would snatch the box from him with a 'No you bloody well won't!' compounding his mystification.

At the checkout, Ben had time to look around. He quite liked being a lone male in the supermarket. It made him feel independent, almost attractive again. The checkout girls joked with him. Sometimes a harassed husband gave him a blokeish grin, the sort that said, 'Lucky you. Bet you got round in half the time!' And occasionally, very occasionally, he was half convinced that one of the slim, athletic women who jogged around the aisles with baskets full of Linda McCartney vegetarian dinners actually fancied him. Well, it was a start.

Tonight, as he was waiting in the queue, a large poster caught his eye. It read:

'Californian-Style Singles Night! Come and sample some American delights, including Tex-Mex Snax and wine from the Napa Valley, while you make new friends! Your local Spenders store will be open from eight to eleven for this special promotion event!'

'Trying to get into her good books again, are we?'

The chirpy voice of the checkout girl startled him. She was staring at the contents of his trolley which he began to unload at high speed, conscious of the queue behind him.

'Is it that obvious?' he moaned.

'Well it could be her birthday, I suppose.'

'Oh God,' he joked. 'When's that? Have I missed it already?'

As Ben drove home he was wondering how best to appease his wife. He was sick of all the arguments, the sullen silences. Maybe if he tried, really tried, they could get back to how they used to be. It was hard to remember those days, but he knew that once they had done this sort of thing – champagne, impromptu meals, nights of passionate love – quite often. He thought of how Shelley had looked as she walked in through the door that evening, pale and drawn, her hair in need of washing. Perhaps an evening of tender loving care, a session in the bath followed by a sensual massage would do the trick and turn the clock back for both of them.

When he got in, Shelley was sitting listlessly in front of the television. She looked surprised, rather than pleased, when he handed her the mixed bouquet.

'Special offer,' he grinned. 'From me to you.'

Her expression, at first tinged with suspicion, metamorphosed into something more hopeful. She gave a smile and began to look pretty again. 'Thanks, Ben. I wasn't expecting anything like this.'

'There's more. You just stay there, put your feet up, while I get us something nice to eat.'

'What have I done to deserve this?' she asked, with a touch of cynicism.

'Maybe absence made my heart grow fonder,' he quipped, taking the shopping into the kitchen. He was still wary of her, knowing she could lapse in a moment from friendliness into irritation or worse. That was how it had become these days, he felt he was walking on glass when she was around. Yet he had to try and break out of it, for both their sakes.

The pizza was a success, the wine even more so. Mellow and relaxed, the pair of them sat on the sofa together to watch a mildly erotic film. Ben began to feel normal again, daring to believe that there was nothing wrong with his marriage that a quiet night in and some indulgence of their basic instincts couldn't put right. The couple on screen were naked and screwing in soft focus, turning him on, and he could tell from the way that Shelley was cuddling up to him that she felt the same. He turned her face to his and gently kissed her.

She responded with startling passion, pulling him down until they were horizontal and unbuttoning his shirt. Her hands roved eagerly around his chest while her tongue probed between his lips, hot and demanding. Ben had been preparing himself for resistance, for having to woo her slowly and cautiously, and he was thrown quite off beam by her enthusiasm. Nevertheless he let her undress him and watched in amazement as she snaked down his body, her lips fastening eagerly on his half-awakened cock.

After being interrupted earlier, in the midst of his auto-eroticism, Ben's libido returned in full force and soon he had a stonker of an erection. No problem there, he thought happily. Shelley tore off her knickers and hitched up her skirt, then sat astride him. He reached up to undo her blouse and impatiently she unfastened her bra at the back, letting it hang loose over the taut mounds of her breasts. He grasped them greedily, fingering the hard nipples and making her squirm with the sudden deepening of her lust.

Shelley lowered herself onto his tumescent organ without ceremony and began to rub her clitoris as she bounced up and down. Ben wanted to do it for her, but he had a feeling she wouldn't let him. Her appetite was rapacious, to put it mildly. She was totally centred in her own mounting pleasure, her face contorted with lust, her body on autodrive. There was something about the look of her that disgusted him, but he was powerless to prevent his own rapid rise towards orgasm. When her vigorous thrustings took him over the edge, he came in a series of violently spasmodic squirts that left him feeling drained.

Shelley remained on top of him while his dick shrank inside her. She was gasping and sweating now as she struggled towards her own satisfaction. It seemed to be taking a long time. Wanting to help her out, Ben gave her nipples firmer treatment, pinching them between his finger and thumb until they felt hard as nuts. He could feel the juices trickling out of her and down his thigh, over his slack balls. She was squeezing him in a vain effort to resuscitate his erection and he wished she would stop.

At long last she came, arching back and moaning aloud as she first speeded up and then slowed her hand movements. The clenching movements of her orgasming vagina made his dick slip out of her altogether and then she flopped down onto the sofa, utterly drained.

Lying beside her, Ben had the uncomfortable feeling that what had just occurred had been nothing whatsoever to do with him. He had been a convenient prick, that was all. A stupid prick, too, for imagining that anything might have changed between them. A quick bang in return for wine and roses wasn't going to rescue their marriage. He frowned in sudden recognition. Those flowers had had sod all to do with it! In retrospect Ben recognised the mood she had been in when she came home: all that prickly energy had come from suppressed hunger for sex, not for food. His wife had been horny after her weekend away, she'd come back dying for it, and he happened to be the only available male.

So what had happened at this 'conference' to make her leap on him in that uncontrolled way? Maybe she'd hoped to get that Duncan into her knickers and it hadn't happened. He knew she'd fancied her boss for ages. It had been obvious that time when he'd phoned her up when she was off sick and she'd gone all love-struck and giggly. Ben had even found a photo of the bastard in her bag. Her explanation had been that he'd asked her to stick one on his pass card for him, and she'd forgotten to return the spare.

'Would you like a coffee?' he asked her.

She stared up at him, red-eyed. 'Just some water, thanks. Coffee might keep me awake.'

He went out and poured two glasses of mineral water. When he returned, she was sitting up with her blouse draped over her shoulders and her knees clutched to her chest, watching a late-night chat show.

Ben contained his annoyance. 'Do we have to have that thing on? I thought we might talk.'

'That's rich, coming from you!'

'Okay, but I wanted to ask you about your weekend. You haven't said much about it yet.'

Shelley wouldn't take her eyes off the screen. 'It was

fine. Some American woman going on about new media opportunities, a bloke discussing copyright, someone on educational broadcasting. All useful stuff, I suppose.'

'What was the hotel like?'

'God, Ben, it was a hotel, that's all.'

'I mean, was it nice? You know, pleasant grounds, good cooking . . .'

'Ben it was *work*, not a holiday!'

'Yeah, but I was thinking maybe we could go away to a hotel sometime. Just for a weekend.'

'Whatever for?'

'A break, for God's sake! We could both do with one.'

'But I've only just come back from a weekend away.'

Ben snorted out his exasperation. 'But that was work, you said so yourself. What I'm thinking of is a chance to relax in a nice hotel, to get away from it all. Some married couples do that sort of thing, you know, from time to time.'

Shelley looked straight at him. Her eyes were sad, but her mouth was set hard. 'Look, Ben, I'm sorry but you're the last person in the world I'd want to be stuck in a hotel with. I'm sorry, but that's just the way it is. We'd get on each others' nerves, the weekend would be a failure and we'd have wasted our money.'

'Shit!' Ben plonked himself angrily down beside her and seized her wrists. He wanted to shake some sense into her, but managed to restrain himself. 'If you aren't even prepared to give it a try, what hope is there?'

She sighed. 'I don't know. Look, please don't hassle me now. I'm dead tired.'

Ben steeled himself to ask the question that had to be asked. He pulled her round to face him. 'Is there anyone else, Shelley? I have to know.'

She hesitated for a second or two then shook her head. 'No, Ben, I'm not having an affair.'

His shoulders sank as he released her. 'Well that's something, I suppose.'

He lapsed into the mindlessness of the chat show, his eyelids growing heavy. After a few minutes he announced that he was going up to bed and expected Shelley to follow. Surprisingly, she remained downstairs for quite a while, leaving him to reflect dourly on the state of their marriage in their empty bed.

When she eventually came up and slipped under the duvet beside him, Ben felt a resurgence of his former lust. It was the first time in months that they'd actually done it, and he was reminded of what it could be like to come inside a woman's body instead of his own fist. Now he wanted to feel that warm, pulsating flesh around his dick again.

Somehow a mouth-to-mouth kiss seemed too personal for what he had in mind. The way they'd copulated earlier, he had felt used. Now it was her turn. Reaching down past her hairy delta he found the still damp lips of her pussy lying half-open to his touch. She moaned as he inserted a fingertip into her entrance and he felt her muscles contract over it. Just above he could feel her rigid little mound, crying out for stimulation. He began to work it back and forth with his thumb. Shelley moaned sleepily and let her thighs fall further apart.

Ben knew he wasn't going to get enthusiasm, but at least she was offering compliance. His prick was rearing impatiently as he felt her get wetter and wetter, but she made no attempt to stroke or kiss him, just lay there like a corpse uttering the occasional moan that presumably passed for encouragement. Fearing that his erection might subside under the psychological weight of his wife's inertia, Ben heaved himself up and found his way into her slack vagina.

The soft envelope of flesh caressed his shaft passively, letting him do what he liked with it. At first all he wanted was to move in and out very slowly, making gentle thrusts with his hips, his head resting between Shelley's spread breasts. He felt small and childlike, coming as a supplicant to the woman who could give him what he needed, a safe haven. Just for tonight he felt safe from her taunts, her moods. She was too tired to be angry with him, too shagged to resist his one-sided stealing of pleasure from her body.

Ben gradually speeded up his thrusts, feeling the gathering rush in his groin, the tension in his balls. He felt lulled rather than excited by the rocking motion, yet all the time he knew that he was slowly rousing himself to that point of no return, allowing the process to develop of its own accord. It was a change not to feel that urgency, not to be willing it to happen. He didn't even care if it didn't happen, he only wanted to be there inside her again. It was some kind of victory just being in that position, and he wanted to savour it.

Shelley had given up. The effort to pull herself back into a state of arousal had evidently proved too much for her and Ben suspected she might actually be sleeping now. He was still caught up in the dreamy momentum, felt he could go on forever just like that as if he were immersed in a warm bath. His easy sliding in and out was automatic now, the see-saw rhythm had caught him in its mesmeric grip and he couldn't let go. His whole body felt strange, almost anaesthetised, dulled to both pleasure and pain.

It was a peculiar sensation, as if he might drift away into an out-of-the-body experience. He'd never had one, but from the descriptions he'd read this strange detachment might have been a precursor of that mysterious severing of body and soul. A numbness was creeping through him like a paralysis, but it was not unpleasant. Perhaps it was the result of extreme emotional fatigue. Sometimes he felt utterly drained by the tedium of his unemployed life, his dreary stay-at-home existence and the routine meaninglessness that his marriage had become. Could he possibly change things? Maybe this would change things, this admittedly futile attempt to inject some passion into their relationship and pretend that they could become lovers again. He speeded up, more out of desperation to restore some feeling to his body than anything, and Shelley gave an indecipherable groan that could have been one of pleasure, pain or protest.

Then, without any forewarning, he had a weak ejaculation, accompanied by a feeble buzz that went down the length of his dick from his balls. The anti-climax was over in a second, leaving him limp and bemused. He withdrew his already flaccid penis and lay down beside his wife who acknowledged his presence by turning her back on him. Ben put his arm round her and felt the squashed side of her breast. It comforted him to hold it in his hand while he waited for sleep and she didn't try to stop him.

In the last few minutes of consciousness Ben found himself going back to the beginning, remembering how it had been when they had found each other exciting. They'd screwed in every room of the house when they'd first moved in, by way of making it their own. He had made her put a frilly apron over her nakedness and taken her from behind at the kitchen sink with her arms elbow-deep in washing-up liquid. They'd done it with her sitting on his lap while he sat on the environmentally-friendly, replaceable hardwood toilet seat. She had been sweet to him on every piece of their three-piece suite, served herself up for him on the dining table, let him mount her on the stairs. Each time had seemed newer and more stimulating than the last and afterwards the house had been humming with energy, so bright and vibrant that Ben had joked it might run without need of electricity.

Yet all that beautiful wild energy had slowly drained away along with their enthusiasm for each other, leaving them entombed within dead walls. Now, lying there in the dead of night, Ben found the atmosphere oppressive and draining. It seemed incredible that where they both lay, in that same double bed, he and Shelley had more than once made mad, passionate love from sunset to sunrise. Memory and imagination struggled within him to recall and recreate that early romantic rapture, when every time they'd made love had been like the first time. But superimposed on all Ben's attempts was that recent sad apology for a screw. What he had just limped through in their marital bed had been about as exciting as doing it in a cat litter tray, with or without the benefit of a feline companion.

Chapter Three

Shelley was dreading returning to work on Monday. After her passionate night with Duncan, his snubbing of her had been painfully humiliating. Yet she must continue to work in the same environment as that snake, pretending that everything was still okay and that she was well used to bed-hopping.

To ease the hurt, she'd first told herself that the rapturous feelings he had induced in her were merely her body's response to sexual abstinence. The fact that her husband had failed to take her to similar heights contradicted that argument. Unless, of course, her marriage really was on the rocks. The contrast in her responses to the two men was forcing her to draw that obvious conclusion.

As Shelley entered the studio where they were shooting a commercial, Duncan greeted her with surprising warmth. His eyes raked over her trimly suited figure with more than a hint of interest and Shelley was caught off guard.

'Morning, Duncan,' she said, very coolly indeed.

'Hullo, Shelley. Did you enjoy the weekend?'

His voice was low and faintly amused, challenging her to respond in kind. She fixed him with as blank a stare as she could manage. 'I thought it was quite useful, overall.'

'Useful?' She had the distinct impression he was laughing at her. 'I was hoping you'd say "enjoyable".'

'Yes, it was quite pleasant.' His brows shot up. 'You chose a good venue, Duncan.'

He laughed, a rich chuckle that forced her blood more rapidly through her pulses. Shelley felt a dull fury building up inside her. Did he imagine that, just because he was her superior at work, he could act condescendingly towards her?

'I'd like to see you in my office when we take a break,' he told her, moving away before she had time to reply.

The business of filming the commercial began, and Shelley was soon absorbed in the direction The product was breakfast cereal and there was a child involved, so it was trickier than usual, especially as the little brat was refusing to co-operate.

After several temper tantrums and some silly larking around they managed to get some decent footage in the can by late morning, then Duncan called a break. 'Forty-five minutes, studio! Be back here by one, or heads will roll!'

'I'll give you three guesses whose!' remarked Steve, the cameraman, under his breath. He was one of several free-lancers that they often used. Shelley smiled at him and he grinned back, his eyes surveying her in a way that gave her spirits an instant lift. He fancies me, she thought, not for the first time. Well her ego could do with all the boosting it could get, right now.

Shelley made her way to Duncan's office. He was sitting down with coffee and a half-eaten doughnut on his desk before him, looking very smug.

'God, Shell, you were amazing with that kid!' he began, gesturing for her to sit down on the padded leather chesterfield.

'Was I?'

'Yes. You did really well to get anything out of Jeremy at

all. He's notorious when he's in that mood. I don't know how he still gets work.'

'I think he'll be fine. It's a difficult job we're asking him to do. I imagine it's not easy to turn a bowl of cornflakes upside down on your head without giggling, and we've made him do it over and over again.'

'You're right, I'm probably expecting too much. Which brings me, rather neatly, to what I wanted us to talk about. Look, if I acted out of order on the weekend, I apologise. I don't know quite what *you* were expecting, but you made it pretty damn obvious that you were sulking next day . . .'

'Sulking!' She rose indignantly to her feet and placed both hands on the desk, towering over him. 'You spend all day totally ignoring me, and flirting with that American woman, and then you accuse me of sulking!'

He took her right hand, squeezing it slightly, and Shelley felt her womb respond with an aching swoop. The way he was looking at her now she could forgive him anything. Scenes from their lovemaking played over in her mind's eye like movie clips.

'Nothing happened between me and Fay, I promise you.' He got to his feet, putting his hands on her shoulders and turning her to face him. 'I'm sorry if you believed I was neglecting you, Shelley, but I thought I'd made it clear that the rest of the weekend had to be purely business. We'd already had more than our share of pleasure, I think you'll agree.'

Shelley felt herself blush. Her eyes slid away from his, afraid of what they might reveal. She wasn't sure herself what she felt. Her anger had almost melted away, but not quite. Duncan's voice continued, slow and seductive, soothing her into acquiescence.

'The last thing I wanted was to upset you, Shelley. What we shared was very special, and I don't want you to think I undervalue it.' His hand touched her forearm lightly, just below where her sleeve ended, and bristling electricity ran down to her fingertips. She was willing herself to remain upright, fighting the urge to sink helplessly as her knees grew soft as putty.

She looked into the calm grey of his eyes and saw her own feelings reflected there, if anything even more strongly. It was impossible to say who instigated their next move. It was as if they were directing their own love scene, acting according to a pre-arranged script. Duncan took hold of her and drew her to him at the same moment that she leant towards him, and their mouths met halfway.

They seemed to pick up exactly where they'd left off on Saturday morning, like a scene that had to be held over until the following day. Feeling his lips brush teasingly against hers, Shelley allowed her tongue to protrude between them, just a little, until she could taste the sugar from his doughnut. His tongue fenced with hers for a few seconds before plundering her mouth, making her feel the full force of his hunger for her.

It took a few seconds before she realised that he had started to undress her. She took a step back, murmuring her protest, but already one full breast was being wrenched out of its protective upholstery and her nipple was subjected first to the rough stimulation of his fingers and then to his voracious mouth. As he sucked hard on its burgeoning rigidity, Shelley arched her neck back in sensual abandon, already too far gone to resist. She wanted him badly, and she knew he was equally hot for her. A surge of triumph went through her as she thought of that Fay woman, and how Duncan had only been interested in the influence she wielded in her field. It was

Shelley he lusted after, Shelley he couldn't wait to possess. She almost laughed to think how jealous she'd been.

'Come on, let's move over here,' he urged, gruffly, undoing his shirt as he manoeuvred her onto the sofa. She stripped off what remained of her garments and he did the same, reaching over to lock his office door as a precaution.

They sank back onto the leather upholstery and began to caress each other's nakedness, their hands passing quickly over shoulders, belly, thighs. Shelley felt her blood warming, the sultry fire of her passion heating her up so that when she shivered it was from desire, not cold. Between her thighs she was more than ready for him, liquid and swollen, all the nerves in her tender places tingling with sharp sensation.

'God, Shelley, I could hardly wait to do this again,' Duncan growled, his thick penis probing between her labia. Finding her entrance already open to him he thrust in quickly, making her cry out with delight as the hard flesh slid between her inner lips and her inner walls. He paused for a moment, letting them both savour the intimate contact, before he began a slow, smooth rhythm of intercourse, stroking the enlarged bud of her sex with his shaft each time he pulled out or plunged in again.

Shelley gradually abandoned herself to the pleasure. She forgot entirely where she was as the intense stimulation of their coupling blotted out everything else. He was penetrating deeply now and she tilted her pelvis to accommodate him. The thickness and length of his organ was profoundly satisfying, taking her quickly through the preliminary stages of arousal and on to a plane of pure bliss where she was content to stay awhile. Duncan bent his head to her breast and nibbled at her nipple with his lips, filling her with shudders of delight that evoked trembling echoes from her womb.

'Ah!' Shelley heard herself utter the long, sighing syllable as the first thrilling stages of her orgasm began. She let the swirling current of ecstasy lift her up and up, her whole body arching against Duncan's accelerating drive, and he grunted in accord with her as the squeezing action of her vagina brought him swiftly to his own climax. Then, just as her upwardly spiralling bliss reached its zenith and began to melt away, she felt him inject all his wild energy into her and sighed again.

'God, I needed that!' Duncan exclaimed. He withdrew and wiped himself with a tissue from a box on the desk, throwing her a couple more. 'Sometimes a quickie is just what you want, isn't it?' He glanced at his watch. 'Fifteen minutes left. Good.'

Shelley looked up at him through incredulous eyes. How could he spring up from the couch like that and immediately return to work mode? It disturbed her.

As she slowly wiped her still throbbing vulva, Shelley felt let down. He hadn't even kissed her afterwards, told her how nice she was or anything. Now he was tucking into the remains of his doughnut and brewing more coffee, his attitude jaunty, apparently oblivious of her presence. Her previous fears about the man returned, despite all her attempts to tell herself that the time and the place precluded any kind of prolonged intimacy.

Shelley dressed and accepted the coffee that he offered her. Sitting down on the sofa again, she took her own packet of sandwiches out of her bag. She felt tacky, both inside and out, but there was no time for a shower. She'd have to make do with one of those feminine wipes you could get out of the machine in the Ladies.

As she munched her way half-heartedly through her lunch, with Duncan going on about child psychology, Shelley knew she would have to say something about what had just occurred between them, since he seemed determined to pretend it had never happened. But she had to be tactful. Despite the pressure that was building up in her, she had to retain a good working relationship with him at all costs.

'Well, I suppose we'd better be getting back,' he said at last, picking up his clipboard.

'Yes – Duncan, about what happened just now. I hope you don't think that's what I want. Quickies in your office at lunch-break, I mean.'

He looked at her quizzically, running a hand through his glossy dark hair. 'Of course not. I liked spending the night with you. It was great.'

'But it would be nice to do something else together, too. Go for a meal, perhaps, or see a movie.'

He frowned. 'We have to be very careful, Shelley. You know how rumours spread in a small company. I can't take the risk.' He glanced at his watch again. 'Look, I really must dash. You can take a few extra minutes if you like, I won't comment. See you!'

He whirled through the door, leaving her gasping in his wake. She might have known there would be a bitter aftertaste to the sweetness of their love-making. The man was offering her nothing but an occasional opportunistic screw. Well, that wasn't what she wanted. Much as she appreciated his sexual technique, that wasn't all there was to life. The very idea of a relationship that consisted of work and sex with nothing in between was depressing.

The afternoon passed drearily, with takes and re-takes, the stroppy child growing more and more fractious. The overtime they were having to put in was eating into the budget and, by the time they had enough film to end the session, Duncan was fuming, muttering under his breath that this was the last time he would use this particular brat. Shelley sensed it was no time to suggest a quiet chat over a drink. Besides, she was knackered and longing to get home.

When she finally arrived at her suburban semi, Shelley wanted to shower straight away. She was longing to rid herself of the unpleasant dregs of Duncan's lovemaking which was making her feel soiled and used once again. Much to her surprise, for once Ben was not stuck in front of his computer screen when she entered. He greeted her with a kiss, and delicious smells wafted through from the kitchen.

'I've cooked something a bit special for us tonight,' he said, proudly. 'But it'll be a while yet. You go on up and have your shower, then I'll bring you some champagne.'

'Champagne! How lovely!'

His solicitous behaviour was making her feel guilty. Ben could be very sweet, when he wanted to be. Shelley ran the shower, stripping while she adjusted the temperature, then stood under it for a few seconds letting the warm water splash onto her face, breasts, stomach, thighs. When she was wet all over, she took the bottle of luxurious shower gel that Ben had bought her for Christmas and squirted a large dollop into her palm.

As she proceeded to rub the sticky substance into her warm, wet skin, it foamed up and became sleek and sensuous. Shelley loved the scent and feel of it. She was soon squeaky clean but she kept on smoothing it around with languid strokes, feeling her breasts and buttocks grow taut and aroused. The session with Duncan that afternoon had been all too brief, a snack rather than a meal, and it had left her unsatisfied. She wanted to bring herself off in the shower, but Ben had said he would be up with a drink in a minute so she would have to postpone it. Sometimes she quietly pleasured herself in bed, when she was sure her husband was asleep, so she would wait till then.

Going through to the bedroom, Shelley reached for the body mousse on her dressing table. It was the same luxurious scent as the shower gel, and there was talc to complete the set. She pressed the pump and a dab of white foam oozed out, like vanilla ice-cream. Rubbing her palms together, she began to stroke the velvety stuff over her arms.

'Why don't you let me do that?'

She turned to see Ben smiling in the doorway, holding two glasses of champagne. He set the glasses down on the bedside table then picked up the body foam. Shelley took a long sip from her glass, then lay face-down on the bed with relief. It was so good to sink her face into a soft pillow and unwind completely.

Ben started at her feet, caressing them lightly at first as he covered them with a smooth film. Then he covered the soles with his thumbs, circling around with firm pressure so as to stimulate all possible points on the meridians that formed a subtle network in her body, linking to her organs. Shelley felt the niggling worries that had kept her on the verge of a headache all afternoon simply melt away. She sighed, wriggling against the fluffy duvet, as she felt Ben's hands creep up her calves and thighs, moisturising her skin with the mousse. Beneath his firm ministrations her muscles achieved a deeper level of relaxation, turning her into a floppy doll.

By the time he came to knead the slack mounds of her buttocks, Shelley was lost in a world of pure repose. He covered her back with long, slow strokes, untied the knots in her shoulders with the full force of his knuckles, and then asked her to turn over. She soon lay open to him, eyes closed, the slow tide in her ready to turn from sensuality to sexuality, if he wished to take her in that direction. But she wasn't sure what he wanted of her.

Ben massaged her shins and knees with his capable hands before starting on her thighs. He stroked first the outer edges then the inner ones, where her skin was more sensitised. Shelley let out an involuntary sigh as his fingers just brushed against the hairy bulge of her mound, but he didn't linger there. Instead he moved to her hands and arms. The fleeting arousal of her desire was dampened down and she returned to her previous state of complete letting go.

It was impossible to remain unmoved, however, when he returned to stroke the smooth dome of her stomach. Again his hands were making brief contact with her pubic hair, this time at the top of her delta, and she couldn't prevent the first urgent pang of desire from flushing through her. Hoping it would not recur, she tried to regain her equilibrium but now he was moving up towards her breasts. Once he started there, she would be lost.

For a while Ben merely skated around the lower slopes, carefully avoiding her nipples. The scented oil was reaching her nostrils, its delicious perfume seducing her with its rich aroma of jasmine, rose and narcissus. Already her breasts were taut, the nipples straining with yearning and paradoxically even more aroused than if he'd been fingering them directly. Try as she might, Shelley couldn't shut her mind to her desires. All the frustration engendered by her earlier, short-lived session with Duncan came back at her with full force. She could feel her clitoris, the ultimate barometer of her lust, pulsing away hotly at full throttle.

Ben's voice broke into her silent world of longing. 'Do you want me to touch your nipples or leave them alone?'

Shelley was well aware of the sub-text. Her husband was asking her if she wanted to turn this into some kind of sexual encounter. Well, if it happened now, it would save her the bother later. She made an inarticulate noise in her throat, cleared it, then hoarsely whispered, 'Mm, please.'

The suspense continued for a few moments longer as Ben's fingertips wound round the outside of her breasts, his nails scratching lightly across her tense skin. Shelley was fully awakened now, in every sense, and sharply focused on the area he was so casually spiralling around. Suddenly Ben stopped and took both of her generous mounds in his hands, lifting them up and squeezing them gently, evidently enjoying their solid weight. He bent his head and licked the very tips of her nipples, one after the other. She gasped with surprise, both her russet buds throbbing with renewed feeling. His mouth closed over the one on her right breast and, as he sucked on it strongly, Shelley felt her womb contract. She wanted him to lick her down there, where she was more than ready for him.

Yet Ben seemed reluctant to move away from her thrusting globes with their provocatively rearing crests. His fingers were working one nipple into a frenzy of tingling sensation while he continued to manipulate the other with his lips and tongue. Shelley's body began to undulate with frustrated craving, her thighs brushing each other impatiently while she wriggled her pelvis too and fro, arching her back and wiggling her bottom in a desperate attempt to bring some relief to the lower part of her body.

At long last Ben answered her need. While his mouth moved to the other breast, kissing the plump smoothness of her skin, his hands skimmed their way down her sides and fell to rest at her hips where he stroked her softly. They moved across to her mound and then down to part her thighs wide enough for him to see her open pussy. Shelley knew it would appear moist and deep pink, like the flesh of a succulent fruit. She knew he'd be unable to resist it.

She was proved right when his mouth left her breast and came to join his questing fingers at the place where his eyes were already feasting. Dimly Shelley tried to recall the last time her husband had gone down on her and found she couldn't. As his tongue found its way in through her meltingly soft flesh, probing as far into her vagina as it could reach, she lay back against the pillow and wallowed in pure selfish pleasure.

Ben had forgotten none of his technique, she was glad to discover. As he brought her slowly but surely towards a climax, she let go of all her inhibitions, grudges and reservations, enjoying the experience whole-heartedly. Thanks to Duncan keeping her mechanisms ticking over, she was well able to respond and her practised clitoris carried her swiftly and easily towards the consummation she longed for. When the sweet convulsions began she clutched at Ben's head with her thighs and cried out in a series of little exclamations, 'Oh, oh, oh!' Dimly she heard her husband crooning, 'That's it, my beauty, my love!' and the incongruous thought hit her that he was addressing her like a horse.

The intrusive absurdity of that idea brought her down abruptly, spoiling the last few, precious seconds of her orgasm. Oh, why did he have to say such stupid things at crucial moments! Irritatedly Shelley turned over on the bed, hiding her face from him. While the heat dissipated from her, along with her bliss, Ben gently stroked her buttocks but even that was annoying to her and, when he spoke, his voice grated.

'Would you like some more bubbly, love?'

Feeling that she was being unfair to take umbrage against him for nothing at all, she turned onto her back. 'Mm, yes please.'

Eagerly she sipped the champagne, hoping it would elevate her mood. Ben replaced the top on the bottle of body mousse and stood up from the bed, taking his glass with him.

'I'll pop down and see how the dinner's getting on,' he smiled. 'Should be about ready.'

A few minutes later he called up the stairs to tell her he was dishing up. Shelley was glad, she felt starving. Quickly she drew on the long orange linen robe she'd bought in a Moroccan market, not bothering to wear anything underneath. Her body still smelt of the sultry Rochas toiletries, the spicy undertone now reinforced by her own fresh musk.

'So what's this all about?' she asked, amused, seeing the table lit with candles, adorned with flowers.

Instantly she regretted it. Ben turned from setting down the dishes, his face pained. 'What do you mean? I wanted it to be nice for us tonight. Especially tonight.'

Feeling as if she'd been caught up in some devious scheme of his, Shelley frowned. 'Why tonight, for heaven's sake?'

'You mean you'd forgotten? Don't you know what day it is?'

She shook her head, trying to recall the date. Suddenly it dawned on her and she realised what a fool she'd been, and how cruelly she had mocked his preparations for the evening. 'Oh my God! I'm sorry, Ben, really I am! How incredibly stupid of me. It's just that I've been so busy lately . . .'

'Yes, well you don't have to rub it in. I know you're the high-powered career woman and I'm the one with all the time in the world. Time to remember trivial details like wedding anniversaries.'

Shelley hugged him, murmuring her apologies, her thanks, trying to hide her acute embarrassment as best she could. Ben shrugged it off, but she could tell he was deeply hurt underneath. Although she tried her best to enjoy his carefully cooked food, a slow depression was creeping up on her. It seemed somehow symbolic that she had been the one to forget their anniversary, as if it meant more to him than to her. Poor Ben had tried really hard to make it a special evening but she'd gone and spoilt it. Guilt invaded her soul, like a clammy sweat.

'That was lovely, Ben. Delicious!' she pronounced, pushing away her plate.

He looked at her, mute appeal in his brown eyes. 'Coffee? Liqueur?'

'That would be nice.'

She began to clear away the things but he told her to sit down by the fire and leave everything to him. The guilt-fever in her veins thickened. She'd never felt this physically sick over something she'd done before. It was how she imagined someone might feel if they hurt a helpless animal and then repented.

While he was out of the room, however, Shelley realised why she was over-reacting. The guilt wasn't simply about her stupid oversight. It was compounded by the way she'd behaved with Duncan, not only at the weekend but today, of all days, and in such a sordid and functional manner. All the time they'd been so crudely fucking on that sofa, poor Ben had been planning their anniversary meal, shopping for food and champagne. She felt horribly ashamed.

Maybe I can make it up to him, she thought, pulling up the

hem of her *djellabah* and stretching out her silky-smooth legs. After her relaxing session upstairs, she was in the mood for something a little more strenuous.

When Ben returned she was pleasantly anticipating how she would make amends for her clumsiness. They sat companionably before the fire, Ben on the rug with his head against her knees. 'How did it go today?' he asked. 'Busy?'

'Of course. We had a real little brat to deal with in the cereal ad. Steve, the cameraman, called him "The Flake". He seemed to take delight in doing the exact opposite to what he was told to do.'

'But you do enjoy it, don't you? Working for Harcourt Productions, I mean.'

'Yes, I do. Of course there are off-days, but that's life. I don't feel the need to change.'

'That's good.' He looked up at her, his eyes darkly vulnerable. 'Only I'd hate to think that you were just working to pay the mortgage. Oh, I know you have to. One of us has to, that's for sure, and I wish it could be both of us. But if you wanted to look for another job, I think you should.'

'It's okay, Ben, I'm no wage slave! I enjoy my work, honestly. I just wish I could say the same for you. I used to be able to, when you were with Paravox.'

They fell silent, the spectre of Ben's redundancy in the air between them. The firm he used to work for had pioneered a computer voice reproduction system that had been superseded by rival technology. Some of his colleagues had been offered posts in the other firm, but Ben's field had been too specialised, too tied to the now obsolete system, to enable him to transfer.

'Have you applied for any more jobs lately?' Shelley asked, injecting a note of false brightness. For a long time she had stopped asking, since it was demoralising to both of them to realise just how few potential jobs there were for him.

'Well, I picked up one or two through the Internet.'

'Really? What were they?'

'Both below my position at Paravox, but I have to expect that now.'

'I suppose so.' She leaned forward, putting her arm around his shoulder. 'Did you apply?'

'Yes, again through the Net. Should hear in a couple of days whether they want to take it further.'

'That's good news, love.'

Shelley shuffled down onto the floor, cuddling up to him. She could sense that he still didn't quite trust her, probably thought she was just being nice to him to make up for her earlier faux pas. Maybe the only way would be to make love to him, to show him by deed, not just by word, that she was sorry and wanted to make amends. She began to kiss his cheek, his neck, undoing his top button so that she could plant her lips in the hollow at his throat. He sat on, impassively staring into the fire.

Slowly Shelley unbuttoned his shirt and pulled it out of his jeans. He smelt of clean sweat, strong and animal. She felt her libido rising and kissed all over his hairy chest, lingering at the tiny points of his nipples. Still he seemed unmoved. She put her ear against the sculptured curve of his breast and listened for his heart. It was beating with a dull, steady thud. Although Shelley had the urge to tell him that she loved him, somehow she had the feeling he wouldn't believe her. He was acting very strangely. Evidently the cogs of his mind were turning over some issue that he couldn't speak of yet. Perhaps she could manage to distract him.

Slowly Shelley unfastened the heavy brass belt buckle at his navel and then undid the button beneath. She slid down the zipper and pulled his jeans down far enough to expose his red underpants, but was disappointed to find little sign of life in there. Returning to his lips she tried to coax them into kissing her, pressing her mouth to his with insistent fervour. At last he turned his head to the side and tried to push her away.

'Don't, Shelley. I'm not in the mood. Okay?'

'I'm sorry. Is it because of me forgetting our anniversary?' He shook his head. 'Maybe we shouldn't have started talking about work, then. It was bound to upset you.'

'It's not that!' he snapped.

Shelley stared at him in consternation. 'What, then? For God's sake tell me, can't you?'

The look he gave her then made her wish she hadn't asked. She knew what was going through his mind, knew that he feared her reply and yet had to ask the question. And she knew she was going to have to decide whether to lie or tell the truth.

'All right, I just want you to answer me straight. Are you sleeping with anyone else?'

Shelley panicked like a creature in a forest fire, not knowing which way to jump. 'I . . . er, no. Not really. I mean, I haven't exactly been entirely faithful, but it wasn't . . . it didn't mean anything.' She covered her prevaricating face with her hands. 'Oh God! Yes, I suppose the answer has to be yes. I did sleep with someone, but it's over. Finished. And it was never remotely serious or significant.'

'I see. Just a one-night stand then, was it?'

She glanced through her fingers at him. He was still motionless, staring into the red heart of the embers. 'Something like that. Look, Ben, I'm really sorry. I thought there was no hope for us, and I just felt so wound up and frustrated. He happened to be on hand.'

'Who was it, someone at work? At that conference.' She nodded, seeing no reason to deny it. 'Was it that Duncan fellow?'

'Does it matter who it was?'

'Not to you, perhaps. I knew you fancied him. Well, did he live up to your expectations?'

His tone had turned bitter, cruel even. She got up, feeling vaguely threatened. This was the first time she'd cheated on him and there was no knowing how he might react.

But the long, brooding silence continued, straining her nerves to the utmost. 'I'm sorry, Ben,' she repeated, but the effort was futile. 'Perhaps I'd better sleep in the spare room tonight. I'm very tired. We'll talk in the morning if you want.'

He said nothing, so she left him there in his misery. If there was any healing to be done to their marriage, it could not take place right then, not while he was still set against her in cold anger. Shelley crept upstairs and fell into the spare bed, without even taking off her robe. It would do as a nightgown. She lay there waiting for him to come up, but the night wore on and there was no sound of him moving from the front room. Deep in her breast her heart felt leaden. She recalled with shame her abandoned love-making with Duncan. Had it really happened on the same day as this? And how was it that she was able to throw herself wholeheartedly into having sex with that unfeeling bastard while the man she really wanted to love couldn't turn her on? Was she psychologically perverse in some way?

At last she heard the familiar noises of doors being locked downstairs and knew that Ben was on the way to bed. Shelley sighed with relief and turned on her side. Maybe, now everything was out in the open, they could start to rebuild their marriage. But, lying there alone in the dark hours before dawn, it seemed a forlorn hope.

Chapter Four

Ben was alone in the house for three days, while Shelley visited her mother. Work had been slack at Harcourt so she'd taken some leave and since Ben was not particularly fond of his mother-in-law (it was mutual) his wife had gone off to Dorset on her own. Besides, as Shelley had said, it gave both of them a breathing-space to consider what they wanted out of life. And whether they still wanted each other.

The fact that she'd slept with another man still rankled, yet Ben couldn't pretend he wasn't somehow to blame. Since losing his job he'd become a bore and a slob. He would be the first to admit it. Ben knew he had to do something to restore his self-esteem, or his marriage would break up and then he'd feel even more of a loser. He knew he was starting on a hopeless downward spiral, where it would become increasingly hard to recover from each setback.

Meanwhile, however, there was always the Internet. Ben spent the whole of Monday communicating with individuals that he suspected were similar no-hopers to himself. Who else had the time to surf the net all day? Only skiving students, the disabled or the unemployed, presumably. There could be a few idle rich out there but, somehow, he doubted it. Added to

which, the general level of electronically transmitted conversation was about as stimulating as a teenage fanzine or an
unremitting diet of Adrian Mole.

Even those alt.sex news-groups had lost their appeal.
Adolescent porno ravings, most of them, each trying to outdo
the other in outrageousness. Ben still read them, though, just
in case. And occasionally he was rewarded. Like today.

His attention was caught by a presumably female (although
you never knew for sure) user who had decided to bare
all, soul-wise, to whoever was into 'alt.sex.femdom'. Her
name was Trix, which Ben soon realised must be short for
'Dominatrix', and her accounts of how she lived with her two
sex-slaves proved very diverting.

'I have two slaves, one male and one female,' she began.
*'They are both entirely dedicated to my service and spend every
weekend with me, without fail. Although they both hold
positions of power in the business world, they obey my every
whim. 'Thing' is a hunky, well-built young male, with blonde
hair and blue eyes, the kind any woman would love to take to
her bed. 'Stuff' is a beautiful woman with long dark hair and
brown eyes. They make the perfect couple and, if they were not
both totally devoted to me, they would probably get it together.
Yet they are so afraid of my displeasure that they would never
dare to meet outside our weekend meetings.*

*Last weekend was fairly typical. Thing and Stuff got into
their costumes as soon as they arrived. Thing wears leather
cuffs and anklets together with a leather harness that loops
round his balls but leaves his dick free to expand. I like Stuff to
wear sexy, feminine clothes and she makes her own. She's very
handy with a needle and surprises me each time. This time she
wore a black halter-neck top in shiny nylon that came below her
bust and showed off her lovely tits, pushing them up like a*

corset. She also wore pink velvet hot pants with poppers underneath, black fishnet stockings and knee-high boots in soft, crinkly black leather. Fabulous!

As usual I lounged on the antique chaise longue in my back room with a box of chocolates while the pair of them did my housework. I love watching Thing's bare arse shaking as he puts plenty of effort into scrubbing out the grate, or polishing the floor. Stuff usually does the more delicate work, like dusting my porcelain collection.

From time to time I ordered them to stop working on the house and work on Thing's erection instead. He is particularly well endowed and I like to see his thingy up and ready. Even though I might have no intention of doing anything about it, it's there just in case. So I made him stand, legs apart, from time to time while Stuff knelt and gave him a good tonguing just to restore his thingy to maximum proportions.

Anyway, they both slaved so hard at making my house spick and span from top to bottom, that I decided they deserved a reward. I don't usually do rewards, it being more in my nature to dole out punishments, but I'd finished all my chocs except for two disgusting strawberry creams and as I was about to ask Stuff to throw them in the bin I had a better idea.

'Come here, Stuff!' I snarled. 'Take this and stuff it into your little box.'

She obeyed unquestioningly as always, squatting down then undoing her poppers so that she could insert the strawberry cream into her pussy.

'Now Thing, lick it out!' I commanded him.

Stuff lay on her back with her tits pointing upwards where I could reach down and feel them whenever I wanted. Her legs were wide apart and her shaven lips were smooth and juicy. I saw the gleam in Thing's eye as he went down on her, but just in case he got carried away I tightened the harness around his balls making his eyes water.

'I want it all licked out, every last bit,' I warned him, menacingly.

I've never seen his tongue extended so far into Stuff's quim before. He gobbled and slurped as the chocolate juice ran out of her and into his mouth. She wriggled and moaned until I told her not to, then she just lay there like a taut wire, ready to snap at any moment.

'Can you still feel it inside you?' I asked Stuff, after a while.

'Yes, Mistress.'

I delivered a well-aimed flick of my whip across Thing's buttocks, just above where his balls dangled. 'You must do better!'

He took his stained mouth from her brown-streaked quim for a few seconds, keeping his eyes cast down. 'Yes, Mistress. Sorry, Mistress.'

With renewed enthusiasm Thing began sucking again but it was soon obvious that Stuff, like a prize idiot, had stuffed the choccy too far up her chuff and he was only getting at the melted bits. So I ordered her to use her inner muscles to expel the thing into Thing's mouth.

Stuff took a deep breath and then pushed with all her strength. The choc flew out of her with the force of a ballistic missile and caught Thing at the back of the throat, half choking him. He coughed and spluttered for about five minutes and I had to slap him hard on the back to prevent his asphyxiation. What a good job I chose a soft centre, I thought. Think what damage might have been inflicted with a hazelnut crunch!'

Ben giggled over the ludicrous account. There was no way of telling whether it was true, of course. The Internet was a wonderful vehicle for fantasy. Even so, it gave him food for thought. He began wondering if that was the kind of relationship he would like to develop with Shelley. He already felt in a subordinate position, with no income of his own, no real function. Maybe there would be some emotional gratification in being his wife's sex slave, in obeying her every wish instead of kicking against the pricks or acting sullen and resentful. Was he capable of playing that totally subservient rôle?

The thought of subjecting himself to that degree of degradation was weirdly fascinating. Scary, too. Then he wondered if he would enjoy the reverse, having his independent and successful wife turn into a compliant submissive the minute she arrived home. Now that was an altogether more attractive prospect!

Slowly Ben built up a fantasy as he lay alone in bed that night. He imagined Shelley arriving home and going straight upstairs to change into her costume. A French maid's outfit would be nice, with a very short black skirt and nothing up top except the bib of a frilly white apron that scarcely covered her pretty, freckled breasts. She would wear the obligatory black stockings and high heeled shoes, of course, and when she turned round the skirt would have a hole cut in it to show off her bottom cleavage. That would be especially nice when she bent over to be spanked. She would be wearing no underwear of any description, since her stockings would be held up by garters.

Savouring the image that he had conjured up in his mind, Ben let his hand drop to fondle his balls for a while. The familiar heat began to curl slowly through his loins, pumping blood into his prick and making it stir a little. Now he imagined himself sitting in the front room, perhaps reading the paper with a drink at his elbow, waiting for his wife to appear. When she did it would be on all fours. She would crawl over the carpet towards him and lick his boots, by way of salutation.

The thought of her boobs hanging heavy beneath their inadequate covering, and her pink buttocks showing through the window in her skirt, hastened the progress of his erection. He would devise little tasks for her, just waiting for her to make some small mistake like spilling a drop of his drink or creasing his newspaper. As soon as she did he would pounce on her with a cry of, 'Naughty, naughty girl! You must be punished!'

Humbly she would bend over his knee, presenting her trembling behind to his bare hand for chastisement. As he slapped her hard the flesh would wobble and redden. Then he would send her into the kitchen to prepare his meal. If she did that well, cooking the food and serving it up faultlessly, she would be spared further punishment and instead he might offer to reward her. She would be so grateful, her face would light up as she prepared to do what she most loved doing in all the world.

Carefully she would take down his trousers and ease his throbbing erection out of his pants. Then she would sit beside him, her beautiful breasts on full display so he could fondle them at will, and bend her pretty lips to his penis. Ben felt the organ in question swell to its fullest extent beneath the duvet and he grasped it with his right hand, beginning the regular firm strokings that he knew would bring him swiftly to his climax.

Shelley would take infinite pains over her act of fellatio, for she knew that if she failed to please him she would be punished. She knew exactly how he liked it, delicate fingers at first and not too much friction to the sensitive glans, only gradually introducing the end of his prick into her soft, capacious mouth. She would spend some time licking around the shaft and easing him in and out of her mouth, simulating intercourse. Only later, when he was fully aroused and eager for more action, would she take the whole of his pulsating member into her mouth and let him thrust right into her throat without gagging. Keeping her sharp little teeth well out of the way so they only grazed his flesh, not bit into it, she would contrive to keep him hovering on the edge of an orgasm for up to half an hour before finally coaxing him over the edge and letting him come deep in her mouth, shooting his white juice right down into her stomach, the way she liked it.

As the fantasy had the desired effect, Ben felt himself spurt into the warm reaches of the bed and he groaned aloud with the relief. He had been ready for that all day. While the dying spasms filled his limbs with tingling he smiled to himself at the absurdity of his dream. Shelley couldn't bear him coming in her mouth. As for the rest, it wasn't even worth thinking about except as a visual aid to masturbation. Still, it had worked a treat for that.

The following afternoon Ben paid one of his obligatory visits to the Job Centre. How he hated those condescending women, with their niggling little questions: how many letters of application, how many replies have you received, how many interviews? He didn't even bother to pretend any more. They were talking of sending him on some daft scheme – 'Workfit' they called it, or 'Workshy' or 'Fit for Nothing' maybe. They talked as if he couldn't even sign his name without someone guiding his hand. The fact that he'd once held down a highly technical and prestigious job seemed to have slipped their minds.

After waiting around for hours in a dingy, depressing room Ben returned home to find nothing much to eat. He cheered up at the thought of going to the supermarket. Bright lights, sweet music and spend, spend, spend . . . whoopee! Fortunately Shelley was still letting him pay for groceries out of their once-joint account despite the fact that she was the only one putting any money into it these days.

Normally, on a Tuesday night, the supermarket would be quiet but tonight it seemed unusually busy. Giant red heart-shaped balloons were floating above the door, and there was a banner proclaiming 'Singles Night'. Ben remembered the poster he'd seen and smiled. This should be fun! Just for once he could pretend to be unattached and maybe he'd get away with it. Shelley wasn't due back until tomorrow night, so he might even score!

The thought was rather scary, but exciting too. If his wife could screw someone else, why shouldn't he have some fun? As he went in through the doors, wheeling his trolley, a pretty girl handed him a long-stemmed red carnation. 'For you to donate to the lady of your choice, Sir,' she explained, with a smile. Romantic music was coming out of the walls and there were hearts and flowers everywhere together with recommendations for aphrodisiac foods, seductive cocktails, breakfasts-in-bed. Some couples had already got into the swing of things and were actually waltzing up and down the aisles.

Once Ben had got used to the party atmosphere, he began to eye up the talent. Some of the women looked so predatory that he avoided their eye and hurried past surveying the shelves, pretending to be there just for the shopping. Then he saw someone he fancied, over by the frozen peas. She was small and slim, with short blonde hair and a neat little bottom shown off by skin-tight jeans. She looked young, no older than twenty, and when she glanced up at him her face gave a welcoming smile.

'Hullo,' he grinned back. 'Anything good in the frozen cabinet, then?'

He cursed himself for such a lame remark. As a chat-up line it was not the most sophisticated he'd ever uttered, but she didn't seem to mind. 'Ice cream on special offer,' she told him. 'And some yummy cakes. I was just wondering whether to have the lemon gateau or the double choc.'

'I'm afraid I'd have to go for the chocolate. I'm a bit of an addict.'

'Me too,' she confessed.

Emboldened by the warm glint in her brown eyes he suggested that they might buy one between them and share it, then they needn't feel quite so guilty.

'It would take a while to defrost,' she said.

'That's okay, I've got all night. How about you?'

She giggled, held out her hand. Every finger had a ring on. 'My name's Carol.'

'And I'm Ben. I haven't eaten yet, have you? To tell the truth, I'd forgotten this was going to be Singles Night.'

'Great idea, isn't it? Mr Broadbent, the manager – he's my neighbour, well my Mum's actually – anyway he got the idea from an episode of 'Baywatch'. They do this sort of thing a lot in America, apparently. Have you ever been?'

'To America? Yes, I have.'

'Ooh, lucky you! I'd love to go. I can't afford it this year, but I'm saving up for next summer. What's it like?'

Ben frowned. 'Hard to say, really. I went on business, so I spent most of my time in Silicon Valley.'

'Is that near that place where all those tall red rocks are? The ones they show in all the Westerns?'

'I don't think so. It's in California. Where they do computer research.'

'Oh, do you work in computers then?'

Her tone had gone flat, along with Ben's mood. He didn't want to be reminded of his old job, especially not after that afternoon's session. 'Not any more. Look, I was going to suggest that you might like to eat with me tonight. We could go to a restaurant.'

'I'd rather we got some food here. Then I can pick out what I like, if that's okay. Can we take it back to your place to cook it, though, because my flatmate's got her boyfriend there and it's a rather small flat and, well, you know.'

Ben was cheered by her openness, her trust. He didn't want to refuse her, but he was afraid that the minute she walked in through his door it would be obvious that he was married.

'All right,' he agreed at last, too overwhelmed by the ease with which he seemed to have scored to argue. He was flattered that she felt comfortable enough to go home with him on their first date. It was a most promising start to the evening.

He followed her tight little butt around the supermarket, assessing the size of her breasts beneath the pale pink sweatshirt, happy to let her throw anything she fancied into his trolley. It reminded him of the early days with Shelley, of gleefully wandering around Waitrose together, discovering each other's likes and dislikes.

When they arrived at Ben's house, laden with groceries, Carol was impressed by the mock Tudor splendour of his semi. 'Is this it? It's quite posh, isn't it. I'd love a house like this.'

'Where do you live then, Carol?'

'In a really grungy flat over a betting shop. Still, it's all I can afford on my money.'

She looked around as they went in. Ben did the same,

searching for clues to a feminine presence. Apart from Shelley's jacket hanging on the hall stand and a pair of women's shoes tucked underneath, which Carol appeared not to notice, he could find nothing on the ground floor. The bathroom would be a dead giveaway, of course. He showed his guest into the front room, excused himself and hurried upstairs to sweep all the tell-tale toiletries into a cupboard.

Afterwards Ben felt guilty. If Carol asked whether he was married he wasn't going to lie to the girl, but he told himself there was no point in jeopardising their first evening together. He was expecting nothing more from their encounter but light diversion, and so far there was no evidence that Carol had any higher expectations. If she did, the time would come when he'd have to let her down gently.

Ben put some music on the CD player and then went into the kitchen. Most of the food they'd chosen was easily heated up in the microwave. He placed a bottle of white wine in the fridge, then returned to the front room where Carol was looking very at home with her bare feet tucked under her on the sofa. She commented on the music, the décor, the plants, but Ben had little to say at first. He soon realised how unused he was to chatting up girls – or just to chatting, for that matter. His lifestyle had become essentially anti-social, since he saw none of his old work mates and Shelley tended to go out with her own friends rather than inviting them back home. There were a few mutual friends they saw occasionally, for old times sake, but on the whole Ben led a more or less solitary existence.

'Do you like watching telly?' Carol asked eventually, evidently stuck for something to say.

'Actually I spend more time on the Internet, these days.'

'Oh, that's computers again, isn't it?'

It was obvious that she knew very little about the information super-highway. Once they'd polished off their meal, Ben decided to educate Carol about the joys of cybersurfing. It also seemed an excellent way to get their minds focused on sexual activity. He switched on the computer and, after a brief introduction, started scrolling down.

'Look, there's the alt.sex stories,' he told her, as if he'd only just discovered them. 'Shall we see what's going on there?'

She giggled, excitedly. Slowly he scrolled through the subgroups, where all the sexual fetishes known to man (and woman) were represented – and probably many unknown as well. Alt.sex.alien.abduct looked interesting. All those weird grey beings with long probes that went into every orifice. Then there was alt.sex.bagpipe, (which he knew from previous browsing referred to the quaint custom of armpit fucking) alt.sex.ringpulls (presumably they weren't talking beer-cans), alt.sex.sporran (so that *is* where they keep it!), and alt.sex.subaqua (Ooh, those rubber wetsuits and phallic snorkels!).

'Let me know if you're interested in anything, and I'll download it,' Ben told her. It occurred to him that this was a useful way of sussing out a potential bedmate's sexual preferences.

Unfortunately the one Carol eventually picked was alt.sex. megadongs. Ben was not amused. Although by no means under-endowed, he could not compete with 'tadgers like truncheons', 'didgeridoodles' or 'trouser snakes like anacondas'. She giggled her way through the accounts of male prowess and then asked if he could download her alt.sex.deepthroat, which sounded a lot more promising.

What followed were detailed instructions on how to give a blow job. Carol was paying serious attention. In fact, she looked like she was taking mental notes. Ben found himself becoming somewhat embarrassed, not to say aroused, and went into the kitchen to brew some coffee. By the time he came back, Carol had finished reading the item and was sitting on the sofa, smiling.

'Well, I've learned a thing or two today!' she told him, taking her coffee.

Ben felt bolder. 'Feel like putting theory into practice, then?'

He laughed, making light of it, but to his amazement she took him seriously. 'Okay. When I've drunk my coffee.'

He wasn't used to women being so matter-of-fact about sex. On reflection he realised he'd been out of circulation for almost six years, so times had probably changed a good deal. Or was it just that women who went to 'Singles Nights' were less inhibited?

Ben settled onto the sofa beside Carol and put his arm around her. He already had a hard on. It was a novelty to be with someone smaller than his wife, more compact, and he liked the way her small breasts pressed close to his chest as he cuddled her. Tentatively he put his right hand on her left breast and squeezed it gently through her pink sweatshirt. She responded eagerly, turning her face to his to be kissed. Ben's lips closed slowly over hers, enjoying the way her mouth yielded at once to the pressure, opening a little. He slid his tongue between the moist flesh of her lips, aware of her fingers toying with the thick layers of his hair, gradually penetrating further into the warm cavern of her mouth where her tongue waited to greet his.

Encouraged, Ben slipped his hand beneath the loose sweat-shirt and felt smooth, naked skin. He moved up to her bra, which felt like one of the minimal variety, two skimpy triangles joined together which allowed him to feel the contours of the shapely mounds they contained. Through the thin nylon her nipples stood out like ornamental studs and Carol squirmed with delight when he took one firmly between finger and thumb and gave it an experimental squeeze.

'That feels good!' she murmured, interrupting their kiss. 'Wait a sec, I'll take my top off.'

Quickly she stripped to her bra and Ben's eyes went straight to her chest, confirming what his fingers had detected. Although small, her tits were round and firm, needing little support. Smiling seductively Carol reached round her back and undid the garment.

'Nice breasts,' Ben commented, feeling suddenly self-conscious. He was unused to being intimate with strange women. It brought back recollections of teenage fumblings, memories calculated to sap his confidence.

Yet Carol seemed to have confidence enough for both of them. She began to unbutton his shirt, dotting his neck with light kisses while her hands spread eagerly over his exposed skin, feeling the muscles and the light covering of hair. She kissed his nipples briefly, making his stomach contract with longing, then undid the belt of his jeans. Ben felt the weight of her breasts in his hands as she bent over him and began gently pulling at the downward pointing nipples. She murmured with pleasure. Her hands pulled at his zipper until the front of his pants was exposed and his penis was making its presence known in a very obvious way.

'Lovely!' she sighed, the minute his tumescent organ came into her grasp. She proceeded to give it a thorough inspection. 'Yours is a nice pink colour,' she declared. 'I hate them when they're all white and pasty-looking. It's a good size – I don't like them *too* big – and there's a nice head on it, too, with a good straight shaft.'

She sounded like a member of CAMRA trying out a new ale. Ben didn't know whether to be flattered by her compliments or disturbed that she seemed to have such a wide basis for comparison.

As soon as she began stroking his dick, with long plucking movements of her fingers, all Ben's misgivings disappeared. He could feel the blood rushing to fill every spare inch, extending his erection even more, and he settled back to let her get on with it in her own enthusiastic fashion. She rolled his penis between her palms, massaged it with her fingertips in tiny circles, alternated firm friction at the root of his shaft with gentler touches near the top. Soon his glans was covered with a film of sticky fluid and messages were winging their way through his nervous system in throbbing code, signalling 'Yes, yes!' and 'More, more!'

Carol was obviously getting excited herself and after a couple of minutes she took off her shoes, unzipped her jeans and stripped to her underpants. Smiling cheekily over her shoulder she said, 'I like having my bum felt, and you can touch up my pussy too, if you like. Only I never remove my panties on a first date, okay?'

'That's fine by me,' Ben assured her, amazed they'd even got that far.

So while Carol knelt astride him, facing south, and bent her blonde head to deliver tip-of-the-tongue licks to his impatiently thrusting cock, Ben pushed his hands down the top of her bikini-style pants and felt the plush skin of her taut little bottom against his palms.

Carol opened her thighs a little and arched her back like a sensual feline creature, her bum spreading wide. Holding her stretched buttocks, Ben let his thumbs trail along the divide in between. He was scarcely in control of himself any more, his

penis playing a dangerous game of brinkmanship in response
to the rhythmic licking it was getting. Recklessly he let his
right hand slip below the lower curves of her bottom and,
before he knew it, his finger was probing between her tumid
labia. He waited with bated breath for her to tell him to stop
but no such instructions came, so he delved further into the
sticky wetness until he found the dark entrance his finger was
blindly seeking.

Deep inside her cunny Ben felt the walls contract, squeezing his finger tightly, and the sensation was just too much for
his self control. The unstoppable rush towards orgasm had
begun. Sensing his extreme arousal, Carol was now letting
him thrust hard against the soft palate of her mouth and soon
she was making inarticulate gurgling noises as his milky juice
shot into her throat and Ben's mind exploded into pure
sensuality. Fierce, hot energy waves enveloped him, flowed
around and through him, lifted him up to the peak then left
him to slowly sink down again in weary bliss.

'God, that was fantastic!' he breathed, as his de-tumescent
penis slid out of Carol's mouth and his finger withdrew from
her pussy. He lay back on the sofa, still panting, while she
snuggled up to him.

'I like giving head,' she said, frankly. 'I can't understand
why some women don't, really.'

After a while Ben recovered enough to ask her whether she
wanted him to return the favour. In the old days he would
simply have tried it on and wait to be encouraged or rebuffed
but Carol seemed to prefer a more verbal approach. Besides,
from what he'd heard about date rape, women these days
practically wanted you to sign a contract before you touched
them.

To his dismay, she looked at her watch. 'Look, it's half

eleven so I think I should be going. I promised my flatmate I'd
be back by midnight. We've got this stupid burglar alarm, see,
with it being over the shop and everything, so it has to be set at
a certain time and her boyfriend's staying the night so she
wants me to do it when I get in.'

'Sounds a bit restricting.'

'Yes. We've asked the landlord to change it, but it's his shop
and . . . anyway, I've got to go. But it's been great, Ben. I'm
glad I went shopping tonight!'

'Can I give you a ring? I'd like to see you again.'

Carol rose, starting to dress. 'I'm not actually on the phone,
and Hamid doesn't like us to use the shop number. But if
you'd like to give me your number, I'll ring you at the
weekend.'

Ben felt downcast. He didn't like leaving the ball in Carol's
court. On the other hand, she hadn't exactly refused to see
him again. He wrote the number down in her address book
and then offered to drive her home.

'That's okay, I can get a taxi. Can I use your phone?'

'I'll do it!' Ben leapt up, remembering that his wife's clothes
were on the hall stand with the phone. He went out into the
hall, praying she wouldn't follow, and called the cab.

After Carol had gone, Ben sat in front of the television but
his mind was miles away. Much as he had enjoyed the evening,
it seemed to present him with more problems than it solved.
Obviously he couldn't invite Carol back to the house when
Shelley was there, but it sounded as if they couldn't use her
place either. He was reminded of the frustrations of his
teenage years, of gropings at parties and furtive screws while
girls were 'baby-sitting'. Maybe he would just have to come
clean about being married and hope she didn't mind becoming
his mistress and having assignations on neutral ground. Some

women found such affairs exciting, or so he'd heard. It would certainly be a welcome diversion for a frustrated out-of-work house husband whose wife was also screwing around!

Chapter Five

Ben had definitely been acting strangely lately, Shelley decided as she drove to work. It wasn't anything she could put her finger on, just a brighter edge to his presence. She'd heard him whistling in the kitchen the other day, something she couldn't recall him doing since they were first married. And he'd gone shopping in the West End and bought some Calvin Klein underpants, two snazzy shirts and a cashmere sweater, using their joint account. Not that she had the heart to query it. She was pleased that he seemed to be taking interest in his appearance again, but something told her it was not just in order to improve his image at job interviews. Could he possibly be having an affair?

The idea both amused and disturbed her. Shelley felt she couldn't blame him if he was getting a bit on the side. She hadn't been an enthusiastic bedmate for ages, and no doubt his ego had taken a battering when he found out about her fling with Duncan. Yet where could he possibly meet other women – at the supermarket, amongst the washing powders? The thought of Ben discussing biological stain removal with his supposed lover made her giggle as she pulled in to the staff car park of Harcourt Productions.

They were filming a training video that day and, as she entered the studio, Shelley was pleased to see that Steve Lord was one of the cameramen. It made her job easier if the agency sent staff she'd already worked with, and Steve was one of her favourites. He had an easy-going manner that made the atmosphere in the studio a lot more pleasant.

Today he greeted her with a grin, his blue eyes lingering on her body, taking in the details of her curves beneath the pink velour top and black pants. 'Hi, Shelley. I gather it's going to be talking heads most of today. Not much room for my famous creative camerawork there!'

'We can't all be David Bailey!' she laughed. 'Anyway, make Cecil Barker and his pals look good and you might get some freebies.'

'What, a doll with a willy? No thanks!'

Barker Toys made anatomically correct dolls. Shelley had a feeling that the training video for their sales staff was going to be hilarious, but she would have to keep a straight face. That meant she would have to avoid Steve's eye, at all costs!

The morning's work was relatively straightforward. Cecil Barker gave his introductory pep talk and then followed a couple of dramatised sequences on a set designed to look like a toy shop. The Barker sales rep was extolling the virtues of the dolls to a shop owner, and Shelley's fears turned out to be well-founded: the selling pitch was ludicrous. The earnest female rep sounded like a crusading evangelist as she condemned the 'complexes' that generations of children must have acquired through playing with dolls that had no genitalia.

'Children without brothers or sisters secretly believed they were deformed,' she asserted. 'And as for Barbie and Ken, their relationship could never have been anything other than platonic. Nowadays, with so much more openness about sex, parents are demanding lifelike detail in the dolls they buy for their children.'

'Steve, did you get a good enough close-up on the doll that time?' Shelley asked, once the scene was shot.

His mouth twitched at her, barely containing his amusement. 'I'm not sure it was anatomically correct enough, Shelley.'

She stifled a laugh. 'Okay, let's take a couple more shots and edit them in afterwards. That's a wrap, the rest of you. See you back in the studio at two sharp.'

Soon only Shelley and Steve remained. As the cameraman moved around the set getting the best camera angles on the dolls, the atmosphere was quiet but strangely tense. Shelley realised that the air was filled with an electricity that had nothing to do with the studio. She'd been aware of the spark of attraction between her and the handsome cameraman for some time but never before had it struck her quite so forcefully. She stood aside as he bent low to capture the dolls, his lithe body moving here and there with an animal grace, wholly focused on the task in hand. Then, when he'd got all he wanted, he turned and smiled.

'Okay, that's it,' he said, his voice warm and husky. 'Buy you a drink?'

Shelley felt her heart lift. 'That would be nice. I'll get my bag and meet you at the door.'

They didn't go to the King's Arms over the road, where everyone else went. Instead Steve took her to the *Bon Viveur* round the corner, where they drank white wine and ate seafood. Shelley found herself becoming secretly aroused as she sat close to him in the crowded wine bar, knees touching under the table, and the alcohol loosening her inhibitions a little.

'I don't think I'll be doing this sort of work for much longer,' Steve told her, after they'd discussed the morning's filming.

'I'm getting to the stage when I can afford to pick and choose I'd rather take the more creative assignments.'

'Really?' Shelley was disappointed. She'd come to rely on him turning up regularly at the studio. 'Well, I'll miss you Steve. It makes my job a lot easier when I know the crew.'

'Of course.' He smiled, enigmatically, running a hand through his casual mop of dark blonde hair. 'Same here. I've always liked working with you, Shelley, you know that, but Harcourt don't provide the kind of stimulating work I need. If I hadn't had my own projects to work on these past few years I'd have gone nuts!'

'Your own projects? That sounds interesting.'

He looked as if he'd already said too much, and Shelley wasn't going to press him. But then his expression changed. He leaned forward and said, confidentially, 'I've set up a studio in my flat so I can do glamour photography.'

'Really? What, "page three girls" and stuff?'

'Something like that. It's what I really enjoy doing. I've built up quite a few outlets now, and it won't be long before I can give up this sort of job altogether.'

'I see. Well good luck to you, Steve.'

He hesitated a moment, his blue eyes searching hers. 'Actually I was wondering if you'd consider modelling for me, Shelley.'

She laughed incredulously. '*Me*?'

'Yes. I think you'd be very photogenic.'

'But I've had absolutely no experience of that sort of thing.'

The idea excited her nevertheless. As he talked, Shelley was aware of the flush rising in her cheeks, the animated tone in her voice. There was no way she could pretend she wasn't interested in taking up his invitation. Even as a child she had fantasised about being a model, and the dream had never quite faded. Besides, she knew that, if anyone could make her look good in front of a camera, Steve could. There was a rapport between them that would guarantee spectacular results, and what woman could resist being transformed into a pin-up?

'Are you free tonight?' she heard him say. 'If we dropped into my flat I could show you some of the work I've done and maybe take a few test shots. Then, if you wanted to continue, we could make an appointment for another time.'

Shelley didn't take long to make up her mind. 'I'd like that,' she said, quietly.

Steve looked pleased. The sexual tension was still there between them but was put on hold as they got themselves back into the right frame of mind for the afternoon's work. They discussed it briefly as they walked back to the studios. They parted with an agreement to meet in the car park after the day's shooting.

At the end of the afternoon Shelley went off to the cloakroom to repair her make-up. She looked at herself critically in the mirror: large, wide-set eyes that hovered between grey and blue; a mouth that seemed soft and vulnerable when tinted, as now, with glossy peach; skin that appeared matt and flawless when she used a honey-toned foundation; hair that had been called 'carrot' when she was a child but which had, thankfully, deepened to a subtle auburn so full of rich highlights that she didn't have to dye it. Overall, Shelley liked what she saw and she guessed that Steve did too, or he wouldn't have asked her to pose for him.

But was his interest in her purely professional? She wondered about this as she made her way to the front exit. A large part of her rather hoped not – she had always fancied Steve. Since her last ignominious encounter with Duncan, she'd been avoiding her boss as much as possible. She had vowed not to mix business and pleasure ever again, but if Steve was unlikely to work for Harcourt in future that was no longer an issue. Yes, she mused, a half-smile forming on her newly glossed lips, an affair with Steve might suit her very well indeed!

They travelled in separate cars, Shelley doing her best to keep track of his as they shunted through the rush-hour traffic. Eventually he drew up outside a thirties-style block of flats.

'This is it,' he grinned, coming to open her car door. 'Welcome to Horatio Court.'

Steve led her through the swing doors and up in the lift, where Shelley felt the attraction between them heightening with their proximity to each other, making her feel weak-kneed and forcing her to lean against the padded wall. She was relieved when the lift stopped at the fifth floor and they got out. Following Steve along the corridor, Shelley knew that if he made a pass at her later she would have no will to resist.

His flat was dominated by French windows leading onto a balcony that overlooked that part of the city. While she admired the view, Steve poured them each a drink and then took her through to his studio. He had converted the main bedroom, blacking out the window to create a totally enclosed world. There were lights and cables everywhere, tripods, a full-length mirror mounted on castors, large white umbrellas, various other props and a huge mahogany wardrobe.

'This is it, Studio Steve!' he announced, with a sweeping gesture of his arm.

Shelley began to examine the photos on the walls. They were all of women in various erotic poses, some more suggestive than others. She saw a red-haired girl kneeling on all fours on a leopardskin rug with her back arched and her pretty face contorted in a snarl. One arm was raised, the fingers curved like claws. It was powerfully eloquent, her black-fringed eyes looking straight out at the viewer with primitive energy, and yet there was a tongue-in-cheek aspect to it as if she didn't expect anyone to take her seriously.

Steve stood at her elbow, to give her a commentary. 'That's Danni, she works for a top model agency now. I helped get her on the ladder. Wonderful personality, great body, I knew she'd go far.'

'Who's this?' Shelley pointed to a chubby sexpot, her pink nylon negligee artfully arranged over her ample breasts. She looked as if someone had just surprised her in the bedroom.

'Oh, that's Janella. Page Three Girl. You may have heard of her.'

'Janella Hawkes?'

'You have heard of her.'

'Of course, hasn't everybody? I suppose you gave her her first big break too.'

Steve smiled, smugly. 'Don't say that in her manager's presence! Recognise this face?'

Shelley stared at the sophisticated beauty in the G-string, holding a single lily between her shapely breasts. Despite the classic proportions of her face and figure the woman looked nervous and a bit incredulous, as if she couldn't imagine why anyone should want to photograph her. 'It's not Melody James, is it?'

'The very same!'

Shelley let out a breathy whistle. The woman had just been voted Top Model of the Year. 'I'm impressed!'

'So you should be. She posed for me as a favour, long before she hit the catwalk. I was getting my portfolio together at the same time as she was doing hers, so we struck a deal.'

Staring at the gallery of beautiful faces Shelley suddenly felt humbled. 'But why on earth did you want to photograph me, Steve, when you could have all these lovely models to choose from?'

He grinned, fixing an aggressive-looking lens to one of his cameras. 'I told you, Shelley, I photographed all these girls at the beginning of their careers, long before they became famous. I'm not interested in established models.' He came over and held her by the shoulders, peering intently into her face, thinking hard. Then he relaxed a little, going on to explain, 'What I like to capture is camera shyness. The quality that a woman has when she's still unsure what the lens is going to make of her, when she lacks confidence. It's a kind of virginity, in a way. Once a girl has had her naked body probed by the camera a few times, that particular quality vanishes, melts away, never to return. Can you understand?'

'I think so.' Shelley looked back at the photos on the wall. There was a certain uniformity in the expressions of those women, now she came to think of it, a nervous apprehension that belied whatever efforts they were making to strike a confident attitude.

'I've been thinking about how I'd like you to pose,' he said, making her heart-rate suddenly accelerate. 'We'll just take a few with you in your underclothes, to see how it goes. You needn't undress entirely.'

Oddly enough, Shelley felt disappointed. She'd braced herself to bare all for the camera, and now it felt like an anti-climax. Mentally she reviewed her underwear: black padded 'shaper' bra with plenty of uplift, and matching briefs cut high over the thigh. Could have been worse!

While Steve fiddled with filters and lined up his lights, Shelley went into the bathroom next door. She was feeling extraordinarily roused and sexy. Quickly she stripped to her undies and then combed her hair in the mirror and applied a new coat of gloss to her lips. Steve's voice called, 'Ready when you are!' and she took a deep breath before going back into the room.

'Lovely!' he smiled, as soon as she appeared. 'We'll have you looking like the girl in the Wonderbra ad in no time!'

The lights were shining on a small stepladder draped with a bedspread. Steve suggested she sit on it so her legs could be at different heights. Before she knew it he was snapping away, telling her to change position all the time, making her dizzy with the speed at which he was working.

'Now bend forward a little to accentuate your cleavage . . . great! Smile, now, and lean back on your hands, that's lovely. Now turn round and look back at me over your shoulder, a bit surprised . . . good! One more, but smile this time . . .'

Shelley's head was spinning by the end of the session. Steve came up and put his arm around her bare shoulders, kissing her briefly on the lips. 'I think you're going to be pleased with the results, Shelley. You'd better get dressed now, though. I can't spare any more time today, because I've someone coming for some calendar shots at eight.'

Again Shelley felt disappointed, but she told herself that it had been good of Steve to fit her in to what was obviously a busy schedule. She fought against the frustrated longings that were swirling around in her and went back into the bathroom. When she came out Steve was on the phone, making another booking. He was evidently much in demand. Before him on the desk was his diary and it looked pretty full.

'Maybe we should make another appointment too,' he suggested with a smile as he put the phone down. 'Are you free on Thursday evening?'

'I could be.'

'Fine. Shall we say eight o'clock, then? I'll show you what we took tonight and then we can discuss how to proceed. Presuming you'll want to, of course.'

Shelley glanced at the photos on the wall. 'I'm sure I shall. I've always wanted to have some glamour shots taken. Well, I suppose it's every woman's dream really, isn't it?'

Steve smiled but said nothing, and Shelley sensed it was time to leave.

On the way home Shelley decided to tell Ben nothing about her photo session. She still hoped that she and Steve might end up in bed together, so it was better that her husband knew nothing about him. She had no wish to rub his face in it.

When she arrived the front door was ajar and she could hear Ben on the phone in the hall. Shelley paused to listen. She was not in the habit of eavesdropping but something about her husband's tone had made her suspicious.

'I might be able to see you on Thursday afternoon,' she could hear him saying. 'If you can get the time off . . . yes, that would be nice. I'd like that.'

She entered quickly, watching his reactions. Guilty as hell, he covered the mouthpiece and said hurriedly, 'Must go now. 'Bye.'

'Hullo, Ben,' she smiled. 'Who was that?'

She saw the cogs of his mind spinning furiously, trying to weave a lie. 'Oh, just someone trying to sell us double glazing.'

'Really?' Shelley gave him an unblinking stare. 'So they're coming round on Thursday, are they? Didn't you tell them the house is already fully double-glazed?'

'Er . . . yes, of course. But she – they wanted to check that it had been properly done. Said there were a lot of cowboys about. I thought, might as well.'

Shelley enjoyed seeing him squirm, but enough was enough. Now she had the proof she needed. 'Look, Ben, you can see who you like for all I care. Invite them here on Thursday night if you want, I shan't be home till late.'

'What do you mean?'

'I mean, if you want to have an affair, you don't have to hide it from me. We're both free to do as we like.'

'I'm not . . . I mean, I don't want to upset you.'

'Oh Ben!' Shelley walked into the kitchen and put the kettle on. She was tired of it all, the excuses, the lies. Maybe it was time for them to both accept that their marriage was over.

Ben followed her into the kitchen with his tail between his legs. 'Shell, this is not what I wanted. When you said you'd screwed that Duncan I was so mad I went out and picked up a girl, but . . .'

Look, Ben, I've had a long tiring day and now is not the time to discuss this, okay? Do what you like on Thursday. I'm seeing someone in the evening and I may not be back till Friday night.'

'Is it Duncan?'

'It's none of your business.'

Ben looked wild, almost desperate, and for a moment Shelley was afraid. He blurted, hoarsely, 'I just want to know. Is it him?'

She shook her head. 'I'm not seeing Duncan any more. I learnt my lesson, no more hanky panky with people at work. Now I think I'll take a bath, I'm tired.

Shelley could tell he was perturbed but there was nothing she could do about it. She thought she should let Ben get used to the idea that she was seeing other men in his own good time. As long as she didn't complain about his affairs, he didn't have a leg to stand on.

Yet once she was alone, lying in a hot bath, Shelley felt sadness soak into her like penetrating damp. Would she ever find again the kind of happiness she and Ben had shared in the beginning? Not with Steve, that was for sure, yet she needed him to tide her over until someone more promising came along. Sex without love was all she needed at the moment, and he seemed the best prospect on the horizon.

As the time for her Thursday night appointment neared, Shelley felt herself getting keyed up. She was looking forward to seeing the results of the previous session as well as posing for some more photos. Steve had finished his stint at the studios, so she made her own way to his Beckenham flat, snatching a meal in an Italian-style pizzeria en route. She had taken a lot of care over her make-up and hair, checking them in the car mirror before she presented herself at his door.

'Come in, Shelley!' Steve beamed at her, a glass of wine in his hand which he waved in the air. 'Will you join me? Have you eaten? I could rustle up a snack...'

While they sipped the cool New Zealand Chardonnay, Steve showed her the photos he'd taken of her. Shelley was impressed. He'd made her look good, there was no doubt about that, even though she had that same air of slight apprehension that she'd noticed in some of the pictures on the wall. There were two shots that she was particularly pleased with: a casual pose that showed off her long legs and had her looking straight at the camera with a challenging smile, and a languid, over-the-shoulder shot that had caught her in a wistful mood, making her look distant and romantic.

'You can keep both of those,' Steve told her. 'I rather liked you in this one, too.'

He had singled out the one that made her feel uneasy

because it was the most blatantly sexy of the poses. She was sitting on the top of the stepladder, leaning forward with her legs wide apart and her fingertips on the platform just in front of her crotch. The way she was squashing her breasts together had resulted in a deep and fleshy cleavage, and while her eyes were half closed her mouth was half open, sending out an unmistakably seductive message.

'Do you want it?' he asked. She took it with a smile. It was the one she'd been a bit too reticent to ask for, but she secretly loved its 'Hollywood sex siren' look.

'I don't know what you want to do tonight,' he said, rising with a casual air. 'But there's a whole load of props and costumes in that wardrobe. I suggest you have a browse while I get another bottle of wine out the fridge.'

Shelley opened the wardrobe with glee. She'd loved dressing up when she was a girl, and now the sheer volume of clothes and accessories dazzled her. She flicked through the outfits on the rail and began pulling out those which appealed to her: a long pink feather boa; a spangly purple and gold G-string with matching nipple tassels; a pair of black leather hot pants and a peephole bra; a slinky full-length red dress in clingy satin that was slit to the waist on one side. She hardly knew which to try on first.

'Try mixing and matching,' she heard Steve say, coming into the room, as if reading her mind. He picked up the hot pants, the tassels and the boa then handed her a glass of wine, which she sipped thoughtfully. She was already feeling extremely randy, and the way he was looking at her, assessing her body, imagining her in the sexy clothes, was turning her on even more.

'Want to get into them?' he said, huskily. 'Might as well start. I can't wait to see how you look through the viewfinder.'

This time Steve had placed a couch and some cushions where the steps had been. Shelley undressed quickly, not bothering to leave the room. She got into the hot pants and draped the boa around her neck, but then she was stumped. 'How do I put these things on?' she asked, holding up the nipple tassels.

Steve grinned. 'Well, your nipples need to be erect, for a start.'

He came up and, before she knew it, was gently stimulating her nipples by rolling them between his fingertips. His eyes looked into hers, bold and knowing, setting off wild flurries in the pit of her stomach. Oh God, she thought, I must have him tonight or I'll burst!

'There, now they'll just hook over,' he smiled, twisting the elasticated loops over her very hard and prominent nipples so that the golden fringe swept down to caress the slopes of her breasts beneath. Steve gave them a playful tweak and they swung, shimmering. 'Maybe you can do a belly dance later, and we'll video it,' he smiled.

Somehow Shelley knew he wasn't joking. The thought that he might make a video of her as well set her insides quivering sensually. Just what *was* this guy into, altogether? The prospect of finding out filled her with both excitement and apprehension.

Steve put on some muted jazz and turned up the lights, making a bright stage of the sofa. Shelley took her glass with her and arranged herself in a reclining pose, her left leg bent over the arm of the couch and her right leg dangling onto the floor.

'That's nice,' Steve murmured. 'Turn your top half a bit more this way, can you? That's it.'

After that he took her sitting astride the back of the sofa, kneeling on all fours on the seat, leaning on the top with her back to the camera, sitting cross-legged with her arms spread along the top. Then he suggested that she should take off her hot pants and pose naked, with just the tassels and boa.

Shelley was swept along as he made his curt suggestions, doing whatever he said, trusting him to get the best out of her with his camera. The wine had made her head fuzzy, blurring her judgement so that she couldn't think straight anyway. Besides, she was caught up in a pornographic vision of herself, a sequence of increasingly suggestive poses and images that were partly his idea and in part her own.

It was Shelley's idea to put the string of feathers over her shoulder, down between her tasselled breasts and then between her legs. Giggling she trailed the feathery tendrils around her swollen labia, heightening her erotic tension. She loved the delicate tickling of her clitoris that ensued as she gently pulled the downy boa back and forth. Half oblivious of Steve's presence she kept on doing it, rousing her throbbing button even more, stimulating it towards a climax.

'God, you are a sexy woman, Shelley!' she heard him say as he clicked away. 'I've got the most fantastic hard on, just watching you. But hey, I've got an idea.'

He darted towards the wardrobe and pulled out a large cardboard box. Dim-eyed and still experiencing sensory overload, Shelley paused too. Her clitoris continued to throb demandingly, so she placed her cool hand over her mons to ease her frustration while she found out what Steve wanted her to do next.

'You might like to play with one of these,' he suggested, holding up a large ivory-coloured dildo. 'I've several different kinds.'

At first, Shelley was taken aback. 'What, for the camera?'

He nodded, smiling as he handed her the vibrator. 'Only if you want to. But you look as if you're in need of this thing anyway.'

Shelley would rather he satisfied her himself but, since that didn't appear to be an option right now, she would settle for what she could get. Steve had correctly divined her need, and if he was going to take pictures of her masturbating, what did it matter? He'd already assured her that the photos were for her own private and personal use only.

She switched on the vibrator and it whirred into life. Feeling her need deepen, Shelley sat back on the sofa, drew up her knees and opened her legs wide for the camera. There was something delightfully liberating about exposing her pussy in that way and Shelley realised, with a faint shock, that it was something she'd always wanted to do. Steve took a few shots of her split beaver before she applied the bulbous tip of the dildo to her still-pulsating clitoris. The friction stimulated her instantly, making her already moistened labia run with fresh juice.

'Oh, God!' she moaned, as the relentless drive towards orgasm continued, urging her to put the fat nose of the dildo right into her hungry quim. She thrust it inside, feeling it with her walls, and the sensations that were spiralling through her intensified rapidly. She could hear the whirring of the camera continue as she threw back her head and wriggled around but she was long past caring. It seemed as if this climax had been building for days and she could wait for it no longer.

The sheer explosive force as she hit the peak almost expelled the dildo from her vagina. Shelley gasped and flung the thing aside as shock after shock of acutely pleasurable sensation engulfed her, filling her with a rich sense of utter gratification. She had turned herself on with her suggestive poses, and now she was reaping the delicious fruits of her fantasising.

But what about Steve? Faintly she returned to awareness of him as the blissful feelings subsided. He had stopped filming and was sitting on a chair sipping wine and waiting for her to recover. How could he sit there so coolly, she wondered. Now that her frenzy of self-pleasuring was over she felt awkward, exposed.

She wanted Steve to say something reassuring, but all he said was, 'Would you like some more wine?'

'Yes, please.' Shelley took her full glass back to the sofa where she sat wondering what would happen next. Steve showed no sign of being interested in either sex or photography. Maybe she'd better just leave.

'Do you want to do any more tonight?' she asked, at last.

He raised his brows as if he'd only just become aware of her. 'Do you?'

'I'm not sure. I feel rather drained, as a matter of fact.'

'I'm not surprised.' He rose and came towards her. Shelley wondered if he would take her in his arms, make passionate love to her. But all he did was take her hand, looking down at her. 'I'm tired too. Let's call it a night, shall we? But if you'd like to do some more we could meet again, maybe in a week's time.'

'Fine.'

Shelley got up and went to where she had left her clothes. She put them on slowly, unsure whether she wanted to leave or not. Steve's manner was so vague, so ambiguous that she had the feeling he would be open to seduction if she really came on strong. Except that she really did feel drained, and what she wanted now more than anything was the warmth and comfort of her own bed.

Chapter Six

Ben had been looking forward to his Thursday afternoon meeting with Carol. She arrived at the house looking smart in a navy blazer and pleated skirt, explaining that she'd taken the afternoon off work.

'Just for me?' Ben grinned, as they walked through to the kitchen. 'I'm flattered.'

She took off her jacket and hung it on the back of a chair, revealing a semi-transparent white blouse that showed the lace of her bra beneath, a feature Ben found very titillating.

'Oh, I can work more or less the hours I want. My boss is good like that. He doesn't mind when I come and go as long as I do the work.'

'Great!'

'How about you?'

Ben stared, realising that they hadn't talked about such mundane subjects as work last time. They'd been too busy doing other things with their mouths. 'Well, I ... work at home.'

It was true, Ben told himself. He worked pretty hard hoovering and dusting, shopping and laundering! But Carol was looking curious. 'What do you do, then?'

'Oh, computer stuff.'

'Ah!' She came up close, putting her arm around him and pursing her lips. 'Aren't you going to give me a kiss?' she said.

He obliged instantly, relishing the sweet mintiness of her mouth. At once his desire for her grew, pumping up his erection. To his surprise Carol reached down and felt his hard cock through his trousers. 'You are pleased to see me, aren't you?' she smiled. 'Maybe we'd better go straight up to bed.'

Ben had already neutralised the upstairs rooms, hiding his wife's toiletries in the cupboard again, putting any of her stray clothes away and locking the wardrobe. Their wedding photo, which normally sat by the bed, had been consigned to a drawer. He must remember to replace it after Carol went, or Shelley would be suspicious. He wondered, briefly, how she'd react to him having a mistress. Maybe she would accept it, given that she'd already taken a lover, but he preferred to be on the safe side for the time being.

'Mm, nice room!' Shelley bounced on the bed. 'Did you choose the duvet cover and curtains?'

'Well . . . yes.'

She looked faintly surprised. The design was a Laura Ashley floral style, more feminine than a man would be likely to choose. Ben realised that hiding Shelley's presence was harder than he'd imagined. Were there other give-aways? He racked his brains, mentally going through every room, but everything was so familiar to him it was hard to see it objectively.

Carol was removing her clothes in an uninhibited fashion, piling them neatly on a chair, until she was down to her underwear. Then she lay on the bed and leaned back on her elbows with a smile. Her breasts were already straining against the lacy confines of her bra, the nipples roused into provocative points. She watched him, smiling, as he unbuttoned his shirt and stepped out of his trousers.

'It was your turn last time, now it's mine,' she told him, as he came towards her naked.

'You mean you want me to lick you?'

She nodded, pulling down the triangle of her pants to show her light brown hairy mat. Ben felt his dick spring up, thudding lightly against his stomach. He couldn't stop looking at the fleshy divide beneath her pubic mound, the tempting fruit that was making his mouth water. Carol undid her bra and exposed the small breasts with their large, demanding nipples. Then she pulled the knickers down over her slim thighs and, once she was free of them, opened her legs wide. 'Come on, don't keep me waiting!'

Eagerly Ben knelt on the bed and parted her labia with his fingers. The pink corrugations of her vulva were exposed to his view and he examined her eagerly, noting how she was different from Shelley. The whole of her sex seemed more tightly furled, more compact. He placed his fingertip into the damp well in the middle and it came out glistening. Carefully he touched the top of her labia where her clitoris was hiding beneath its hood. The tiny red tip emerged and he bathed it with her juices, then bent his head to add his saliva to the balm.

'Aah!' Shelley sighed her satisfaction as he covered the whole of her pussy with one long lick before flicking the end of his tongue across her swelling clitoris. The bud was growing in response to his careful treatment, evidently producing keener sensations as it did so because Shelley began moaning loudly, her hands reaching for the taut mounds of her breasts. Looking up her supine body, Ben could see the way she was caressing herself, stroking her tits and scratching her nipples lightly with her nails. She seemed to know exactly what she was doing. Well, he would leave her to it. He had plenty to get on with himself!

While he continued to use his tongue to good effect, Ben stroked her thighs and stomach, tangled with her pubic hair, teased her bottom crack with his gently probing fingers. He could feel her responding to him, her little button throbbing beneath his lips, her pussy growing wetter. He knew she wanted him to penetrate her but he guessed she wasn't ready for full-scale intercourse yet. Experimentally he put one finger at the entrance to her vagina and moved it around, making the juices squelch as they seeped over her soft tissues. Carol wriggled wildly, murmuring her assent.

Ben could feel his penis at full strength now and beginning to strain at the leash. He wanted to feel her lips enclosing his glans, like they had last time, so he manoeuvred himself round until his cock was within reach of her mouth. Fortunately she took the hint but, instead of fellating him, she began to masturbate him with one hand while continuing to stroke herself with the other. He thrust vigorously into the small hollow made by her curved hand. She tightened over his shaft, making a better fit of her palm, and Ben knew he wasn't far off coming. The way she was moaning and writhing was a real turn-on.

In the end, though, Carol beat him to it. She started on a long crescendo of ecstasy and when he thrust into her vagina he could feel the strong spasms closing rhythmically over his finger. Imagining what that might do to his prick, he pushed harder into her half-clenched fist and felt his own orgasm arriving, taking him into a succession of forceful ejaculations that almost ripped him apart with their fiery power.

Ben lay back, exhausted, and closed his eyes. Dimly he heard Carol ask, 'Have you got any tissues?'

'Mm. In the drawer, I think . . .'

It was only when Ben heard the drawer being pulled that he remembered. His eyes shot open but he remained staring at the ceiling, holding his breath and praying that she wouldn't see it. But then she said, 'What's this?' and he knew she had.

He tried to sound nonchalant. 'Oh, just my wedding photo.'

'You're married?'

'Only technically.'

'What's that supposed to mean?' She put the photo down on the bedside cabinet, where it belonged. 'Are you divorced?'

'Not yet. We're still living together, but we lead separate lives.'

It was the truth, but it pained Ben to say it. He realised that he hadn't properly faced up to his situation before and a bleak emptiness overtook him. Carol rested on her elbows, back against the pillow, frowning. She seemed to have forgotten about the tissues.

'I'm not sure I like the sound of this. I've never broken up anyone's marriage, and I don't intend to start now. Why didn't you tell me last time, Ben? Now you're making me suspicious.'

'There's no need. She's probably with some other man this evening. She said she might not come home. Honestly, Carol, it's all over between us.'

'Are you getting divorced, then?'

'We haven't actually discussed it yet.'

'What does she do, your wife, does she work?'

'Yes, for a production company. They make videos, commercials, some TV programmes.'

Carol was looking quizzically at him. 'While you stay at home, looking after the house?'

'Sort of.'

She laughed, which he took to be a hopeful sign. 'You're a house-husband, then! Does she make you do all the housework?'

Ben was irritated. The delightful feelings that she'd induced in him just minutes ago had completely evaporated, leaving him drained and edgy. 'She doesn't *make* me do anything, Carol. It just makes more sense for me to do the shopping and stuff since I'm here all day.'

'Working, huh?'

He didn't like her tone so he ignored her, getting up to go for a pee. When he returned she had got dressed again. Her face was set in a cold expression and Ben knew he'd blown it. He sat on the bed, waiting for her to have her say.

'I think I'd better go, Ben. It's been nice knowing you, but if I'd realised from the start that you were a married man I'd never have come home with you.' She started towards the door, then snapped over her shoulder, 'It was supposed to be a *Singles* night, if you remember!'

Ben let her go without protest, then lay back on the pillow and closed his eyes, listening to her hurry downstairs and out of the front door. Well, it had been good while it lasted, and at least he knew he could still pull a bird when he needed to. Yet as he thought about what Carol had said, a dark mood descended on him. His marriage was in limbo and, as long as that continued, he couldn't hope to start something serious with anyone else. Maybe it would be better to make a clean break of it, after all.

Not that he would be much of a prospect, even if he were divorced. At the moment he was living comfortably, supported by Shelley, but if they divorced and sold the house he would have to live on half the proceeds until it ran out. When he thought about the practicalities of his situation, it was quite unnerving. Was he just hanging on with Shelley because the alternative was even more depressing?

Ben put on his dressing-gown and went downstairs. He poured himself a whisky, then switched on the TV for a late-night film. It was past midnight when he heard Shelley's key in the door. Much to Ben's surprise, he felt relieved that she'd come home. Going into the hall to greet his wife, he noticed at once that she was holding something under her jacket – a brown envelope. She looked embarrassed as she caught his eye, then hid it with a smile.

'Hullo, Ben. Still up? Must dash to the loo.'

He guessed that she'd gone upstairs to hide the envelope in her usual place. Ben had long ago discovered where she put things she wanted to surprise him with, birthday presents and the like. At the back of the wardrobe, in the spare room. He'd check it out tomorrow after she'd gone to work.

When she came down again Ben offered his wife a whisky and, rather to his surprise, she accepted. They sat in the front room with the television on but neither of them really watching it, both of them lost in thought. Ben felt an overwhelming sadness as he remembered how they used to cuddle on the sofa as a preliminary to making love in bed. Now they sat in separate chairs, locked in their own isolation.

The distance between them seemed even greater when they lay in bed, close but not touching. Ben wanted to embrace her but he was afraid of being rebuffed, and he didn't know how to express what was in his heart. He didn't want to lose Shelley, yet he didn't know how to win her back. Their marriage was like a roller coaster that had gone out of control: it would go whizzing round the same old track pointlessly until it finally ran out of steam.

In the morning Shelley was up early as usual and out of the house almost before Ben had opened his eyes. Once he would have been up with her, snatching a hasty breakfast, making hurried arrangements, giving her the usual kiss before they went their separate ways to work. It seemed like a lifetime ago.

While he was drinking his coffee, Ben suddenly remembered the brown envelope. He went back upstairs and groped in the back of the spare room wardrobe. Yes, there it was. For a moment he felt pity for Shelley, who clearly believed that her 'secret' hidey-hole was inviolable. Then he opened the envelope and drew out what he soon realised was a set of photographs.

The sight of his wife in those pin-up shots first amazed and then intrigued him. Who had taken them? And what on earth had possessed her to pose semi-nude? The one that caught his eye showed Shelley sitting on some kind of platform with her legs splayed, leaning forward to show off her cleavage. The expression on her face was blatantly sexual. She was looking straight at the camera through heavy-lidded eyes and making a kissy mouth with her brightly painted lips. But who was the photographer?

Ben took the envelope and its contents through to the bedroom and got back into bed, wanting to study them more closely. The background looked like a real studio and the portraits were well lit, suggesting that whoever had taken them was a professional. Someone she had met at Harcourt, perhaps. Not that Duncan, surely? He looked again at the three photographs spread out on the duvet. Two of them were fairly innocuous, it was the third which worried him. The look on his wife's face suggested that if she hadn't had sex with the photographer in the last ten minutes, she was certainly going to in the next ten. But what disturbed him most was the intimacy of her expression. She was looking at the camera the way she used to look at him, in the privacy of their own bedroom, and it filled him with an infuriating sense of betrayal.

As he continued to look at it, Ben grew aware of a stirring in his groin. It was absurd to be turned on by a photograph of his own wife but that was undeniably what was happening. He pushed back the duvet and untied his bathrobe, giving his penis more room to expand. Shelley's face stared up at him, bold and seductive, in her black underwear. He could see where her erect nipples were filling out the lacy cups of her bra, and between her thighs the slit pouch of her sex could just be detected, with a few stray pubic hairs peeping from the legs of her panties.

Seizing his eager penis, Ben brought it up to full strength with a few firm strokes. The tingling warmth spread throughout his pelvic region, making him feel good. He was pretending his wife was someone else, not Shelley Derwent with her career and her money and self-confidence and thinly-disguised contempt for him, but a woman who used her sexuality to pleasure her men as well as herself, who knew how to make a man feel like a king. She was his fantasy lover, the woman he'd fallen in love with so many years ago, and that one photo had brought it all back.

Swiftly Ben brought himself to a climax, feeling in the rush of elation that accompanied his orgasm, the powerful assertion of his masculinity. Afterwards he realised that he'd shot his load all over the photograph. Swearing, he reached for some tissues and wiped the sticky mess off her face and body. There was still a light film over it. He took another tissue and wet it with his tongue, removed the residue, put it back with the others then replaced the envelope in the wardrobe.

For the rest of the morning Ben felt a weird mixture of shame and satisfaction. He tried to come to terms with his feelings by confessing via the Internet. An account headed 'I wanked over my wife's photo' appeared under his net-name of 'Bender' in the alt.sex.confess user group. It sat happily between 'Wifey takes it up the bim' (sic) by Ivor Biggun, and 'Sex Doc cured my frigid wife' by Thaddeus. Once it was all written down, though, Ben saw himself in the context of all the other sad cases and became depressed.

He was eating his solitary ham sandwich in the kitchen when there came a knock at the back door and a cheerful voice called, 'Ben, are you there? It's only me, Anne from over the road.'

At once Ben cheered up, glad of some company. He liked his opposite neighbour, who was divorced with two teenage kids and worked part-time as a secretary. Anne was in her mid-thirties and still attractive, with the intriguing combination of a petite frame and large, well-shaped breasts.

Ben invited her in at once and put the kettle on. 'I don't want to disturb you,' she began. 'But I wondered if you and Shelley had anything for a car boot sale. The PTA is running one on Sunday week and I could do with a few more items.'

'I'm sure we could find something,' Ben smiled. 'What sort of stuff do you want?'

The conversation flowed easily, moving on from school fund-raising through the general state of the economy to Ben's being out of work.

'It must be hard, staying at home all day while your wife works,' Anne commented. 'That sort of situation can put quite a strain on a marriage.'

'It already has,' he admitted. 'Shelley and I are drifting apart. We seem to lead more or less separate lives these days.'

'Do you think you'll divorce?'

'Probably. Eventually.'

'I'm sorry, Ben.' Anne looked genuinely sad. 'It's never a good experience, but at least you've got no children.'

She started talking about her own failed marriage, and it was three o'clock before she glanced at her watch and jumped up. 'Oh Lord, the kids will be back in an hour and I haven't done the shopping yet!'

'Can I give you a lift to the supermarket? I was intending to go myself.'

She accepted his offer and Ben found himself happily exchanging shopping tips as they drove down the High Street. Anne was easy to talk to and relaxing to be with. It occurred to him that he'd never seen her with a man in the six months she'd been living nearby. Did she prefer her own sex? It seemed unlikely, but with the new breed of 'lipstick lesbians' you couldn't spot them so easily. Maybe her divorce had led her to become celibate rather than risk further heartache. If so, it was a pity. A woman like her, in the prime of life, deserved better. Glancing at the way her breasts thrust proudly either side of the seatbelt, Ben felt his prick stir.

Since Anne was in a hurry they moved quickly through the supermarket. Ben drove her home in time to see her two gawky teenagers dawdling down the road. He wondered what they would think if they saw their mother being driven around in his car, but as he let her out she said, casually, 'I'm at home on Tuesdays and Fridays, if you feel like dropping in for a coffee and a chat, Ben.'

'Thanks. I might just do that.'

Her hazel eyes surveyed him briefly for a moment, smiling muted encouragement, before she turned to face her two children with a different kind of smile. Ben greeted the kids with a wave and then walked up his own path feeling jaunty. After his somewhat humiliating encounter with Carol, his neighbour had miraculously succeeded in making him feel like a desirable male again.

The weekend passed, as it usually did these days, with Ben and Shelley following their separate pursuits. For Shelley it was a whirl around the clothes shops, a meal out in the evening with a friend whose husband was abroad and then, on Sunday, a protracted visit to her sister in Notting Hill. Ben mowed the lawn on Saturday afternoon, spent the evening slumped in front of a hired video with a microwaved curry and spent most of the next day on the Internet. By the time his wife returned, at nine on Sunday evening, the idea that they might as well be living apart had only been reinforced in Ben's troubled mind.

By Tuesday morning acute boredom had set in and it was only when Ben glimpsed his next-door neighbour, Nosey Rosie, hanging out her washing that he remembered Anne's standing invitation to coffee. It had been several days since she had come in to ask him for some stuff for next weekend's car boot sale and he'd done nothing about it. Quickly he scoured the house, coming up with some CD's they never listened to, some kitchen gadgets they never used and several unwanted gifts. Now he had the perfect excuse to drop in to his neighbour's house.

Anne's face lit up when she saw him, and as he handed her the large plastic bag full of jumble her smile broadened even more. 'It's very good of you, Ben. Maybe you could help me price the stuff. I've no idea what to charge.'

She took him through to her kitchen. Ben had never been inside her house before and it was strangely familiar. Everything was the other way round, like a mirror image.

Anne had been baking. A large batch of scones stood on two cooling racks and she put one on a plate for him with some butter and jam while she poured coffee. Ben bit into the still-warm scone with a blissful smile. 'Mm, delicious!' he murmured, through the crumbs. 'Why can't my wife cook things like this?'

'I don't suppose she has the time. I've never wanted to work more than part-time, not until the children leave home. I enjoy domestic activities like cooking.'

Ben said he did, too. Somehow there seemed no stigma involved in admitting it to a woman like Anne. They talked about cooking for some time, then moved into the back room where she kept all the car boot stuff.

'Now these are the ones I've already priced up,' she said, kneeling on the floor before the assorted items, her breasts swinging forward heavily beneath her blouse. 'Perhaps you could check them over, see if I'm asking too much, or too little.'

Ben squatted down on the carpet beside her. The room was quiet and still, with a view of the sunny garden beyond and washing flapping in the breeze. Suddenly Ben felt absurdly carefree, filled with the sudden conviction that he and Anne would soon be starting an affair. It was inevitable because she wanted it as much as he did. Now he could smell the fresh, clean scent of her and see the downy hairs on the nape of her neck just below the sculptured curve of her short, light-brown hair.

'I think you could charge a bit more for that vase,' he told her, picking up a monstrous chunk of green glass. 'It's Fifties' Art Deco. Very collectable.'

She took it from him, frowning. 'What do you reckon, then – ten? I think it's hideous myself.'

'Try fifteen. And this should be more too.' He picked up an ashtray adorned with a Guinness toucan. 'At least a fiver.'

'So I'm not asking too much for anything, then?'

They were very close as she looked up, her eyes wide with enquiry. Ben felt lust make a sudden lurch in the pit of his stomach. He was already rock hard. Silently, he shook his head, temporarily unable to speak.

Anne made a slight, hesitant move towards him. Scarcely perceptible, it was enough to convince Ben that she wanted what he wanted and he moved at the same time, narrowing the gap between them. Their lips touched minimally, a light brushing that sent tingling messages all down his spine. He reached out and put a hand to her head, pulling her to him. At the same time his mouth came down on hers with crushing force.

She was moaning as they kissed, giving him the impression that she'd been hungry for this for a long time. She clutched at his biceps then began to caress his back. Ben's hands dropped to Anne's small waist, revelling in the contrast between the bare handspan there and the substantial mounds of flesh he could feel pressed against his chest. His curiosity was aroused and he longed to see her naked.

'Oh Ben!' He heard her sigh as his lips left hers to trace a path down the side of her neck. 'It's been so long!'

He paused, looking down at her flushed face. 'Are you sure you want this?'

Anne nodded, starting to unbutton her blouse. Ben felt his

cock pushing against the tight cotton of his pants and a surge of adrenaline went through him. He stared intently as she opened the front of her blouse to reveal her white bra, fully stretched, and the deep ravine between her breasts. Mesmerised he watched her take off first the blouse and then the bra, until her incredible breasts were on full view. She looked at him with shy pride, as if she were used to men paying tribute to her natural assets.

Enormous as her boobs were, they supported themselves pretty well. They were pale-skinned and freckled, surmounted by large brownish nipples that, even as he watched, were puckering into a state of arousal. Beneath her bosom the tiny waist seemed almost too fragile to support all that weight up top.

'What fantastic breasts! You're in great shape for a woman who's had two kids, Anne.'

She seemed pleased. 'I try to keep fit. I go swimming twice a week.'

Ben drew her into his arms, suddenly touched by her air of vulnerability. As he kissed her, his hands wandered to her mammoth globes and stroked their yearning tips, making her moan again. His solid penis was pressing against the hard swell of her mons, clearly defined beneath her tight-fitting skirt.

They kissed deeply, Ben sensing Anne's growing desire for him as her nipples hardened in response to his repeated fingering. So he wasn't surprised when she broke out of his embrace and scrambled out of her skirt and pants before throwing some cushions on to the carpet. 'I think we'll be more comfy down here,' she smiled.

Ben tore off his shirt and then the rest of his clothes. Although it was a north-facing room, Anne had the central heating on and it was quite warm. He saw her eyes on his erection as he pulled off his pants, and her smile widened. Slowly he knelt down beside her and ran his hands over her smooth stomach and down her thighs. When she lay down, her breasts fell to each side like pillows pushed apart in the night. He bent his head and caught one taut nipple between his lips, making her squirm.

'Oh Ben, this feels so good!' she murmured. 'May I touch you . . . down there?'

'You've no need to ask permission. He's dying for you to touch him, can't you see?'

She gave a kind of whimper as her hands enclosed his rampant organ. Evidently she'd not been this close to a man in a good long while. Her hands grabbed at him quite mercilessly at first, bringing him dangerously near the brink, but then she settled down into a gentle stroking that pleasured him more slowly, taking him only gradually towards his peak.

Now her own pleasure centre was within his reach, and Ben tentatively parted the curly strands of her pubic hair to reveal the pale lips beneath. While he held one ample breast to his mouth and suckled on the nipple his other hand dived into the wet canyon of her pussy and began to explore. Anne gasped with a sharp intake of breath as he found the central powerhouse of her sexuality, throbbing with raw energy. He stroked around the hard little trigger warily at first, not wanting to over-stimulate it, but it was soon obvious from the way she was wriggling to maintain contact with his elusive fingertip that she was ready for stronger stimulation. Taking his mouth from her straining breast, he re-positioned himself so that he could lick her pussy while she continued to stroke his grateful cock and balls.

The sleek lips parted to allow access to his tongue, and Ben was soon tonguing her deeply, relishing the sweet taste of her fresh juices. She was responding eagerly, lifting her tight little bottom off the floor as the sensations became keener, more acute. Despite her own arousal she was not neglecting him, and her delicate fingering of his shaft and balls was bringing him rapidly towards the peak. He could feel the first drops of fluid lubricating his glans and, just as he felt he could hold out no longer, he heard her say, 'Ben, do you have a condom?'

The intrusion had a slightly deflating effect on his erection. 'No, sorry!' he uttered, in a hoarse whisper.

'Neither have I, what a pity!'

In a way, Ben felt relieved. At least he now knew where they stood with each other and there could be no embarrassing misunderstandings. Intensifying his efforts, he flicked his tongue rapidly back and forth over the hard pellet of her clitoris and was soon rewarded by the touch of her lips on his glans. She took half of him into her mouth and he shuddered with delight as the warm, wet softness enveloped him. Thrusting along the velvety plane of her tongue, he soon felt the unstoppable rise towards orgasm begin, his penis tensing for the delivery. When the first electrifying warmth spread from his shaft through his lower body, he pulled back from Anne's mouth, not wanting to subject her to the full force of his ejaculation.

As Ben drew back the milky substance spurted all over the heaving slopes of her breasts. He gasped, at the same time thrusting a finger deep into the chasm of her vagina where she was alternately tensing and relaxing in rhythmic self-help towards a climax. He nibbled softly at her enlarged button while his finger continued to work its way deep inside her, squeezed by her impatient walls until he was suddenly caught in a series of softer undulations that he knew must signal the onset of her orgasm.

Flinging her head back, Anne uttered one long, continuous moan that soared in harmony with her climax then slowly faded into silence. Ben slipped his finger out and lay his head between her mountainous breasts, heedless of the sticky mess he'd made of them. He could feel her stroking his hair as she came down from her pinnacle, and then her hand relaxed as she fell into a doze.

They must have slept for twenty minutes or so, then Ben awoke to find his head was on a real cushion, not a fleshy one. He could hear Anne humming in the kitchen as she made them a drink, and for a while he just lay there with his eyes closed, savouring the feelings of complete relaxation and contentment that were flowing through him.

'Tea or coffee?' he heard Anne say, at the door.

'Tea would be nice, thanks.'

In a few minutes they were sitting on the sofa fully dressed, almost as if nothing had happened. Anne still looked flushed, her hair dishevelled, and there was a girlish gleam in her green-brown eyes. She talked excitedly of the new computers the PTA planned to buy with the proceeds of the car boot sale.

'You've got one, haven't you? I don't know anything about them, but Paul and Sally would like me to get one. I know they use them at school, and they play games on their friends' computers, but I don't know whether to get them one of their own. It would have to be second-hand, of course, but I don't know how you tell what kind to get. Maybe I should ask Mr Simonds, their computer teacher...'

Sex, it seemed, made Anne garrulous. Ben sipped his tea in silence, letting her rabbit on. After the almost desperate passion of their love-making he wanted to be alone again, to get back to his own computer and the silent, undemanding communication of the Internet. When he'd finished drinking, Ben put his cup down and got to his feet.

'Look, Anne, I'm sorry to interrupt but I really wasn't planning on staying this long and I've several things to do this afternoon.'

'Gosh, I'm sorry! Of course you ... well, I didn't plan it either, and ...'

The poor woman began to blush. Ben gave her a gentle kiss on the lips. 'It was lovely, Anne, really, but I have to go now.'

They began to walk out into the hall. Ben could sense her nervousness, knew she was wondering if she'd done the right thing. She turned at the front door with her hand on the latch, her face one big, silent question.

'I'd like to see you again,' he said, softly, bringing a smile of relief to her lips.

'I'm at home on Friday. Every Tuesday and Friday, like I said. You're welcome any time.'

'Friday it is, then.'

She smiled, reaching up to kiss his cheek and whispering, 'Well don't forget to bring our little friend Johnny next time.'

Chapter Seven

Duncan called an impromptu meeting in the studio gallery on Monday morning. Everyone was on edge, and Shelley had a sinking feeling in her stomach. Rumours were circulating that business was slack. If it didn't improve, Harcourt Productions would be in deep trouble.

'Look, I don't want to keep you long,' Duncan began in his usual brusque way. 'Fact is, we don't have enough work this week to keep all of you busy so I'm going to put half a dozen of you on standby. If we need you, we'll let you know by nine in the morning at the latest, okay?'

There were anxious murmurs. Bob, the floor manager, asked what would happen if the same situation arose next week. Would there be any redundancies?

'Not at this stage, that I can promise you,' Duncan smiled. 'We've two commercials on the books for next week. That means that those of you who are not needed this week will definitely be working next week.'

'Put us out of our misery then, for God's sake!' Bob called. 'Who's going to be laid off?'

Duncan visibly controlled himself. 'No one will be "laid off" as you put it, Bob. It's not a question of that yet, as I said. I'm just asking the following people to be available if needed.'

Shelley's name was on the list of those not required that week. Somehow she'd guessed it would be, which did nothing to allay her paranoia.

'Now I don't want you to be too alarmed about this,' Duncan continued, smoothly. 'This is a temporary measure until things pick up, that's all. As you know, we've put in a strong tender for the new Telmax sitcom and if we get that we'll all be working our rocks off for the next two years. So let's hope we get it, eh?'

'When will we know?' Bob asked.

'Within the month, hopefully. Fingers crossed, folks!'

Shelley left the studio feeling dejected. The thought of a week at home with Ben was less than appealing and she'd already visited her mother and sister recently. Instead of going home, Shelley spent the morning in the National Gallery, had lunch at a nearby pub, then thought of Steve. She rang him and explained that she was probably going to be free for the rest of the week.

He sounded pleased. 'How about coming round this afternoon, then? I've got some more photos to show you and I think you're going to love them.'

Shelley made her way to Steve's flat in a lighter mood. He met her at his door, wearing a short black kimono that made his slightly exotic features look even more oriental. Taking her into his arms, he gave her a warm kiss of greeting on the mouth that filled her with subdued excitement. This time, surely, they would get it together.

He led her through to the studio, where the photos he'd taken of her last time were spread out on a table. Shelley was startled to see herself in such blatantly sexy postures. The ones where she was masturbating with the vibrator were particularly shocking. Steve had taken one obviously at the point of orgasm, where her head was thrown back in the throes of ecstasy and a pink flush was spread over her throat and breasts. Now she blushed again.

'They're very ... blatant,' she murmured, but then a disturbing thought struck her. She turned to Steve with a worried frown. 'You wouldn't do anything with them, would you? I mean show them to anyone, or anything.'

'Of course not.' His open smile was reassuring. He reached out and stroked her hair. 'They're just between us, our little secret. I'll even give you the negatives if you like.'

'It's not that I don't trust you, Steve. I just don't want anyone else to see them, even by accident. That's all.'

'It's okay. Of course I *could* find a commercial outlet for them. I've plenty of contacts in the business. The camera loves you, Shelley, and you're very sexy. This one in particular is quite wonderful.' He singled out a photo showing Shelley with the feather boa snaking down between her tasselled breasts and legs, her laughing face showing the kind of *joie de vivre* that had made Monroe so photogenic. 'But I would only proceed with your full consent,' he continued, solemnly. 'I can promise you that.'

'It's not what I wanted, Steve. I thought it was just going to be between us.'

'That's fine by me. I've got plenty of other models on my books. I just thought, with things being a bit dicey at Harcourt, you might want to line up some alternatives.'

Despite her initial qualms, Shelley couldn't deny she was tempted. 'I'll think about it.'

He gave her a brief hug. 'Good girl! Now how about doing some more?'

Shelley began her third session wearing a 'baby doll' nightie and lounging on the bed that had been left in the studio after a previous shoot. It was a luxurious double bed with silken drapes and lacy pillows. As she went through a series of coy poses, revealing more and more of her naked flesh, Shelley began to imagine herself and Steve making better use of the bed and her desire for him grew. The short kimono was revealing quite a bit of his body, especially when he bent over to peer into the viewfinder. She could clearly see the musculature of his semi-exposed chest and strong thighs, glimpse the covering of dark hair. Only the central area of his body remained concealed beneath the tie at the waist. Shelley wondered if Steve was as aroused as she. As she pictured a sturdy penis pointing up towards his navel beneath that black silk, her insides gave a shuddering lurch like hunger pangs.

'Hey, Shelley, this is really good! You're looking fantastic,' he said, smiling over the top of the camera. 'But it's getting harder and harder for me to keep my distance, I can tell you!'

She thought, wickedly: Yes, I bet it *is* getting harder and harder! Curling her legs under her, she pulled the short top of the nightie back down over her provocatively erect nipples, affecting a prim and proper air. 'Is this better?'

Steve laughed, taking a couple of shots. 'Nice idea, babe! Sometimes the sexiest poses are the ones that conceal more than they reveal.'

Shelley pulled her hair back experimentally, scraping it into a more severe style. 'Maybe I should try the "strict governess" look?'

'Well, if corporal punishment's your thing, we've certainly got the props for it. But that's one scenario where it's really best to have a partner.' He gave an impish grin. 'I don't mind volunteering!'

'You mean, you want me to smack your bottom?' Shelley giggled.

'I'll smack yours, if you'd prefer.'

'I can think of one or two things I'd rather you did to me,' she murmured, amazed at her own daring. He fiddled with his camera then came forward, untying his belt as he did so and making Shelley's pulse rate increase dramatically. The kimono fell open, revealing the full extent of Steve's erection. His penis was shortish but very thick and with a glans the size of a golf ball. It reared from its bed of black curly hair with an air of jaunty confidence.

Shelley groaned softly, unable to take her eyes off his uplifted prick. She could feel herself flooding in the concealed crevices of her pussy, readying herself to receive his rampant organ, and knew that if he rejected her now she couldn't bear it. From the look on his face, he was equally determined that they should consummate their relationship at last. She leaned back against the high pillows, knowing that the pink crests of her nipples were revealing themselves beneath the see-through nylon of her top. The dark vee of her mons was equally visible through the matching panties.

'Get up on all fours,' Steve told her, as he came on to the bed.

Thinking he was going to take her from behind Shelley obeyed, arching her back and spreading her thighs as she thrust her rump up into the air. His hands grasped her buttocks and she gasped with the sudden contact, but then she was aware of his hair brushing against her thighs and before she realised what he was doing his tongue had begun to probe into her engorged labia, licking the length of her vulva from beneath and making her wiggle with sudden excitement. She moaned aloud when he found the fleshy protrusion that was silently clamouring for his attention, and began to concentrate on tonguing it as he rubbed her thighs.

That particular method of stimulation was short-lived, much to Shelley's disappointment. Steve's mouth withdrew and he began to kiss her thighs and then to make his way up her spine, pushing up the flimsy top as he did so. His hands moved round her sides until they found the hanging globes of her breasts and he started fingering her tense nipples. The tingling spread instantly down to her clitoris, evoking a sympathetic throbbing. Shelley soon became aware of the thrusting movements his cock was making as it slid up and down the crack between her bum cheeks and her arousal grew to an almost unbearable pitch.

'God, Shelley, I want to get inside you!' she heard him grunt in her ear. There was a brief pause while he delved beneath the pillow and produced a condom in its plastic envelope. Turning, she saw him tear at it with his teeth, then extract the cream coloured ring.

'Will you do the honours?' he invited her, his eyes darkened by lust.

She nodded, kneeling to handle his prick. It felt warm and lively against her palm. Carefully she rolled the rubber over his glans, retaining the teat, and slowly unfurled it down the length of his shaft. When she released his cock it leapt up, spring-loaded and raring to go.

Steve reached towards her and lifted the top of her nightie right over her head, then pulled down the frilly nylon pants until she was stark naked. Shelley lay back with her arms around his neck. His mouth came hungrily to her left breast while he squeezed the right one. The need to have him penetrate her came more urgently, more insistently, so that she seized hold of his thick shaft, feeling the slight ribbing of the sheath that encased it, and tried to pull it towards her yearning pussy.

'Steady on,' he muttered. 'I want to be sure you're ready first.'

'I'm ready all right! I've been ready for ages, and I reckon I'll go off the boil if you keep me waiting any longer.'

Her words came out more impatiently than Shelley had intended. Fortunately he took her outburst for what it was, a token of her extreme desire for him. Without wasting any more time, he positioned himself between her thighs and pushed straight between the tumid outer lips and in through the wide open entrance to the welcoming haven beyond.

The instant Shelley felt him slide inside her she gave a sigh of relief followed by a long muscular squeeze of his penis. Steve withdrew again, very slowly, until the head of his organ was only just in contact with the outer rim of her vagina. He proceeded to make very small thrusting movements, which produced the most exquisitely titillating feelings in her as her clitoris responded to the stroking and stretching of the sensitive skin of her labia.

Opening her eyes, Shelley saw him poised above her on his strong arms, the long shaft of his penis clearly visible as it continued gently probing her below the dark mound of her pubic hair. She could feel the tremulous onset of her climax gradually gathering force, recognised the voluptuous heat that made her limbs heavy and her flesh quiver with delight at the slightest stimulus. She abandoned herself to lazy sensuality for a while, content to wallow in that delicious suspense between relaxation and arousal.

But Steve unexpectedly leaned forward and tweaked both of her nipples at once, triggering the full flush of her orgasm. Shelley was almost disappointed as she was propelled into the maelstrom of overwhelming sensation, realising from the vigour of the paroxysms that her pleasure would be over all too soon. She was only dimly aware of being enthusiastically shafted, the thick rod delving repeatedly into her throbbing flesh until Steve also reached his tumultuous climax. By then she was floating back down, utterly satiated.

They collapsed together on the bed for a few seconds, then Steve got up and went to the bathroom. It left Shelley feeling vaguely uneasy. In retrospect, there had been something odd about their coupling, a lack of spontaneity. She had felt as if Steve weren't quite into it, as if his mind were elsewhere, and the whole episode had felt as if it were being choreographed. The matter-of-fact way in which he had risen from the bed only seconds after they'd both climaxed only confirmed her doubts.

'Want something to drink?' Steve asked as he returned, clad again in the black kimono. 'There's juice, beer, tea or coffee.'

'I'd like some tea, please.'

He disappeared to the kitchen and Shelley went into his bathroom to wash. Somehow she had the impression that it would soon be time for her to leave. By the time Steve returned she was fully dressed and he didn't raise an eyebrow as he handed her a steaming mug.

'Well, we should have some more good shots for you to see next time,' he smiled. 'That was quite a torrid session, wasn't it?'

Shelley stared at him. 'You don't mean you were taking photos all the time we were . . .'

He laughed. 'Of course! Didn't you realise?'

'But how? You were on the bed with me.'

'I had this remote control for the camera set up. It fires automatically every twenty seconds. Don't look so alarmed! Like I said, no one else has to see the pictures unless you want them to.'

Shelley recalled the faint clicking sound she'd heard at intervals during their lovemaking. A feeling of disgust overwhelmed her. 'Is nothing sacred, Steve? Do you regard the whole of life as some kind of performance for the camera?'

'Hey, don't be like that babe! I'm a photographer, it's what I do, okay? I thought you'd like to see what a great pair we make when we're in action together. If you want, I could develop them right away.'

Despite herself, Shelley was curious. 'How long will it take?'

'Not long. You can have a look through some of my other work, if you like. I had an exhibition in Amsterdam last year. They compared me to Robert Mapplethorp. Imagine!'

Shelley took the folders that Steve produced and laid them down on the coffee table in the lounge while he went into his dark room. She opened the one labelled 'Dutch Exhibition' first. It was obvious at once that the quality of the work was high, 'art' photography, but Shelley was taken aback by some of the subject matter. There was a whole sequence showing a pair of bodybuilders, a black male and a white female, flexing their muscles while posing in a variety of sexual positions. Although she found the sight of the man's enormous cock arousing, there was something cold and impersonal about the way he was relating to his partner, as if she were just so much meat.

Shelley flicked quickly through and found another subject: two naked women playing with flowers. One appeared to have a hyacinth growing out of her vagina while her partner brushed her nipples with a pair of daffodils. In a second photo the pair were spreading their thighs to show red roses growing out of their sex. Shelley hoped they were the thornless variety. Another photo showed a woman tied to a tree with a strong creeper while a man dressed in a leopard skin swung over her head, Tarzan style, his penis and balls visible under the short pelt. The bondage theme was continued in a study of three naked women bound, back to back, in the middle of a wood while three small hounds frisked and barked around them.

The images were all bizarre and somehow disturbing, yet Shelley could not deny their artistry. She opened another folder and saw photographs of quite a different kind. They were all of women, fully clothed except for one small, erotic portion of their anatomy that was shown through a hole cut in their garments. It was not difficult to see these photographs as pleasingly erotic, for the women were all beautiful and the clothes exquisite. A Chinese girl in a turquoise silk mandarin jacket and sheer black tights was revealing a tiny portion of her shaven pussy lips through a split in the crotch. A blonde woman in a pink evening gown showed the tip of one pink nipple, so near in colour to the shade of her dress that you didn't notice it at first. A brunette in a short white dress had a fuzzy black heart cut out over her mons. It looked weird, as if it was stuck onto the material rather than sticking through it.

'What do you think of them?' Steve asked her, suddenly appearing.

'They're very clever, very artistic.'

'But do you like them?'

'I'm not sure. I mean they're all interesting, but they're not conventional pin-ups by any means. There's something a bit sinister about some of them.'

'That's what I want to convey, Shelley. The hidden weirdness behind posing for the camera. I mean, it's such an unnatural act, don't you think?'

Shelley shrugged. 'I wouldn't know. But what about the ones you took today?'

'They're drying. Want to come and see?'

She followed him into the small area of his studio that he'd partitioned off as a dark room. When he switched on the light, she saw the processed photos hanging up like washing on a line, fastened by small clips. Slowly she walked along the line, examining each in turn.

The first few were of Shelley alone, posing in the Baby Doll pyjamas. She was used to seeing herself in pin-up poses by now, but already she could see that her facial expression was more controlled, her eyes and mouth showing a more confident relationship with the camera.

'Not bad for an amateur,' Steve commented.

Then came the first of the poses with Steve. Shelley couldn't help feeling acutely embarrassed as she saw the way he was kneeling behind her with his stonker of an erection, his head half hidden between her thighs. There was worse to follow. Shots of her rolling a condom onto his organ with loving care, of him stretching out her nipples with his fingers while his dick was half inside her. Now she knew why he'd seemed to be holding back from her, it was so that the camera could get the best possible view of his extended penis.

'Of course, these are essentially candid action shots,' he explained, casually. 'Those photos you've just been looking at were another story entirely. They were very carefully posed, took hours to get exactly right, some of them.'

Suddenly Shelley felt claustrophobic in the tiny room, her heart thudding wildly. She turned towards the door, saying she wanted to go to the bathroom. As soon as she was alone, she sat down on the loo and tried to stop her panic reaction. It didn't take her long to work out why she'd felt that way. Now Steve had clear photographic evidence of him screwing her, would he try to use it against her in some way? Had she walked straight into a trap?

She came out of the bathroom feeling shaken. Steve offered her more tea, evidently satisfied with her explanation that she couldn't tolerate confined spaces. While she drank her second mug of hot, sweet tea, Steve told her that he shot videos too.

'I have one entered in the erotic video Oscars, taking place in Hamburg next month,' he told her, with some pride. 'It's called *Rubber Dollies*. Would you like to see it?'

'No thanks,' she said, hurriedly finishing her drink. 'I really should be going.'

'Another time, perhaps.'

Shelley rose, still feeling agitated, then plucked up the courage to ask him if she could have the photos they'd taken that afternoon, plus all the negatives. Steve put on a hurt expression. 'Don't you trust me, babe?'

'I don't know if I can or not, Steve, but you did say I could have the negatives if I wanted.'

He shrugged. 'That's fine. But I must say I'm disappointed. I was hoping you might do some commercial work with me. You're an excellent model, Shelley, and you could go far. But maybe you'll change your mind when the shit hits the fan at Harcourt, eh?'

She followed him as he strode towards the dark room. 'What do you mean?'

'I don't think that outfit's going to last much longer, do you? I mean, here you are laid off for a week and it's not the first time. If they don't win a few fat contracts soon . . .'

He gave a thumbs-down signal, and Shelley sighed. He was only voicing her own fears. Yet the thought of working for Steve, making porno videos, filled her with dismay. There surely had to be a better alternative for her than that!

True to his word, Steve handed over all the negatives and photographs that he'd taken of her. Shelley felt bad about not trusting him but it was too late now. Whatever there had been between them by way of attraction seemed to have evaporated once she'd said she wasn't interested in working with him any more. As she drove home, Shelley felt duped. All those sexy glances he'd given her when they were working together in the studio must have been cool and calculating. All the time he'd been seeing her through the eye of a camera, assessing her potential for making money. His personal feelings had hardly entered into it. What a fool she'd been to think she could build a normal, loving relationship with a man who was basically a pimp for his camera.

The next few days proved surprisingly pleasant. Shelley was not used to being at leisure in her own home. The weekends were usually a high-speed round of shopping and socialising and the house had become little more than a place to crash in. But even Ben's presence didn't irritate her as much as she'd thought it would. He was being rather sweet, cooking her meals, bringing her flowers, taking drinks out to her in the garden where she was enjoying relaxing in the spring sunshine with a book. If only she could get her worries about her job out of her mind, she would be perfectly content.

On Thursday afternoon she decided to join Ben in a bit of gardening. He had made quite an effort with the vegetables, as well as re-stocking their two flower beds, and Shelley was impressed. Gardening was not a skill that she would have associated with her husband. But while they were weeding, Ben suddenly remembered he had an appointment with the dentist and he went off, leaving her on her knees amongst the flowers.

The sun was hot for April, making Shelley think of lying on a beach somewhere. Maybe a holiday was just what she needed. Then a mental cloud loomed, obscuring her pleasant thoughts. Once she would have planned to go with Ben, but perhaps a holiday away from him was more appropriate now. The thought saddened her. Despite the relatively relaxed few days she had spent with him that week, they had still not made love, nor even discussed their relationship. Her marriage, like her job, seemed stuck in limbo. Both parties were reluctant to make the decision that would put them out of their misery.

Suddenly Shelley was startled to hear a voice call 'Coo-ee!' over the garden fence. She knew at once who it was: Nosey Rosie, their neighbour. The woman was a notorious gossip, having nothing better to do with her time, and Shelley usually tried to avoid her. Today, however, she was a sitting target.

'I wonder if you have a moment or two,' Rose called. 'Maybe you'd like to come in for a cup of tea?' No, I wouldn't, Shelley thought. She was trying to think up an excuse when her neighbour continued, 'I think there's something you ought to know, Shelley.'

Tempted as she was to tell the woman to keep her nose out of other people's business, Shelley was nevertheless intrigued. This time Rose had made it sound as if the information was personal to her.

'Well, just for a few minutes then,' she agreed. 'I want to finish weeding this bed before Ben gets back.'

The kettle was already boiling when Shelley arrived in her neighbour's kitchen. Rose made tea and sat the fat brown pot on the table with the crockery and a plate of biscuits. Her boot-button eyes were set close together, giving her the air of some inquisitive little rodent.

'I saw Ben go off and leave you alone,' she began. 'That's why I thought this was the right time to talk to you. We don't get much of a chance to chat, do we, with you being out at work all day? Are you off sick at the moment, dear?'

'No, no. I just thought I'd take a bit of a break.'

'Not going on holiday or anything, then?'

'I've no plans at the moment, Rose. Now what is it you wanted to tell me? As I said, I don't have a lot of time this afternoon.'

Rose poured the tea, her thin lips pursed. Then she sat back, clearly relishing in advance what she was about to say. 'It's about your husband, as a matter of fact. Now I don't usually take much notice about what's going on round here . . .'

Like hell you don't! Shelley thought.

'But I couldn't help noticing that Mr Derwent has been spending rather a lot of time with that woman opposite. Now don't get me wrong, I'm not suggesting they're having an affair or anything like that. But Anne Meredith has been on her own for a long time, and she's still quite young and attractive, and . . . well, a man only has so much self-control, doesn't he?'

Shelley had to think quickly. 'He did say something about Anne collecting stuff for a car boot sale,' she told her. 'I'm sure there's no more to it than that.'

'Well I certainly hope so. I wouldn't like to see you two in any kind of trouble. It must be hard enough already, what with him being unemployed and you having to be the bread-winner. I mean, that's not good for a man's pride, is it?'

'I'm sure Ben will find another job before long.'

'Yes, dear, I'm sure he will. How long has it been now, nearly a year? They do say that the longer you're unemployed the harder it is to get back into a job. I'm just grateful that Philip is in no danger of that. However much the world changes, we're always going to need undertakers, aren't we?'

Shelley decided it was time to get her own back. 'I hear that DIY funerals are becoming all the rage. They're selling self-assembly cardboard coffins, you know.'

Rose vociferously pooh-poohed the idea and went on to describe the lavish funeral that Philip had arranged for a local dignitary the week before. Of course, being Rose, she couldn't help mentioning that both his mistresses had been present as well as his first and second wives! While her neighbour nattered on, Shelley found her mind wandering back to the thought of her husband and their other neighbour. She couldn't help recalling how jaunty he'd seemed over the past couple of weeks. Had he really been knocking off the very well-endowed Anne Meredith while she was out at work?

At last, after making her excuses, Shelley returned to her own home to finish working in the garden. When Ben returned she was just finishing and he offered to make her some tea. Shelley knew she had to confront him with her suspicions, and the sooner the better. It wasn't the kind of information she wished to nurture, allowing it to fester in her bosom. Better to have it out in the open straight away.

'I've been talking to Rose next door,' she began, as she sipped her second cup of tea. 'For once, the gossip she's peddling is about you, Ben.'

'About *me*?' At first he seemed genuinely surprised, but then she saw a light dawn in his eyes and they turned shifty. 'What did she say?'

'She thought you might be having an affair with Anne Meredith.'

'Anne over the road?' He was obviously playing for time,

confirming her suspicions. 'Well, I have been over there lately. With the car boot things. I told you.'

'Yes, but she seemed to think you'd been spending a lot of time there.'

'She did offer me some tea, as a matter of fact. It seemed only polite to stay a while.'

'So there's nothing between you then, is there?'

His manner suddenly became truculent. 'You know, you've got a nerve questioning me like this, Shelley. You know what they say about "sauce for the goose". I know perfectly well you're not only sleeping with someone else but letting him take disgusting photos of you too.'

'Photos! What do you mean?'

'You know very well. Horny shots of you and some well-hung porn star. I couldn't believe my eyes when I found them in the back of the wardrobe.'

'What were you doing snooping around?'

'I was turning cupboards out, for God's sake. Looking for stuff to give to Anne for the sale. She could probably have got a good price for that little lot, too.'

Shelley turned white. 'Ben! How could you even think of such a thing!'

'Don't worry, they're still safe in their hiding-place. I wouldn't have mentioned it only you started accusing me.' His shoulders slumped and he looked suddenly quite dejected. 'Okay, I did have a bit of a thing going with Anne. I see no point in denying it, since it doesn't really matter any more. It's pretty obvious that our marriage is on the rocks, and has been for some time. Maybe we'd better start thinking about making it official.'

'You mean, divorce?' He nodded, his eyes downcast. 'Is that what you want?'

'God, no! If I thought there was any hope for us, I'd want to keep going. But you seem to have someone else, and . . .'

'Not any longer, Ben. I told the guy who took those photos that I didn't want to have anything more to do with him. He gave me the negatives, to set my mind at rest. It's over between us.'

'And Duncan? What about him?'

'He's a bastard. That's finished too. Right now, there's no one. But as to whether we can make our marriage work, I honestly don't know.'

It was so frustrating: the will seemed to be there on both sides, and yet the practicalities of the situation were against them. Shelley had watched Ben becoming more and more slobbish and demoralised since he had lost his job, making him less and less attractive to her. It was no wonder he had leapt at the chance of a spot of nooky when it came his way.

Their conversation seemed to go round in circles as they tried to work out the best way forward. Shelley didn't even want to think about bringing her own possible redundancy into the equation. With both of them out of work, she was convinced that their relationship would go from bad to worse.

'But what more can I *do*?' Ben moaned, frustrated by all their vague talk of trying harder. 'I can't pluck a job out of thin air.'

'No, but you could do more about restoring your self-esteem,' Shelley said, thoughtfully. 'Look, why don't you give yourself a complete makeover? Get your hair re-styled, it looks a mess. You started to buy some new clothes the other day – get some more. You could do with some new shirts and a couple of decent suits.'

'I'd have to get a bigger size. I've put on at least two inches round the waist.'

'Okay, why not enrol in the gym? I'll pay for a season ticket. That way you're more likely to go regularly. It would do you good to get back into shape.'

'But will it help me get a job?'

'It might, if you look the part. You've let yourself go, Ben, and it's time to stop the rot. You could sign on at that Ex-Exec agency, too. Again I'll pay the fee. Anything to get you back on your feet again.'

Shelley could see Ben becoming excited by the idea of transforming himself. She was quite excited too. If he really looked the part and had the confidence he could walk into another job just like that, she was sure of it.

'It's your last chance, Ben,' she told him. 'I can't go on watching you go downhill like this. You've got to shape up, or ship out.'

Later Shelley wondered if she'd been too hard on him, but she told herself it was for his own good. She owed it to him, to herself, and to their marriage, to give him one last chance.

Chapter Eight

Ben was not too disappointed at having to break off his affair with Anne. They'd only made love three times, but she was not particularly skilled at it. She seemed to think that just because she had big breasts, men would swoon at her feet. She mostly just lay there and let him get on with it. He wasn't even convinced that she came when he was inside her, although she assured him that it was all 'wonderful'.

Besides, Anne had started to show dangerous signs of becoming attached. He had some sympathy for her, a lone mother who had devoted her prime years to looking after her two ungrateful kids instead of finding herself a new sexual partner. But when she started ringing him up and sending him little notes, even buying him presents of single malt miniatures and silk underpants, the alarm bells sounded.

He had broken the news to her the day after Shelley had given him her ultimatum. Anne had made the mistake of ringing him, thinking that he was alone, and he'd arranged to meet her in a café in town. There, over tea and éclairs, he had told her it was all over.

'Shelley and I really want to make a go of our marriage,' he told her uncomfortably, watching her lip tremble. 'She's given up her bloke, so it's only fair for me to do the same. I'm really sorry, Anne.'

'It's all right,' she sniffed. 'I understand. If I were in your shoes I'd do the same. You're so lucky to have a marriage, Ben. The only thing is, it seems so cruel that just as I'd started getting used to having sex again it's all got to stop.'

'Not necessarily.' He took her small hand in his, stroking her fingers. 'You're still a very attractive woman, Anne. Why don't you do something about finding a new boyfriend? You could go to a dating agency, or advertise in a Lonely Hearts column. In five years Paul will be eighteen and Sally will probably have left home. You owe it to yourself to plan for your own future, without the children.'

'You're right,' she smiled. 'I will do something. But I'll always be grateful to you, Ben, for reminding me of what I've been missing.'

He was relieved when it was over. After he'd dropped Anne off at the supermarket he went on to the gym, to enrol as a member. A man called Jeff showed him how to use the various machines, assessing the right seat height and weight, telling him how many repetitions to aim for and writing it all down for him on his personal training chart. There was a pool and sauna as well and so, after Ben had done his first workout, he went into the Scandinavian-style wooden cabin and relaxed in the company of a muscle-bound guy and a girl in a purple swimsuit whose figure was lean and beautifully honed.

'I could get used to this,' he said with a grin. The other two politely ignored him as he lay his head down on his folded towel. His body felt really good, tired but healthily so. Yes, he could certainly get used to the feeling of calm relaxation that followed on from his exhaustion. He glanced at the girl through his semi-closed lids, taking in every inch of her sleek flesh. Although she was not over-developed, there was not a spare ounce of fat on her. Her limbs were shapely and tanned, her torso voluptuously rounded with breasts that were pert and perfectly spherical within the enclosing lycra. To his embarrassment, Ben felt himself filling out his spandex shorts with a very visible bulge.

Then another bodybuilder appeared, his pectoral muscles well defined and his huge arms bronzed and vascular. 'Hi, Brian!' he said to the other guy. 'Had a good workout?'

His mate moved up on the slatted bench to let him sit down. 'Yeah. I got through that stagnation last week by downscaling my reps and poundage. Thanks for the tip.'

'You've been overtraining, that's all. Too many forced reps and drop sets. Try those routines I showed you for a couple of weeks, then you'll get back in balance.'

Ben listened to their conversation in bewildered fascination. He would have liked to question them but he was afraid to show his ignorance, particularly in front of the girl. Perhaps he would buy some of the bodybuilding magazines, familiarise himself with the jargon. Better still, he would surf the Internet. There were bound to be some bodybuilder usergroups. The prospect of acquiring a well-built body really excited him. He'd always secretly admired muscular guys, and now Shelley had given him the inspiration to work on his own physique.

After a leisurely swim, to get himself back into a livelier state of mind, Ben drove home to find that Shelley had cooked for once. He talked about his time at the gym with enthusiasm, and she seemed pleased. He planned a shopping expedition next day, to update his wardrobe, and on Monday he was going to be interviewed at the Ex-Exec agency to see if he was suitable to be taken on by the prestigious employment agency.

'I don't know why I didn't do all this before,' he commented, tucking into the meal that his wife had prepared.

'You were stuck in a rut,' Shelley explained. 'Your confidence had taken a battering when you lost your job and you hadn't managed to pull yourself out of it. But all that's going to change from now on, you'll see.'

Ben felt touched that she, at least, seemed to have faith in him. He felt closer to Shelley now than he had in months and after the meal the pair of them cuddled up on the sofa and started to watch the video of *Four Weddings and a Funeral* which they'd both somehow missed when it came out. The opening scene, where Hugh Grant's character repeats the 'F' word several times, reminded Shelley of something she'd been told at work.

'When this film was shown on a transatlantic flight they decided that "fuck" wasn't suitable for family viewing,' she told him. 'The airline was worried that children might ask their parents awkward questions, like "what does fuck mean, Mum?" So they changed it.'

'What to?'

'Bugger!'

Ben rolled around in paroxysms of laughter and Shelley joined in. It felt so good to be laughing uninhibitedly with his wife again that he allowed his mirth to prolong itself until his ribs felt quite bruised. The effect of all that hilarity was to raise his libido, so that when Shelley flipped the video back on from 'pause' he found he could scarcely concentrate on the action. He was all too aware of his wife's undoubted attractions: the tempting curve of her neck beneath her gorgeous auburn hair; the equally alluring curve of her bosom in her outsize T-shirt; and the slimness of her thighs in those leggings she wore when she lounged around the house. He put his arm around her and drew her close, scenting the warm, sweet perfume that emanated from her body. Nuzzling into her neck he delivered a few soft kisses and awaited her response.

'Ben, I'm watching the film!' she complained, but not strongly. Her tone was that of mild reproach tinged with amusement. In other words, encouraging.

He put one hand up her T-shirt and felt the round smoothness of her breasts in the clingy bra she wore. As he touched her he could feel the nipples hardening and he tweaked them delicately. Shelley gave a half-hearted sigh of reproof, but she didn't try to remove his fingers. He slipped the other hand down between her thighs, into the gusset of her leggings where her sex was soft and spongy. Shelley wriggled a little, her eyes still on the screen, but he could tell that she was already aroused and it wouldn't take much to distract her completely from the film. His head bent down and he raised her top so that he could kiss her cleavage, between the taut mounds of her breasts.

'Ben! Are we watching this film or not?' she asked.

'What would you rather do?'

He managed to pop one turgid nipple out of its pouch and took it between his lips. Shelley moaned, throwing back her head and closing her eyes. Ben responded to her body language by picking up the remote and silencing the video, then he rolled down the elasticated waist of her leggings until her white cotton panties were exposed. He placed his palm over her mound, feeling the springy cushion of hair beneath. Shelley flopped down on the sofa, abandoning herself to him, and he pulled her leggings right off. Then he reached round her back and unhooked her bra. She pulled the T-shirt off and shrugged her arms out of the bra straps until she lay naked except for her pants.

Ben knelt beside her on the floor and kissed first her mouth, then her breasts in turn. Shelley sighed and stretched voluptuously. It was the first time in ages that she'd been this responsive and Ben felt the adrenaline surging through his veins, giving him the confidence he needed to continue. While he stroked the curved undersides of her breasts his lips moved over the rounded swell of her stomach, tasting the sweetness of her skin that smelt faintly of the rose-scented body lotion she used. He was feasting on her, enjoying again the Shelley he had once adored, reviving his appetite for the love they used to share.

While he explored the inner smoothness of her thighs with his mouth, he could feel his wife's hand down the back of his jeans, stroking the tops of his buttocks. Within his designer underpants he could feel the surging strength of his erection growing by the second and longing for some tactile contact with cool fingers or moist lips. He struggled with his belt and zipper until he could ease himself out of the constricting denim. Shelley was quick to take the hint. Her hands reached down to feel the state of his penis and she squeezed him softly, letting him know that she approved.

Her action reminded Ben of how it used to be between them, of the silent code they used in love-making to tell each other how they felt, what they wanted. Now he knew exactly how to proceed. Carefully he removed his pants, feeling the relief as his distended organ was exposed to the light caress of the air and his balls were allowed to swing free. At once Shelley took his shaft between her fingers and began to rub him slowly. He continued to nuzzle around her damp and musky crotch, licking along the strip of skin at the top of her thighs where a few stray hairs peeped from under the legs of her pants.

She had begun to thrust her mons against him, so he knew she was ready for a more direct approach. Although what she was doing to his prick was becoming very distracting, Ben did his best to focus on her needs. He slipped a finger in through one leg to the mushy centre of her quim. Shelley moaned and tried to pull down her pants, so he helped her out until they were a small heap on the floor. Eagerly he got up onto the sofa and, helped by her willing hands, guided his penis straight in through heaven's gate to the paradise within.

And it was heaven, pure heaven. The cushioning folds opened up to accommodate him and his prick sank in right up to the hilt. He began with slow, gentle strokes the way she liked it, letting her get used to him being in her again, reminding her – and himself – of how good it could be between them.

Yet the spectre of last time they'd made love kept returning to mock Ben's enjoyment. He'd felt used by Shelley and then he'd used her in return. This time, he told himself, it was totally different. She was looking up at him with a dreamy smile and her hips were gently rocking to his rhythm, making it easier for him to slide in and out of her. He put his hand down to feel the hardness of her clitoris in its slippery nook and smiled back at her.

'Yes, yes, rub me there!' she urged him.

As soon as he did, Ben thought he could feel the gathering wave of her orgasm, and the proximity of his own overwhelmed him. Gasping in time with his ejaculation, he felt the hot currents spurt through him, flooding his senses with pure, lustful abandonment. Yet he was aware, as the crisis subsided and his body felt warm and relaxed again, that Shelley remained high and dry. He made a few ineffectual thrusts with his fast-wilting penis but it didn't take long before he slipped right out of her.

'Sorry, love,' he murmured, sinking beside her in a state of exhaustion.

'That's okay. I'll finish myself off.'

'No, let me.' Ben reached for her still-dripping vulva but she seized him by the wrist and put his hand aside. 'I'll do it, Ben. It'll be quicker and I'm really tired.'

He didn't argue. Lying limply beside her while she brought herself off with some rapid friction, Ben felt disappointed that he hadn't been able to hold out just a few seconds longer, but it was too late now. What had begun as a glorious reassertion of their attraction for each other seemed to have ended up in the usual unsatisfactory mess. Hearing her gasps and moans subside, he decided not to put on an insincere show of affection but went upstairs and got ready for bed. By the time Shelley joined him he was pretending to be asleep.

Next day Ben changed his mind about going shopping for clothes. It didn't seem a good idea when he wasn't feeling at his best. He had awoken vaguely depressed after the optimism of the previous evening and Shelley had rushed off to work without saying much, so he couldn't tell how she felt about their love-making session. Personally he felt it was an improvement on their previous effort, but on a scale of one to ten it probably didn't rate any more than a four. Gloomily he considered keeping some sort of chart or graph of their marital couplings, persuading Shelley to do likewise so they could compare their perceptions, but perhaps that would only make things worse.

Then Ben remembered that he'd thought of looking up the bodybuilding user group on the Internet. The prospect cheered him up. He scrolled through the various titles until he found one called *Megabrawn*. The list of sub-headings was interesting: 'Pump up the Poundage', 'Shed and Shred', 'Stripped and Ripped', 'Sets and Reps for Lats and Pecs' – it was a jargon he was just beginning to understand from eavesdropping on the guys in the gym.

The pages Ben looked at mostly consisted of bodybuilders passing on tips to each other about their exercise routines, diet or food supplements. Then a striking advert caught his eye. It read, '*Trade Fat for Muscle in just Three Weeks! Take "Nanzanstan" in combination with "Testonor 19" in a wicked new formulation, and achieve unbelievable results in an incredibly short time. I did it, so can you.*' There was a picture of a beefy squarehead grinning, and instructions on how to order the product using a Virtual Account. '*Just fifty dollars secures you a month's supply of this wonderstuff, along with full dietary instructions, weight-ratio dosage and recommended self-development program. Maximise the effect of your workout with this All Gain, No Pain product.*'

The Internet address looked as if it were in Mexico. It was a very tempting offer, but Ben wondered what guarantees there were that if he did as suggested and gave them his credit card number he would get the pills. He left that advert and went on to learn more about ordering through the Internet. Apparently his credit card number could be encrypted, and then his order would be held over until he received the goods. It was a system that he was already linked into through his Internet server.

Ben took out his credit card. Would Shelley miss thirty pounds or so from their joint account? Maybe if he went clothes shopping soon the pills would be lost in the billing of shirts and shoes and such. He found the place where he had to order them and entered his coded number into his computer. Then he sat back with a sigh. He'd done it! He had ordered something through the Net for the first time, and it was going to help him build a fantastic body in a few weeks. Highly elated, Ben went upstairs and had a quick wank followed by a shower. He grinned at himself in the wardrobe mirror, struck a 'Mr Muscle' pose and then intoned in a deep voice, 'Let's go shopping!'

Normally Ben hated hunting for clothes but today he was on a high. Mindful of the fact that his body would soon be totally re-sculptured, he bought trousers that were too tight at the waist, inspiring him to shed some flab, and shirts that were too big round the collar and chest, as encouragement to acquire some meat. Then he set off for the gym to see if he could improve on the previous day's 'Sets and Reps'.

At two in the afternoon, the gym was almost empty. Ben felt slightly self-conscious in the new lycra shorts and vest he'd bought himself. He took in the other occupants of the gym at a glance: a black guy working quietly with weights in the corner, an old guy on the treadmill and a girl bouncing up and down on the stepper – the same girl he'd seen in the sauna the previous day. She was wearing a mauve bodyshaper and minuscule matching shorts, her blonde, sweat-darkened hair was tied back in a ponytail and she had a pair of pristine white trainers on her feet. She'd obviously been using the sunbed as she had a uniform light tan and when she glanced in his direction her eyes were a vivid, piercing turquoise. Within the inner pouch of his shorts something stirred.

Hesitantly Ben threw her a semi-grin and was amazed when she flashed him a smile in return. He'd expected to be rebuffed. Nonchalantly he went up to the fountain and took a draught of ice-cold water, then made his way to the chest press. His record card said the seat had to be in position five and the weight at thirty kilos. He took the peg out of the fifty kilo hole and tried to ram it into the thirty slot but it just wouldn't go.

'Shit!' he exploded, softly, taking the thing out and trying again. He jiggled it around but still it wouldn't go all the way in. Exasperated he went round to adjust the seat then returned to the back of the machine and had another go: still no luck.

'Are you having trouble?'

He looked up at the sound of a female voice and found himself looking into those disconcertingly blue-green eyes. 'Er ... I don't seem to be able to get it in the hole,' he said, feeling an utter fool.

'Yes, they do stick a bit sometimes. Shall I try?'

Ben tried not to stare too obviously as she bent down to the task, giving him a view of two perfectly firm and rounded breasts within her clingy purple top. She wiggled the peg for a moment or two and then it slipped in. She straightened up with a smile. 'There you are. Should be all right now.'

'Thanks, it's really good of you.'

She flashed him another whiter than white grin. 'All part of the service.'

'Service?'

'I work here, I'm one of the instructors.' She held out her hand. 'Sara Morton. If you need any help with your training programme, just make an appointment.'

It was on the tip of his tongue to say that he did need help, oh yes indeed, very much so, but she had returned to her jaunty stepping before he could utter a word.

Ben's membership card entitled him to make as much use of the gym and other facilities as he wished, and it wasn't long before he was going down the road every day for a workout and sauna. There was something about the routine that really excited him, and soon his body was beginning to show results. Shelley began to notice too.

'Your biceps are really meaty now,' she smiled, feeling his upper arm as he flexed it for her. 'And your chest has fleshed out a lot. It's amazing what a few visits to the gym can do, isn't it?'

'Why don't you join me?'

She pulled a face. 'No time. Anyway, I'm shattered when I get home and there's so much to do at the weekends.'

Ben didn't push it. He was quite relieved that his wife wasn't going to join him at the gym. It had become his own thing, his private domain, and he didn't want anyone he knew to see him working out. Besides, as long as Sara Morton was on the staff, he couldn't help ogling her lithe body as she worked the machines. If Shelley were around, he would feel inhibited. He'd got to know the times when the sexy instructress was in the habit of working out, usually when she came off duty, and daydreaming about her had become part of his routine.

As he did his stint on the rowing machine, he could often see Sara in the wall-mirror, developing her already magnificent chest or honing down her already lean thighs. It wasn't difficult to imagine how that firm, youthful body would feel, and soon Ben would have a full-sized erection which he was powerless to conceal in his skin-tight shorts. Once or twice he caught her glancing at it in the mirror with a faint smile on her lips, and he nearly creamed himself. Despite his intention to put more energy into his marriage, Sara Morton was, quite unwittingly, giving Shelley some serious competition.

Eventually the steroids that Ben had ordered came in the post, much to his relief. He hadn't quite trusted the system, but once he had the pills in his hand he was prepared to order some more from the same source. There was an advert in

Megabrawn for 'Ultraboost', a drug that was supposed to 'inhibit excess fat storage' and 'increase metabolic rate for leaner, meaner definition'. Ben sent off for some of that, too. Although he had made great strides at the beginning of his training, after three weeks he seemed to be stagnating and he thought he could do with some help.

The obvious course was to consult someone about his programme but Jeff, his original instructor, was on vacation and he felt inhibited about approaching Sara. In the end, however, it was she who approached him.

'I've noticed the way you use the Abdominizer,' she told him one day, coming up with a friendly smile. 'I hope you won't take this the wrong way, but it's better if you keep your head up throughout. That way you get more pull on the abdominals. Shall I show you?'

Ben tried not to stare too obviously at her heaving breasts and bulging crotch, but he couldn't help becoming aroused at the sight of that exquisitely moulded body in motion. When she stopped and invited him to have a go, the electricity between them seemed intense. One look from those gorgeous eyes increased his body heat by a couple of degrees. He sat down and grasped the handles over his shoulders, acutely aware of the visible outline of his prick under the close-fitting shorts. As he looked up, he could see Sara glance down to check his sitting position. He knew she couldn't help but notice his erection. Was he imagining it, or did a slight tinge of colour deepen the ruddy tan of her cheeks?

'That's good,' she encouraged him, as he did a few pull-downs. 'Keep your neck as straight as you can. That's fine.'

Ben did twenty repetitions and then stopped. There was an awkward pause as they realised that her job was done, and yet something kept her hanging on there. Sara gave a quick glance round the gym, cleared her throat, then asked, 'Are you having problems with any other apparatus?'

Cheered by the fact that she wanted to prolong their contact, Ben quickly invented a whole host of 'problems' and ended up spending an hour with her. Although they were officially discussing his progress, or lack of it, on the machines, their body language was telling a different story. Sara seemed to take every opportunity to touch him, on the knee or the arm, and every time he felt a quivering sensation in his loins that increased his lust. At the same time he could sense that she was equally attracted to him, her eyes sending smouldering messages to his even as she talked about his training in a cool and professional manner. By the end of the session he was convinced that if he asked her out she would not turn him down.

Deciding to keep it low-key at first, he said he was going to have lunch in the snack-bar and asked if she would join him.

'I was going there anyway,' she smiled, her eyes lighting up. 'Maybe it would be a good opportunity for us to discuss your diet.'

And the rest, Ben thought, determined to get to know this gorgeous woman better.

He showered and changed in record time, found them a table in the snack bar and waited for Sara to appear. She looked fresh and delectable in a pale blue T-shirt that showed the hard tips of her nipples peaking on her well-formed breasts, and slimfit jeans that displayed the tight rotundity of her buttocks. Soon they were sitting opposite each other eating healthy food and talking lifestyles. Ben told her that he spent a lot of time sitting at a computer and felt the need to take more exercise. He didn't mention the steroid issue. From the way in which Sara kept stressing health and fitness, he guessed she wouldn't approve of people taking any kind of drug to build muscle.

When it came to discussing more personal matters, Ben managed to avoid admitting that he was both unemployed and married. Sara had her own flat in Highgate, which seemed promising. When their lunch was over she mentioned that she'd finished work for the day.

'I generally take Jessie, my dog, for a run on Hampstead Heath on my free afternoons,' she told him. 'You're welcome to join me, if you have the time.'

'Sure,' he grinned, feeling a surge of elation in his veins. 'My time's my own.'

He followed Sara's car to her small mews flat and parked in the cobbled street. A yapping sheltie greeted her mistress with unbounded enthusiasm and they all got back into Sara's car to drive to the heath. While Jessie chased sticks with untiring eagerness, Ben found Sara was quite amenable to walking hand in hand across the open spaces or sitting on a bench with his arm around her, and soon he began to hope for more. The sexual chemistry that flowed between them was becoming overwhelming, filling Ben with confident optimism.

By the time they arrived back at Sara's place, sex seemed to be definitely on the agenda. When she invited him in he could hardly control himself, yet it was impossible to say who made the first move. She seemed to fall into his arms at the very moment he opened them, and soon they were kissing with passionate abandon. Sara felt incredibly lithe and compact, her body power-packed yet voluptuously feminine. She was definitely the most exciting woman he had encountered in a long time.

'I wanted you the moment I saw you in the sauna,' she admitted as, sitting quietly together after the first upsurge of mutual lust, they took stock of the situation. 'Only I didn't dare show it. I was afraid I might lose my job if I had an affair with a client.'

'What changed your mind?'

She grinned. 'I made a few discreet enquiries and found out that since you were registered with Jeff it would be okay. One of the other instructors is dating a woman who's registered with me.'

'Great!' Ben drew her close, one hand pulling her face towards him to be kissed while the other sought the enticing curve of her breast. She gave a deep-throated moan as his fingers targeted the stiff nipple inside what Ben guessed was a sports bra. Her lips moved sensually against his then parted to allow access to his tongue, the fresh juice of her saliva mingling with his. They kissed with increasing fervour until Sara, disentangling herself from his embrace, murmured that they would be more comfortable in the bedroom.

Praying that she had a condom, Ben followed her on weak knees into a small room that was dominated by a double bed. At once Sara pulled off her T-shirt to display her uplifted bosom, the nipples filling out the taut white cup into sharply-defined points. Into the V-shaped divide plunged a stunning tanned cleavage that drew Ben's lips like a luscious fruit.

He bent his head to kiss between her close-packed breasts while she fumbled with the zip of her jeans. Her skin was beautifully firm and smooth, smelling faintly of sandalwood, and Sara thrust herself eagerly against his exploring mouth, inviting him to delve deeper. Soon she was naked below except for a pair of white briefs that sat snugly over her pelvic bones.

'Now your turn,' she smiled, her eyes staring unashamedly at his crotch. Ben sensed her excitement, knew she couldn't wait to get a good look at his tackle, and hoped he wouldn't disappoint her.

First he stripped off his shirt, to reveal his arms and chest. Sara placed her palms over his biceps. 'Mm, you're doing well,' she smiled. 'I love the feel of newly-developed muscle. It's different from well-worked flesh, all springy and mould-able as if it really is made of clay.'

She put her mouth to his upper arm and grated her teeth on his contoured bicep, sending anticipatory tingles all across his shoulders and down his back. Ben felt her unbuckle his belt and let her open the button before she knelt to lever down his zip. While he stepped out of his jeans Ben saw Sara take off her bra. He gasped at the way those perfect golden globes jutted out from her chest with their pert nipples inviting his attention, and inside his jockey shorts his penis gave a great lusty leap.

Sara noticed. 'I think we'd better let him out, don't you?' she said, looking up at Ben with a cheeky smile. 'He's like a wild animal in there!'

Carefully she eased the elasticated band over Ben's ram-pant organ. She gave an 'Ooh!' of delight as first the naked pink head appeared, then the solid column of his shaft and finally his swinging balls. She cradled the pair softly with her hands while she gave his glans a brief, tantalising kiss, then let his shaft nestle between her breasts. Smiling, she rolled her tits round with her hands so that they gave his penis a good massage, taking Ben almost to the brink of coming. He exerted all his self-control, not wanting to spoil things too soon, but he knew if she kept that up for long there would be no stopping him.

Fortunately she had the sense to leave off before things went too far. Pushing him gently back until Ben felt the edge of the bed behind his knees, she told him to lie down while she took off her pants. He lay back against the pillow watching her. As she bent over to remove the garment her breasts didn't swing floppily like Shelley's but retained their buoyant firmness and he longed to give them a good kneading while he sucked at those ripe pink nipples. Then she lowered her pants and he saw the trim shape of her pubic hair, light brown and curly, with just a hint of the dark divide beneath.

'Wow, you look amazing!' he breathed, taking in the svelte proportions of her figure.

'I have to, it's my job.'

'And I bet you're really strong, too.'

She grinned. 'Strong enough. What I like most about working out, though, is the way it increases your stamina. I can make love all night and still get up for work in the morning.'

Her words were faintly alarming. Ben glanced at the bedside clock: three-thirty. He couldn't afford to stay longer than a couple of hours or Shelley would wonder where he was.

Sara noticed the direction of his gaze and his look of faint disquiet. 'Don't worry, we don't have to make it a marathon this time. Let's just make sure it's good, eh?'

She felt for a packet of rubbers in the drawer of the bedside cabinet and deftly rolled one down the length of his erection, then she crawled up the bed until she was beside him, exuding a strong scent of female arousal. Ben reached up and pulled the firm breasts towards his mouth as she straddled him. When he was licking eagerly at one of her nipples and softly tweaking the other, she leaned back and felt for his penis where it was jabbing against her buttocks, proceeding to sweep her palms gently along its length.

Sara positioned herself so that his glans was poking into her crack a little way and he felt the tip enclosed by soft mounds again. She had closed her eyes and was moaning quietly, making small circular movements with her pelvis in order to apply some friction to her vulva as it spread open on his hairy abdomen. Ben could feel the faint sticky trail she left as she wriggled round and round, and it was the same feeling he got when he spurted onto his stomach himself. He sucked hard at her nipple and put one hand down to feel the hard kernel of her clitoris. Sara cried out with the sudden increase in stimulation and, almost before he realised what she was up to, she slid back onto his erection and let the length of him glide right inside her. Ben stroked her iron-hard thighs as she began to ride him, loving the smooth solidity of her toned-up flesh.

It was sheer bliss to feel the taut muscularity of her vaginal walls squeezing him, a subtle combination of velvet and steel, and Ben decided to lie back and let her do most of the work. It seemed to be what she wanted too. For once he felt he didn't have to live up to some macho image. If anything, she was tougher than he was, and if they ever put it to the test he wouldn't like to bet on who would prove the stronger.

For a while Sara contented herself with small up and down movements, letting Ben stimulate her externally with his fingers while she let her own roam over his solidly moulded chest. He pressed hard between her labia, making the slippery nub grow firm and protuberant as it hungered for more stimulation and got it. Then she seemed to change gear and the pace quickened. She rose higher and plunged deeper, faster, urging him on towards the climax that he'd been delaying for too long.

Now there could be no more holding back. Ben gasped and closed his eyes as the tension in him rose to its absolute peak, holding him in an agony of suspense until at last, with a great outrush of breath, the energy poured out of him in fierce bursts of pure relief. Following on from that release came a flood of sensual pleasure, filling every vein in his body with erotic warmth and relaxing all his muscles into a state of languid well-being, similar to the aftermath of a good workout.

'God, Sara, that was absolutely fantastic,' he moaned, looking up into her vivid blue eyes. She smiled, giving his penis a brief clench with her vagina and drawing out the last of his seed.

'Stick with me, kid,' she drawled. 'You ain't seen nothin' yet!'

Chapter Nine

Fortunately for Shelley's peace of mind, Steve didn't appear at Harcourt Productions again. She had two busy weeks, working on another commercial, but after that Duncan told her she would have to take a week's break. This time she was not so dismayed. For one thing she'd been half expecting it, and for another she'd had a phone call from her sister, Evelyn, suggesting they should take a spur of the moment holiday together in Greece.

Shelley knew she needed a break. The stresses at work were beginning to get to her and she was worried about where her marriage was heading. Ben seemed very self-absorbed these days and, although he'd smartened himself up considerably and was toning his body up a treat, he seemed to have little time for her. Sometimes she caught him in the shower, his muscled torso gleaming with water and gel, or saw his powerful back and shoulders when he was putting on his shirt, and she wanted to pounce on him like a voracious lioness. But she was afraid of being rebuffed. They just didn't seem to be on each other's wavelength any more.

So she rang Evelyn and said she would go to Rhodes. 'A week's sun and sea will do me the world of good,' she declared, feeling optimistic already. 'You too, Evie. You've had a rough time lately.'

She certainly had. Her younger sister had just been jilted by Alan, her boyfriend of two years, and all her plans for the future had gone suddenly awry. They were to have been married the following June.

The night before she was due to leave, Shelley was packing in the bedroom and couldn't find her bikini. Thinking she might have put it in a little-used bottom drawer, she opened it up and found, tucked beneath some spare linen, two packets of red and purple capsules. She frowned at the unfamiliar labels: 'Testanor 19' and 'Nanzanstan'. The horrible thought went through her head that Ben had been diagnosed as having some dreadful, possibly fatal, disease and hadn't told her. If that was the case, she simply had to know right away.

With her heart thumping wildly, she took them downstairs. Ben was watching television, but she waved the pills at him and his face turned white. 'Are these yours?' she asked.

'Oh, er, yes. They're just . . . for hay fever.'

She was instantly suspicious. 'I didn't know you suffered from hay fever, Ben. You're not sneezing, or anything.'

'No. Well, I'm a bit congested, that's all.'

'Did Dr Mayfield prescribe them?'

Ben looked shifty. 'No, a friend gave them to me.'

'Who?'

'Oh, someone you don't know. Look, Shelley, I was watching this programme . . .'

Still doubting him, she went into the hall. Picking up the phone she dialled the local chemist's number. He would tell her whether the drugs were for hay fever or not.

The pharmacist sounded shocked when she mentioned the brand names. 'They sound like steroids, and they've almost certainly been acquired illegally.'

Shelley was shocked. 'But what are they for?'

'Well, they do have a legitimate use, probably as veterinary medicines. But they're abused by bodybuilders who want to gain muscle quickly. They can be quite dangerous if taken to excess.'

'I see. Thank you.'

She returned to the front room, tense with anger. Flicking off the television she confronted Ben with the information and he didn't try to deny it. 'They're quite safe,' he assured her. 'Lots of people use them.'

'Where did you get them?'

'By mail order.'

She threw the packets down on the sofa beside him in disgust. 'Then you're a bigger fool than I thought, Ben Derwent. I said get yourself into shape, not screw yourself up.'

Ben picked up the pills and rose from the sofa. He glared at her. 'Well, screw you!'

'Stop, Ben, we have to talk about this.'

He strode from the room, ignoring her, and went upstairs. She followed him, seeing him place the pills in the drawer of the bedside cabinet.

'Are you going to stop taking those things?' she demanded.

He turned on her, his eyes filled with fury. 'The hell I am!'

'But there must be side-effects. You could at least talk to Dr Mayfield about them.'

'That old fool? You must be joking.'

She went up to him, tried to put her arm around him but he shrugged her off. 'Please, Ben, you must talk to someone. You could be doing yourself a lot of damage.'

'I stick to the dosage. And all they do is help you build

muscle.' He suddenly grinned at her and flexed his arm. 'Feel my bicep, go on!'

'Don't be ridiculous! Look, I have to pack right now, but I want you to talk to someone medically qualified before I get back from Greece, okay?'

'This is my business, not yours.'

'But I'm concerned about you, Ben. When I first found those things, I thought you had some serious illness. That's how you might end up if you go on taking them without proper supervision. You *must* ask a doctor about taking them.'

He said nothing but strode past her and went back to the television. Shelley knew she could do no more. She'd had her say but, if he wanted to ignore her, that was his lookout. It was just one more thing for her to worry about. God, did she need that holiday!

Because she had to rise at crack of dawn to get to the airport, Shelley slept in the spare room that night. It was hard to sleep with so much on her mind. She was trawling through her memory for anything she might have heard about steroids. Didn't they turn women into men, and vice-versa? Would Ben be developing breasts? Would his dick shrink? Maybe she should find out a bit more about them herself when she returned from Rhodes.

Evelyn was waiting for her at Heathrow, and as soon as they got onto the plane, Shelley felt a weight lift from her shoulders. She was determined not to let worry spoil her holiday. They arrived at midday and were taken to a vast hotel in the middle of nowhere, or so it appeared. Flopping exhausted onto the twin beds, they decided to catch up on their sleep before exploring their surroundings.

In fact the road to the hotel also contained several *tavernas* and small shops, and there was a village about half a mile away. The best thing about the place, though, was the beach. It was sandy and relatively sheltered, with a light breeze that Shelley suspected would provide welcome relief from the hot sun. The sea was a deep, inviting blue.

'Mm, marvellous!' she declared, standing on a grassy patch in her shorts and bikini top. 'Shall we bag a couple of loungers and spend the afternoon here?'

Soon they were installed on the beach between an over-weight German couple and two giggly girls from Bristol. All the women were topless so they followed suit, rubbing sun lotion well into their breasts and nipples. It wasn't long before two local lads appeared, both in swim-trunks, and sat down between the two sisters and the Germans with obvious intent. Shelley was aware of them ogling her naked breasts but she didn't feel embarrassed. On the contrary, she was proud of her boobs and quite flattered to have them so obviously admired.

'Oh God!' Evelyn murmured. 'I think we've been targeted!'

Shelley looked at them covertly, through her sunglasses. 'They're rather nice looking, actually!' she whispered back.

Her sister's hazel eyes looked shocked. 'Shelley! That's not what we've come here for – is it?'

'Well I wouldn't mind a bit of a fling myself. But I'd have to really fancy the guy. I don't think either of these qualify.'

Evelyn looked serious. 'You surprise me. I thought you were happily married.'

Shelley sighed. 'I'm not at all sure about the state of my marriage, to tell you the truth. I didn't want to say anything, especially not when you were planning to marry Alan. I mean, I didn't want to put you off or anything. But ever since Ben lost his job, things have been going from bad to worse.'

'Oh no! I'm so sorry. I had no idea.'

'Well, I've come away to forget all that, okay? I don't want to talk about it any more. Not right now, anyway.'

Shelley lay back and closed her eyes, letting the warmth soak through her skin and right into her bones. It was blissfully relaxing. But after about five minutes she heard a man's voice say, in a heavy Greek accent, 'Excuse, ladies, you have a light, no?'

Unwillingly she opened her eyes to see the hunkier of the two guys looking down at her. He made no attempt to hide the fact that his approach was merely a ploy to get into conversation. 'My name is Nico,' he grinned, holding out his hand.

Something about the cheeky confidence of the man intrigued her. He was also, on closer inspection, rather handsome. His short black hair clung to his head in attractive curls and his dark brown eyes smouldered sexily at her, taking in every inch of her supine body.

She touched his fingers, lightly. 'Hi, I'm Shelley.'

'And this is my friend, Andreas.' The second man smiled pointedly at Evelyn, who rolled over onto her front and ignored him. 'Is nice here?' Nico asked.

'Very nice. But I think we would like to be left alone now, please. We've only just arrived.'

'From England?'

'Yes. Would you leave us now, please?'

'You want us to go?'

Shelley shrugged. 'Maybe we'll see you another time.'

'Oh yes! You stay in hotel, we see you maybe at the disco. 'Bye!'

Although she was relieved that they were not going to be pestered, Shelley also felt a bit disappointed. It would have been nice to flirt a little, maybe make a date. She was in the mood for a holiday romance, even if her sister wasn't.

'Honestly, you shouldn't encourage them,' Evelyn complained, as soon as the Greeks were out of earshot.

'Oh, they don't mean any harm. They're quite polite. Nice boys, really. And you can't blame them for trying it on.'

While she wallowed in the sun, Shelley found her imagination running riot. She fantasised that the beach was deserted except for her and Nico, and went through a whole seduction scene in her mind. First they would massage each other's bodies with suntan oil. At the thought of his hands on her breasts, Shelley felt her insides quiver with desire. Then she imagined him stroking her back, letting his fingers slip below her bikini bottom and into the crack between her buttocks, oiling her there. Somehow he would persuade her to remove the garment, and his hands would then smooth over the plump mounds of her bottom and down her thighs, just a few inches from the secret heart of her sex. She would long for him to touch her there, to ease the hunger she felt for him with his fingers, his lips, and ultimately with the sturdy prick she had already glimpsed beneath his skimpy trunks . . .

This was no good, Shelley decided. Her aroused clitoris was already throbbing and she could feel herself becoming wet. She was getting herself all worked up and with no immediate chance of relief. If she was going to indulge in such thoughts, she should wait until she was in bed at night so she could pleasure herself thoroughly.

'I'm going into the sea, to cool off!' she announced, rising from her sunbed.

The water was deliciously cool although, if she were not already overheated, it would have felt lukewarm. She swam out from the shore to a safe distance, where there were no windsurfers, and then floated on her back for a while, letting the sun's rays fall on her wet breasts.

Suddenly a small dinghy appeared from nowhere and a voice called out to her, 'Hi! It's Nico! You like swim?'

She looked up to see the two Greeks in their boat, grinning at her. Nico dived overboard, leaving Andreas to guard the vessel. He swam up to her, his white teeth exposed in a grin. 'You want to go in our boat?'

'Not right now, thanks, Nico.'

Although Shelley felt she should be annoyed with him, somehow she hadn't the energy. Anyway, he was being perfectly polite. He circled round her like some marine animal eyeing its prey, then dived below the surface. Shelley felt her ankle being seized and kicked out instinctively.

He resurfaced, laughing. 'You thought I was an octopus, yes?'

'No, Nico! I knew it was you.'

'You like to see fish?' He called to Andreas to bring the boat closer. From out of its depths a snorkel and face mask were produced. 'You want to try?' he offered.

Shelley had never tried snorkelling before. She let him put the mask on and adjust the strap, then attach the tube. He showed her how to stare down under the water and soon she could make out small shoals of brightly-coloured fish and the occasional large, lone grey one.

'There's loads of them!' she cried, excitedly. 'Hundreds!'

He laughed. 'Of course! But none of them will bite you. You need not be afraid.'

Shelley spent a happy twenty minutes swimming around and viewing the underwater life. It was incredible to be witnessing a different world, literally under her feet. Nico put on a mask too, and directed her here and there. While she was so engrossed he often touched her arm, or put his own arm around her waist to guide her towards another shoal, but she didn't mind. She was like a big kid, enjoying a new experience, and she was grateful to the Greek guy for giving her the opportunity.

At last Shelley handed back the apparatus and once again declined the boat trip. 'I want to sunbathe on the beach,' she told him.

'I know better beach,' he grinned, predictably. 'No one there. You can only go by boat.'

'Maybe some other time. I have to get back to my sister now.'

'Your sister? She very nice. What's her name?'

Shelley felt sure that Evelyn wouldn't want her to tell these fellas her name. She ignored him and began swimming for the shore.

'See you again!' Nico called after her, and she felt sure she would.

Once she was back on the beach, however, she sensed that Evelyn was cross with her.

'I told you not to encourage them,' she grumbled. 'I can guess what's going to happen. You'll go off with that gigolo and leave me all by myself for the rest of the holiday.'

'No I won't, I promise!' Shelley stroked her sister's brown hair affectionately 'But if you wanted to make up a foursome with Andreas that would be nice.'

'Well, I don't!' Evelyn turned over on her sunbed to sulk and Shelley settled back for another baking session.

They lunched at the hotel bar, which did Greek salads and toasted snacks, then went to their room for a siesta. In the late afternoon they put on cool cotton sundresses and went for a walk. There was one dusty road that led through the village, past ramshackle smallholdings with lugubrious goats, scrawny chickens and wrinkled old women in black. As they were walking along there was a sudden rickety roar and the blare of a horn. Shelley looked round to see Nico and Andreas on a death-trap of a motorcycle, waving furiously and grinning from ear to ear.

'Oh God!' Evelyn moaned 'It's them again. Are they going to turn up like bad pennies wherever we go?'

'I expect they live round here.'

Shelley waved back briefly but then ignored them. They careered off down the road with Nico driving like a maniac and Andreas' shapely bum hanging dangerously near the road over the back seat. Despite her sister's disapproval, Shelley found she was warming to their exuberant charm. It was refreshing to meet young men from another culture, men who weren't afraid of experiencing whatever life had to offer.

After dinner in a nearby taverna, Shelley and Evelyn went to a meeting with the holiday rep and booked three excursions. That would leave them three days for lounging on the beach. The following morning they went on a boat trip to Lindos, where the temperature was even higher than on the west coast, due to the lack of a cooling breeze. The acropolis, perched high on a clifftop, was breathtaking and the village, with its brilliant white houses, was picturesque.

They had talked of trying out the entertainment put on at the hotel that evening, but by the time they got back to the hotel they were both exhausted. After she'd rested and showered, however, Shelley felt quite lively again. They ate in the hotel restaurant then returned to their room.

'I don't think I can manage any more than supper and bed tonight,' Evelyn declared. 'But if you want to go down for the folk dancing, don't let me stop you.'

By ten o'clock her sister was in bed reading, so Shelley went down to the foyer to see what was happening. There were people in Greek costume dancing in the reception area and a bunch of tourists watching. As Shelley arrived, one of the dancers was beckoning to some Germans, trying to get them to join in. She watched their ungainly efforts for a few minutes, then suddenly felt a tap on her shoulder. Looking round, she saw Nico smiling at her. He was dressed quite smartly in an open-necked green shirt and crisp, new-looking jeans.

'You like?' he asked.

She shrugged. 'Yes, quite.'

'Downstairs they have disco, half after ten. You prefer that?' She nodded, and he gestured towards the bar. 'I buy you a drink? You like ouzo?'

'That would be nice, Nico. Thank you.'

Shelley knew that the evening might lead to them making love, and she felt very excited as he took her hand and led her through the tables to a seat. There was something immensely alluring about the man's sensual simplicity, and she longed to explore it further. With Evelyn safely tucked up in bed, she had no need to feel inhibited, and it would be a relief to know that at the end of the week she would never see him again. Not like Duncan, whose presence she must endure every day at work, or Steve, who might turn up again any time to embarrass her.

'This very nice hotel,' Nico smiled, holding her hand as they sipped their drinks. 'I often come here, to drink and dance.'

'Do you live in the village?'

'No, in another village. In the mountains. I come down to the sea when I am not working.'

'Where do you work?'

'My father has a factory. We make ceramics. Very nice. You come and see, maybe?'

'Maybe,' she smiled.

An insistent beat started up somewhere beneath their feet, signalling the start of the disco. Soon they made their way down to the darkened cellar, where a fat DJ in a too-tight silk shirt played yesterday's hits. Nico took her straight onto the almost empty dance floor and held her round the waist, swivelling his hips and looking into her eyes. Shelley smiled, enjoying moving in the quaint, old-fashioned style that her parents must have known. At home it would have seemed ridiculous to be dancing that way, but here it seemed all part of the exotic charm.

As the disco filled up and the atmosphere grew warm and intimate, Nico held her close and she could smell the raw masculinity that he was exuding beneath his cheap aftershave. She put her arms around him and felt the muscles moving in his back, her breasts pressed close to his wide chest. His hips were moving sinuously in time with hers, his pubic bone pressing into hers, letting her feel the hard edge of his fly against her belly. Although she couldn't be sure, Shelley thought she could feel his erection too, padding out the front of his jeans.

Then the DJ put on a slow number and Nico's movements became more slinky. He began to press his lips, first to her hair and then to the side of her neck, which made her tremble with the tickling sensation. His hands dropped to her bottom and he began fondling her buttocks with a lazy, circular motion that was almost mesmeric, lulling her into a mood of sensual languor.

Shelley was scarcely aware of the moment when their kiss began, so cunningly did he creep from her neck to her cheek and then down to her upper lip, which he brushed softly with his closed lips. By the time he came to full mouth-to-mouth contact, she was more than ready for him. Moaning softly, she let her mouth yield to his and tasted the slight aniseed flavour left from his ouzo. His hands pulled her closer in to him, making her unambiguously aware of his arousal and pressing his penis hard into her belly. Shelley trembled, her legs felt weak, and as his tongue began to probe her mouth she felt as if she would faint.

'Please, Nico, let me sit down!' she pleaded.

He stopped at once and led her to a table. 'You want a drink? You want to go outside?'

She nodded. 'I could do with some fresh air.'

'Aha! We walk by the sea for a while. You get good air there.'

It was a relief to be out in the balmy night. Shelley pulled her cardigan around her shoulders but she scarcely needed it. As they walked beside the murmuring sea along the interminable stretch of sand, Shelley was struck by the clearness of the sky and the bright stars.

'It's so beautiful!' she sighed.

'Of course. Rodos is the island of roses, the domain of Helios, the sun god,' Nico smiled. 'But no island can be as beautiful as a lovely woman, Shelley.'

He grinned, his teeth white in the dark skin of his face, his eyes gleaming like jet. Shelley knew that despite his ludicrous attempt at being romantic, despite the fact that she knew scarcely anything about him, she wanted him. There was something so liberating about being sexually attracted to a man on such a purely animal level.

Sensing her needs, he drew her into some sand dunes and they lay down under the stars. The distant beat of the hotel

163

disco and the gently lapping waves were the only sounds to break the silence. Shelley lay back yielding herself up to him, and he lowered his face to kiss her again. This time their tongues met at once, with an urgency that would have seemed out of place on the dance floor. She revelled in sheer lust for him as he began to explore her body with his hands, feeling the curves of her breasts beneath the thin cotton dress and stroking the bare flesh of her lightly-tanned thighs. It wasn't long before he was pushing up her skirt and stroking her belly, his breath coming in short gasps as he discovered each new part of her anatomy.

'Shelley, you are so beautiful!' he whispered. 'I love to make love with you all night!'

She giggled with pure joy at his naive enthusiasm. Reaching up she undid the top few buttons of his shirt and saw the network of black hairs that criss-crossed his chest. He stripped off the shirt and let her hands rove freely over the dark brown contours that were filmed with sweat. Shelley wanted to press her naked breasts to that handsome chest and she drew her dress over her head, exposing her bosom to his gaze.

'Oh, Shelley, they are . . . magnificent!' he breathed in wonder, as if it were the first pair of boobs he'd ever seen. His fingers went out tentatively to stroke them and she felt a warm thrill as his hands brushed her already erect nipples. Gently he kissed each one in turn, then his lips travelled down to kiss her stomach while his fingers moved softly over her breasts. He was being excessively gentle with her, and the effect was electrifying. She felt as if her whole body were being sensitised, her skin responding intensely to the slightest touch.

After Nico had probed her pussy for a while over her pants,

he slipped his finger beneath the lacy top and looked up at her enquiringly. 'May I?' he murmured.

'Yes.' Her answer came out huskily, testifying to her growing desire. She looked at his jeans and added, 'But only if you let me take yours off afterwards.'

He chuckled, a naughty sound in the still night air that increased her enjoyment of the situation. 'Okay, it's a deal.'

His lips followed the scanty material down over her hips and stomach until her pubic triangle lay bare, the downy fuzz glistening in the light from a rising moon. Lightly Nico brushed across it with the palm of his hand, making the skin beneath tingle. Shelley needed to see him now, in all his glory, to know what manner of man this stranger was that he could arouse her so extremely and yet remain so alien to her. She reached out and undid his belt buckle, then slid down his zipper.

Nico helped her to get him out of first his jeans and then the striped pants he wore. Freed from its constriction, his penis sprang up to greet her, tall and proud, the circumcised head round and pale in the silvery light, contrasting with the darker shaft. Shelley made a little inarticulate sound in the back of her throat and bent to kiss the tip, tasting the first savoury musk of seepage from his glans.

They began to lick each other in the 'sixty-nine' position. It seemed somehow appropriate to be doing it there by the sea, with her tasting of fish and him of salt. Nico was as careful as before, his fleshy lips soft against her lower ones, his tongue seeking the hard nub of her arousal. Shelley ran her tongue smoothly from tip to root of his firm organ, feeling the veined ridges that protruded around the shaft and imagining how it might feel inside her. Then she enclosed the whole of his glans in her mouth and sucked gently, making him squirm with pleasure. The action of his tongue grew more rapid, flicking back and forth over her clitoris and coaxing it into sticking further out of her swollen lips.

Shelley felt the soft sand at her back as she moved her hips, undulating them to apply greater friction to her vulva. In reply Nico began thrusting his cock further into her mouth so that she drew back and then swallowed him in, simulating the thrusting motion of intercourse. His penis grew tense and thick in her mouth and then, without any warning, shot a stream of bitter juice into the back of her throat, making her gag and pull away from him.

Nico gasped and moaned, his body shaking as the last drops were expelled onto her breasts. She felt the slimy contact and shivered. Nico's head came to rest between her thighs, its dark curly mass mingling with her own pubic hair. He continued to moan and groan for a while, then raised his head and muttered, 'I'm sorry, Shelley. So sorry.'

'It's all right,' she assured him. 'I take it as a compliment. You were so eager for me.'

'Ah, yes!' he laughed, delightedly, then his expression changed to one of concern. 'But you, you are not finished. I continue, yes?'

'If you like. That would be very nice.'

Shelley found the quaint politeness of their exchanges both comical and touching. It was almost like being with a child, albeit a precocious one. She lay back again with a sigh.

Nico began by rubbing his sticky residue into her breasts, which felt cool and sensual. With the other hand he dipped into her still wet pussy and gently penetrated her, making her wriggle against his invading hand. The hot centre of her desire began to throb again, taking her nearer to her climax as he slowly moved his fingers in and out of her, with his thumb against the protruding clitoris. She felt him massage the viscous juice into her nipples, rolling them languidly and sending quivering signals from her breasts to her vulva. Everything was in slow motion except her racing pulse and the headlong rise towards orgasm that his gentle ministrations were inducing.

For a while Shelley hovered at the edge of complete satisfaction, her consciousness floating on a cloud of voluptuousness, her body in suspended animation. Then he put his mouth to her left nipple and licked it clean of his fluid. The sudden increase in stimulation triggered her release and she plunged headlong into a vortex of bliss, sweeping her at giddying pace into a series of mini-climaxes, each sweeter and more erotic than the last, until she was utterly spent and sank down. Opening her eyes she saw the whirling stars above her, seeming to advance and retreat at a giddying pace, and she felt momentarily at one with the universe.

'Oh, that was so lovely!' she whispered, as the vision and the accompanying feelings faded.

'No, it is you who are so lovely,' Nico insisted, in his pedantic, gentlemanly way. Suddenly, however, Shelley wanted to get away from him. She found his presence cloying, oppressive. Reaching for her pants and dress she stood up, shakily.

'I must get back. Evelyn will be wondering where I've got to.'

Nico looked dismayed. 'Go back to the hotel? But why? The night is young!'

'I'm sorry, but I must.'

She slipped back into her clothes and held out her hand. 'Come on, Nico, get to your feet. We can walk back over the sand.'

167

She knew he was disappointed but there were plenty more fish in the sea. Somehow Shelley knew that what she had experienced that night could not be repeated. She would rather keep her precious souvenir intact than have it tarnished by another, less than perfect, night of love.

Leaving him in the hotel foyer with a vague 'See you around!' Shelley returned to her room. She'd scarcely entered when her sister put the lamp on and confronted her angrily.

'Where the hell have you been? It's two in the morning, and I've been worried sick. The folk dancing finished hours ago.'

'I went for a walk with Nico, if you must know. Now I'm going to shower and get into bed, okay?'

Shelley was annoyed that her evening had to end that way but she suspected Evelyn might be jealous. While she showered, she reflected that her sister would probably have liked a fling herself but felt it would undermine her image as the 'wronged fiancée' licking her wounds. Even so, she vowed not to do anything to upset Evie during the rest of the holiday. She'd had her fun and sated her lust, now she could just relax and enjoy the tours and the beach.

After she'd managed to smooth things over with Evelyn next morning, they went into Rhodes town on the bus and took an impromptu boat trip. Shelley managed to avoid Nico for most of the day but as they were returning to their room after the evening meal, she met him in the foyer.

'Good evening, Nico,' she said, coolly.

He came up to her with an open smile that became fixed when he saw her turn away and follow her sister into the lift. Shelley felt bad for treating him so cruelly, but she told herself she was only being kind. They'd both had what they wanted from each other and he was now free to prey on another female tourist if he so wished.

The rest of the week passed pleasantly, and both women ended up with good tans and a rested air. As they flew back to Heathrow, however, Shelley could feel the tension growing in her. For a week she'd been able to put her troubles on ice, but now she had to face them.

Quick to sense her mood as always, Evelyn asked what was the matter and Shelley told her about the pills she'd found. She knew she had to give Ben an ultimatum: stop using them or I'll leave you. But would it work?

'You know you can always come and stay with me, don't you?' Evie said, giving her as much of a hug as she could manage inside a fastened seatbelt.

'Thanks.' Shelley gave her sister a grateful smile. She might take her up on that offer yet.

Chapter Ten

Ben stared ruefully at his wife's retreating back as she stalked off to her car, carrying two suitcases. Was that it, then, the end of five years of marriage? Four of them had been pretty good, and he'd hoped they might patch it together. But the issue of his anabolic pills had blown up out of all proportion after Shelley had returned from Greece. Then he'd found a photo in the pocket of her suitcase of a hunk with his arm around her on the beach. She'd tried to hide it from him, but it was obvious from her guilty expression that she'd slept with the guy on holiday.

When, in a spirit of tit for tat, she'd dragged up his affair with Anne, the confrontation had worsened. Although he'd finished with his neighbour, his fling with Sara was still continuing, so he couldn't pretend to be guiltless. Consequently he had lost his temper, ranted more than he'd meant to, and ended up saying things he regretted. The upshot of it all was that Shelley had walked out and gone to stay with her sister, strongly hinting that she might never come back.

The fact that he was seeing Sara that evening was some consolation. He realised, too, that there was now no bar to her visiting him at home. Up to now, they'd made love only at her flat and he was fed up with making excuses to keep her at bay.

He decided to phone right away and suggest he cooked for her, for a change.

Sara loved Indian food and Ben was a dab hand at curries. He whistled cheerfully as he marinaded the lamb and chopped fresh coriander, chilled the beer and ground the spices, yet a nagging doubt reminded him that if Shelley did divorce him he would have to give up his comfortable lifestyle. She might try to put a stop on his use of their joint credit card soon. She might insist on him giving up his car, and then the house. With no job of his own in prospect, the outlook for the future was grim, quite apart from the lonely ache he felt whenever he contemplated the idea of divorce, of starting out on his own again.

Promptly at eight Sara arrived, bearing an exotic chutney that she'd found in a deli. Ben's heart always lifted at the sight of her cheerfully pretty face and fabulously sexy body. Although they'd only dated a few times, he was already wondering if they could get serious about each other. She kissed him warmly, pressing her firm breasts against his equally firm pectorals.

'Hi, Ben! Mm, that smells good. Do we have time for a quickie before we eat? I think my appetite for sex is greater than for food right now. I was thinking about you while I was in the sauna after work.'

Ben felt his spirits rise, blotting out the memory of Shelley completely. 'And were you *alone* in the sauna, by any chance?'

She grinned at him cheekily. 'Yes, and I made the most of it, too!'

'Wicked woman. I should spank your bottom for you. If your boss had caught you it would mean instant dismissal.'

Sara toyed with his hair, smiling provocatively. 'But don't

you understand, Ben darling. The danger adds to the fun! Anyway, I could see anyone coming through the glass door.'

'Trouble is, they could see you coming too!'

She play-punched him in the ribs. 'Ooh, Benny! Anyway, I can assure you I was thinking only of you, which is why I'm so disgustingly randy now. Shall we go upstairs or will you take me right here, on the kitchen table?'

Her words triggered off a memory of the time he and Shelley had 'christened' every room in the house. Ben squashed the poignant feelings and grinned. Maybe it was time to exorcise a few ghosts. 'Okay, let's do the show right here!'

Sara eagerly stripped off her embroidered sweatshirt. She wore no bra and her pert, tanned breasts bounced in a delightfully springy fashion as she threw her top aside. Ben had to turn down the oven but when he turned back she was completely nude and pirouetting like a ballerina on the tiled floor.

'Come on, get 'em off!' she commanded. She picked up the bottle she'd brought and brandished it. 'Maybe you'd like to lick me with relish!'

Ben took it from her and surveyed the list of ingredients. 'Are you crazy? Do you want to join "The Order of the Burning Quim"? There's chilli powder in this. Imagine what that might do to your sensitive little tissues.'

'Oh God, I hadn't thought of that! I got chilli up my nose once and it hurt like hell.'

'If you want to make a meal of it, I expect we can find something else,' he said, opening the fridge door and taking out the bowl of mint-flavoured raita that he'd prepared earlier.

Swiftly she helped him out of his clothes and began to fondle his semi-erect penis into more active life while he stroked her breasts. They kissed wholeheartedly until the fresh saliva was flowing, their tongues filling each other's mouths. Soon Ben was eager to taste the other juices she was producing. He withdrew from her for a moment, put a finger between her labia and then sucked on the tip.

'Mm, delicious!'

'What about that stuff?' She pointed to the bowl of yoghurt.

'Even better.'

'Shall I try lying down on the table, then?'

As she started to heave herself up he said, 'Yes, I'm sure we can manage it. This table's just about the right height for fucking.'

'How do you know, have you done it before?'

The note of suspicion in her voice was faint, but there all the same. Ben had told her nothing about his wife and he certainly didn't intend to do so now. 'No, but I can see it's lower than my waist. Otherwise I'd have had to stand on something.'

'But you're going to lick me first, aren't you?' Sara lay back, spreading her lean thighs wide and revealing her folded pink petals, already gleaming with lubrication. 'God, this table's hard on my back and head. Can you give me a couple of tea towels?'

Settling herself back on the improvised cushions, Sara pushed up her breasts with a sigh and urged him to anoint her with the raita. 'It's going to feel so deliciously cool!' she smiled.

Ben spooned some of the yoghurt onto a saucer and dipped his finger in it. Then he smeared it all over her vulva, to the accompaniment of appreciative cries. 'Oh yes, that feels wonderful! Now see what it tastes like.'

He was only too happy to oblige. There was a sourness mingled with sweetness, and a faint taste of mint. Ben slurped his tongue into her gaping quim.

'Put some on your finger and poke it right inside,' she urged him. 'It's supposed to be good for conditioning the vagina. Fills you with acid-loving bacteria.'

'And that's good?' Ben asked, bemused. However, he did as she asked and felt the slippery walls close over his finger. The effect on his penis was stimulating.

'Shall I screw you now?' he asked, bluntly. He knew Sara was turned on by such language.

'Yes, please! I've been dreaming about it all day!'

He clasped her legs and pulled her across the formica table top, closer to the edge. She raised her bent knees until her pussy was at the right angle for penetration. Placing both hands beneath her taut buttocks, Ben managed to position the end of his prick between her plump, slick labia and slide straight in with no problem. He gave a long sigh of relief as first his glans and then his shaft became enveloped by velvety wetness.

'Can you reach my tits?' Sara enquired.

Ben tried. 'Not comfortably.'

'Okay, no problem,' she smiled, taking her nipples between her own fingers. 'But I'd appreciate some help with my clit. It's hard to get it into the right position to be stimulated while I'm lying so flat.'

'Do you want to change position?'

'Oh no, it's great for thrusting! I like it when you go really deep.'

Ben loved the way Sara knew exactly what she wanted, and how to get it. Her uninhibited attitude towards her bodily pleasures was refreshing and very stimulating. He bunched up his fingers and made circular movements over the hard pad at the top of her vulva, making her rotate her pelvis more rapidly.

'God, that's good! Is it okay for you, Ben?'

It was actually putting quite a strain on his thighs but she was enjoying it so much Ben didn't want to spoil it. He reflected, proudly, that a month or so ago he would have found it impossible to keep up that position for long. Even when he was younger, at the start of his marriage, their kitchen-table coupling had been short and sweet. But now his thigh and calf muscles were rock hard, his back and shoulders far stronger too. Revelling in his new stamina, Ben increased the pace and turned his penis into an impressive driving force, eliciting grunts of increased satisfaction from Sara.

Feeling himself close to orgasm Ben warned Sara, in a series of gasps, that he couldn't keep it up much longer. His finger was rotating rapidly on her bulbous clitoris as he strove to bring her off at the same time as himself. She was bucking her hips wildly, making the whole table shake, and squeezing the hard mounds of her breasts with her thumbs while working her nipples to hasten her climax. He watched her flush bright pink and knew, from the first undulating motion of her vaginal walls, that she had reached her goal. Relieved, he gave himself up to his own imminent pleasure, falling forward as he plunged right into her, his face between her breasts. The pulsing sensations continued with escalating force, filling him with exquisite fire, and then began to die away, leaving him utterly satiated.

'Oh boy, what a fucking great fuck that was!' he heard Sara exclaim, breathlessly. 'I reckon that was better than any workout for burning off the calories.'

They went upstairs to shower and dress, then Ben took the

food through to the front room. While they were eating, Sara noticed his computer work-station in the corner.

'Will you show me how the Internet works?' she asked him. Ben had already told her something about the alt.sex. groups, and the bodybuilding ones.

As soon as they finished eating Ben switched his computer on and began surfing the Net. 'Which do you want to access, the sex or the bodybuilding?' he asked her.

'Oh, sex please!'

He found the sex stories and she scanned the titles eagerly. 'Can we try this one?' she asked eagerly, the cursor pointing to *Lezure Centre, or Plezure Centre?* 'Do you think their spelling's really that bad?'

'Hard to tell. Sometimes they use silly spelling for fun, sometimes they're foreigners. But often they're just bad spellers.'

He clicked on the title and, for once, it was accessible. The script appeared on screen, together with a large map of a 'Lezure Centre' showing a pool, jacuzzi, gym, sauna, changing rooms and showers.

'I wonder what this is all about,' Sara said. 'It looks intriguing, anyway.'

The instructions said: *Click on any part of the map for an instant fantasy.* Sara suggested he should try the pool. At once a crudely-drawn picture of a couple copulating underwater appeared. 'Is that all?' Sara sounded disappointed.

'No, there's some text . . . ah, here it is!'

Ben scrolled down so that the story filled the screen and began to read it aloud.

'*Screwing under water was Judy's favourite fantasy, but it wasn't until she met rugged scuba diver Marco that her fantasy became reality. He offered to give her private lessons in underwater swimming at her local pool and wow, did he give her value for money! First he told her to take off her swimsuit so she could get the real feel of being in another element. "Your skin will feel like a fish's," he told her. She noticed, as he removed his own clothes, that he had a huge erection. Feeling wet between the legs before she even entered the water, Judy dived into the deep end and Marco caught her round the waist. He dragged her down with him, down, down, until she was gasping for air, then he pulled her up towards the surface. "You will not be at home under water until you have lost your breath," he told her . . .'*

'God, this is boring!' Sara complained. 'Try the gym.'

A picture of a girl lying on a bench appeared. One guy had his penis inside her while he was holding two dumb-bells, and another naked man had a girl astride him as he worked out on the leg extender. 'This looks more like it,' Sara giggled. 'Let's see the story.'

She sat on his lap as the words unfolded, and Ben could tell she was becoming excited again. Beneath the taut curves of her behind he was growing quite aroused too.

This time Sara began to read the story aloud. '*Introducing our intrepid Lezure Centre staff, Bob and Kath, Bill and Sue. As you can see they like to take full advantage of their equipment after hours. See Bob pump Kath while he pumps iron! Admire Bill's physique as he gets physical with Sue!*' Sara turned to him with an incredulous expression. 'Who writes this rubbish?'

'Anyone who's on the Internet. There's no discrimination. That's the system's greatest virtue – and its biggest drawback.'

'Okay, but if that's the level of the sex stories maybe we'd better write our own!'

'Hey, that's not a bad idea.'

Sara scrolled on down the text. '*Now let's see Bob and Kath working out on the rowing machine. See the rhythmic thrusts back and forth, as she sits in his lap and he takes her from behind. Bill and Sue are looking quite envious. It's time for them to go onto the step machine. They both enjoy doing it standing up while their thighs move in unison . . .*'

'This is beyond belief!' Sara giggled 'I wonder what we'll get if I click on Changing Room'

The screen changed to a keyhole shape through which a semi-naked woman could be seen taking off her stockings. The text invited the viewer to become a Peeping Tom '*Spy on the lovely Marianne as she gets ready for her swim. See those clutchable round buttocks, those gorgeous great knockers . . .*'

'Some other time, perhaps.' Sara closed it and went back to the main menu. She flicked through the various titles. 'Let's see if we can find any bodybuilding info.'

Ben let her find her own way through the lists of sub-groups while he fondled her breasts beneath the loose sweatshirt. She was wriggling on his lap, and any minute now he was convinced that she would want to swap the Internet for some intercourse. But then she found the ad for 'Ultraboost', one of the drugs he was using, and she gave a gasp. 'Shit, they're advertising *steroids* through the Net! That means anyone could order them.'

'Is that so bad?'

She frowned. 'Of course it is. Those drugs should never be taken without medical supervision. They can cause all kinds of problems.'

Ben felt a sudden chill strike his bones. When Shelley had gone on at him, he'd thought she was talking through her arse. Sara, of all people, should know her stuff. Maybe he was being stupid, after all. 'What kind of problems?'

Sara's tone changed. Slipping into her professional persona, she explained, 'Psychological symptoms for one thing – mood swings, depression, paranoia, you name it. The physical effects include heart disease and liver failure in extreme cases. The trouble is, if you just send off for one or more types and take them indiscriminately you don't know what they're doing to you. The effects of combining them are totally unpredictable.' Her voice grew sharp with suspicion. 'You've never been tempted to take them have you, Ben?'

'Oh no, of course not. I just wondered why they were supposed to be so bad, that's all.'

Beneath his calm exterior, Ben's mind was racing. He was remembering how irritated he'd been lately, how his discussion with Shelley had quickly escalated into the row that had led to her walking out on him. He'd also been pretty depressed while his wife had been in Greece. Was he simply suffering the symptoms of steroid abuse?

'Well it's not worth it,' Sara was saying. 'Sure you get results, and fast, but you pay dearly for it in the long run. Far better to proceed at a steady pace like you're doing, Ben.'

'I'm not sure I am proceeding,' he said. 'I don't seem to have built any more muscle for the past few weeks.'

'You could be overtraining. I expect you're a hard gainer. Some people put on muscle more easily than others.' She twisted round to face him and put her hands on his biceps. 'But you still feel awfully good to me!'

They began kissing, and Ben put his worries to the back of his mind. He lifted up her top to expose her golden breasts and pulled the nipples gently into shape. Sara kissed him passionately and then slowly slid from his lap.

'Come on, hot lips,' she smiled, holding out her hand. 'Let's go upstairs and do it in comfort, for a change.'

He switched off the machine and followed her. They went into the bedroom where, once Ben had drawn the curtains, Sara lit a candle to give a romantic glow. She stripped off her clothes and stood before him in the mellow light, lithe and beautiful.

'God, Sara, I don't think I've ever seen a woman's body as gorgeous as yours.'

'Well, I do try!'

'But it's not just your body I like, honestly.'

'Honestly?' She smiled, almost mocking him. 'You don't have to fall in love with me you know, Ben. It's not obligatory. I just like a good fuck, and you certainly provide that.'

Ben wasn't used to such plain speaking. His emotions were in turmoil as he tried to express his half-formed thoughts. 'All I mean is, I don't want you to think I take you for granted or anything. I mean, you're a fantastic person Sara. The sex is great, but I like being with you too, and . . .'

'Oh shut up and give me a kiss!' she laughed, throwing herself at him so that they both collapsed on the bed. She made hungry noises and began to chew at his nipples with her sharp little teeth, making him wince. She was handling his cock too, drawing it up onto his stomach where it lay like some beached creature being resuscitated. Soon her lips were giving it the kiss of life and it was responding magnificently.

'I want you to take me from behind this time,' she told him.

Sara got up onto all fours and arched her back so that her peachy bum stuck right up and he could see the hairy pink lips sagging between her thighs. The sight was irresistible. Ben got up behind her and penetrated her willing cunny straight away. He knew she would be ready for him, she always was. She began to undulate her hips in a slow, sensual dance that sent him half wild with desire.

Ben couldn't remember when he'd wanted a woman so much. Although she made herself available to him she still seemed, at some fundamental level, mysteriously inaccessible. It was as if, by being so open about sexual matters, she kept a shield around whatever lay beyond in the unplumbed depths of her personality, her soul, whatever you wanted to call it.

When he fucked her, Ben wanted to break through that invisible screen, but no matter how long and hard he pounded away, she remained in the safe realm of the physical. Now she was moaning and exclaiming as his leisurely shafting aroused her clitoris and took her higher and higher, into some dreamlike realm of the senses. Tonight he felt unable to follow her there. His mind was too full of thoughts, and his screwing was becoming mechanical. He reached under her lean body and found her plump, swinging breasts, pulling on the distended nipples until she almost screamed out her ecstasy, moving one hand down to give her engorged labia those few encouraging strokes needed to push her over the edge.

Her coming was swift and violent, with much loud noise and frantic movement, but it didn't trigger him. Maybe he was tired. Maybe, even, she wore him out. It was certainly possible. She had an insatiable appetite for sex and, thanks to her developed strength and stamina, seemed practically indefatigable. Ben knew he could carry on going, but he'd simply lost the will. Drawing out his penis, he lay down on the bed and took her into his arms.

'Did you come?' she enquired.

'Not that time, but I don't mind. I think I'm a bit tired.'

'You're not overdoing it at the gym, are you? I've been wondering about you a bit lately. It's really not necessary to work out every day, you know. Three times a week is quite adequate.'

'But I like it. And I've not much else to do with my spare time.'

'What exactly do you do with computers, Ben?' she asked him. He had spun her the same line as he had to Carol.

'Oh, it's a bit technical. Anyway, I don't want to talk about work right now. I'd rather talk about us.'

'Us?'

'Yes, you and me. And where we're heading. I'm starting to think we could get serious about each other, Sara. We see each other every day at the gym, and make love as often as we can, and . . . well, I know it's a bit early to be thinking this way, but . . .'

'Too right it is! I'm not sure I like the way this conversation's going, Ben. We've only been dating a couple of weeks.'

He sighed. 'I know. But I think you're very special, and I'm very flattered that you want to spend time with me, make love with me . . .'

'Bullshit, Ben! I'm with you because I want to be. But if you start trying to tie me down in any way, I'll be out of this relationship before you know it.'

He was disturbed by the hard edge to her voice and his eyes showed it. She softened a little as she turned her turquoise gaze on him. 'Sorry, Ben, but I want you to know exactly where you stand with me. I am not your exclusive property, nor ever will be. I claim the right to go out with other men if I so choose, and I grant you the right to see other women in return. Do I make myself clear?'

This was a new side of Sara, a steely side that he'd sensed existed underneath her bright and breezy surface. It fitted with her determination to enjoy life to the full and gain the maximum pleasure from her fantastic body. But it left Ben feeling bruised and bleak.

He knew he mustn't push it. Whatever he felt for Sara he must keep to himself, or risk being hurt, humiliated and ultimately rejected. She was that kind of woman, he now realised. Curling up beside her he soon drifted into sleep.

Sara went off early next morning and just as Ben was finishing his leisurely breakfast there came a ring at the doorbell. He looked through the front curtains to see who it was and saw Anne standing there. Unfortunately, she'd also seen him. He went to the door in his dressing-gown, feeling decidedly uneasy. She gave him a nervous smile and asked if she could come in.

'I just need someone to talk to,' she said, in a fraught voice. Ben's heart sank, but he led the way through to the kitchen and poured her a coffee.

'What's the matter, Anne?'

To his horror she began to cry. 'Oh, I've been so lonely!' she moaned, between sobs. 'I've tried so hard to find someone else, because I knew you didn't want me any more, but I haven't found anyone.'

He put his arm around her and she snuggled into his chest. 'Maybe you're trying too hard, Anne. Men don't like it if you chase them, you know.'

'But what am I supposed to do? I went to the singles night at the supermarket and no one so much as looked my way.'

'I can't think why not. You're a very attractive woman, Anne. But maybe you lack confidence.'

'Yes, I know I do. I've been off the dating scene too long, you see. But now you've reminded me what love can be like I just can't settle back into celibacy. I need sex, Ben. I know that now.'

'Of course you do.' He was feeling decidedly uncomfortable. 'You're a very sexy woman, Anne.'

Her face turned radiant. 'Do you mean that?' She embraced him passionately, kissing him on the mouth. He tried to remain unmoved, but it was very difficult. Last night's session with Sara had left him with an excess of libido that needed an outlet. He knew he shouldn't give in to this woman, that it would only cause complications, but his dick was rearing helplessly beneath his dressing gown and she was obviously dying for it.

'Can't we do it now?' she pleaded. 'Just a quickie. It won't mean anything, it's just physical. I shan't pester you afterwards, I promise.'

She was taking her clothes off right there in front of him. The pale freckled breasts flopped out of their bra with the brownish nipples already taut and eager. Ben lifted the weight of her great tits and buried his face between them. God, it felt fantastic!

'Take me, Ben!' she was cooing, as he untied his belt and his prick sprang out from the front of his towelling robe.

Hastily Anne wriggled out of her skirt and stood there in her black suspender belt, a pink satin triangle barely concealing her pubic curls. Her breasts wobbled as she pinged the suspenders against her thighs and rolled down the stockings. Ben moved in fast, seizing the chubby mounds of her behind and pressing her hot mons to his rearing organ. She moaned and wriggled excitedly. 'Oh, it's been so long, Ben! I know you wanted to save your marriage and everything, but you left me in the lurch, you really did!'

'Ssh!' Ben undid her suspender belt and put his hand down the back of her pants, sneaking a finger into her crack the way she liked it. Slowly they sank to the floor, aiming for the rug in front of the dresser. It didn't offer much in the way of padding but it was better than bare tiles.

'I'll do all the work if you like,' she offered, climbing on top of him with her breasts swaying. Ben didn't object. He put a folded tea towel behind his head and reached up to twiddle her long nipples while she lowered herself onto his jaunty erection. She gave a long sigh of relief as her well lubricated quim slid right down to the root of his penis.

Once Anne had got into what Ben thought of as her 'bareback' routine, jogging up and down on him as if she were putting a horse through its paces, he allowed his body to go into auto-drive. He would come eventually, if she kept it up long enough, but the experience was less than erotic. She was so relentlessly hearty about it. Ben had no qualms about fantasising while she was at it, his mind full of yesterday's romp with Sara. At last Anne reached her very noisy climax, with much huffing and puffing, freeing Ben to make his weak ejaculation and be done with it.

'Oh thank you, gorgeous man!' she exclaimed, giving him a wet kiss on the mouth. He only just managed to avoid wiping his lips with the back of his hand afterwards.

She slipped off him and pulled her knickers back on, then stood up. Her breasts looked fantastic from below, like great billowy clouds. Would he have even bothered with her if it hadn't been for those outsize boobs? Somehow he thought not. She smiled happily and continued to dress while he lay there pretending to be knackered.

'Hope I haven't exhausted you for the rest of the day!' Anne said, cheerfully. 'Shall I make more coffee?'

Ben got rid of her by eleven, after she'd promised several times that she wouldn't trouble him again. He hoped she would stick to her word. Then, a few days later, he saw her in the supermarket sharing a trolley with a dark-haired man who looked several years younger. Something about the way they were together told him that she'd found her replacement lover already. She gave him a cheery wave and he winked back with a smile. What with Sara going cool on him and Shelley moving out, he'd been feeling vulnerable lately. It was a relief to know that Anne would not be taking advantage of him again.

Chapter Eleven

'It's great having you here, Shelley, but shouldn't you be thinking about somewhere more permanent by now?'

Shelley heard her sister's words with dismay. 'I'm sorry, Evie, I don't want to outstay my welcome. But it's difficult for me right now. I'm not even sure my job is secure and as for my marriage . . .'

She sighed, and Evelyn gave her a hug. 'That's okay. You stay as long as you like.'

But Shelley knew she couldn't go on living in that small flat indefinitely. Not having her own place was beginning to get to her, along with everything else. She hadn't been able to sleep lately, and Evelyn had given her some sleeping pills that she no longer needed. They made life a bit more bearable, but not much. Sooner or later a decision about her future would have to be made.

At work next day it looked horribly as if one decision had been made for her. The hoped-for sitcom contract had not materialised and rumours were flying round that Harcourt Productions would have to downsize to survive.

So when Duncan summoned Shelley to his office she went with trepidation. His smile was friendly enough as she entered and sat in the leather chair awaiting the news.

'Shelley, I think you can probably guess why I wanted to

see you.' Her heart sank, and she nodded dumbly, her throat too dry to speak. 'But it's not quite as bad as you might think. Not yet, anyway. It's true we've lost the contract that would have kept us in business for the next two years, but there are several smaller projects in the offing and I want you to work on one of them.'

She felt her tension ease a little, but his tone suggested it was not all good news. He clasped his hands together on the desk, the way he did when he had to face some tricky problem. His expression was pensive now, the grey eyes cool beneath the well-defined brows. Despite her anxiety Shelley still found him attractive.

'Only one?' she prompted.

'I'm trying to share the work out as fairly as I can, but I must be frank with you. After next month there's not a lot coming in. What I'm suggesting is this. You've already had a couple of weeks of paid leave. I'd like to be able to go on paying you indefinitely but you know as well as I do that it can't be done. I want to put you onto short contract work.'

He paused to let his words sink in and, as they did, Shelley was horrified. 'You mean, I'll only get paid when I'm actually working?'

'It's the way things are going in the industry. A few of our staff will remain on permanent contract but mainly on the admin side. It's so easy to hire cameramen, technicians and – yes, directors, these days.'

Shelley felt a constriction in her chest, almost choking her. What about the mortgage? They would have to sell the house. Then she realised that it would come to that anyway if she and Ben divorced. She made an effort to think clearly.

'How much work do you think I'm going to get on this next project?'

'If you start next week ... two, three weeks. A month at most.'

'A month! With nothing after that?'

'Not at the moment, although I'm hoping the situation will improve. We've stepped up our advertising. But look at it this way, Shelley. I could have fired you on the spot or kept you hanging on in suspense. Now you'll at least know where you stand, have time to look around. And you could always sign on with an agency for temporary work between jobs here.'

She knew he was being as fair as he could under the circumstances. Her tone softened. 'It must be hard for you, Duncan. I appreciate you being straight with me. I'm very grateful.'

Shelley lingered over the last word, only half intending what she was implying, but Duncan picked her up on it at once, his tone friendly. 'Thanks for taking it so well, Shelley.' The look in his eye grew warmer, and slightly predatory. 'Won't you let me take you out to dinner tonight? I've missed your company.'

His hidden agenda was now obvious. Shelley realised that, if she played along, she might stand to gain more favourable treatment from her boss. Smiling brightly she said, 'I'd like that.'

'Fine. We'll meet in reception at seven, then.'

He stood up and offered his hand, which lingered in hers fractionally too long and sent sudden flurries of excitement up her arm and through her body. He wasn't such a bad lay after all, she recalled. Maybe she could have fun and do herself some good at the same time.

The atmosphere on the studio floor was tense, to say the least. Shelley realised that everyone knew the position Harcourt was now in and nobody felt secure. That didn't make for a great working environment. Tempers were frayed, attitudes were half-hearted and, by the time she had survived a day when no one was giving of their best, Shelley was glad of the chance to spend a relaxing evening with sex at the end of it. She had been making do with her vibrator for far too long.

Fortunately there were showers available to the staff, so Shelley went to freshen up before meeting Duncan. She hoped that, by seven, most of her colleagues would have left the building, as she didn't want to be seen with her boss. If they thought – rightly, as it happened – that she was trading sexual favours for preferential treatment they would be justifiably piqued.

Shelley sighed as she stepped into the warm stream of water and squirted shower gel into her palm. The world of television production was a cut-throat jungle and you had to be tough to survive. Maybe it was time she began looking for another company. Steve had been sensibly building up his own alternative sources of income, others, no doubt, had already seen the writing on the wall and were ahead of her in the queue. But while everything around her was falling apart, Shelley was determined to seize what she could from the wreckage. She knew Duncan still wanted her and maybe he could help her regain control of her life. Carefully she planned his seduction, smiling as she remembered how it had been last time ...

Shelley resolved to put her worries and fears behind her as she walked towards Duncan in the foyer, her hair and skin gleaming freshly and smelling of Un Air de Samsara. He looked pleased to see her and as his hand touched her arm she felt a resurgence of her earlier desire for him.

'I thought we'd go to a Greek restaurant I know in Chelsea,' he told her. Shelley smiled. Since that was where he lived she would probably be going back to his flat afterwards. 'I've not seen you in your car lately,' he commented. 'Is it off the road?'

She didn't want to tell him that she'd left home. 'No, it's just easier to come to work on the Underground at the moment.'

The meal of *mezedes* and *feta* salad reminded Shelley of her holiday and soon they were swapping travellers' tales. Shelley realised that she knew very little about Duncan personally. She discovered that he'd been born in Dundee but had moved to Aberdeen when he was five. Although he was happy to talk about himself, they naturally steered clear of any reference to work in general and Harcourt Productions in particular.

When the meal was over, he invited her back to his place. She was looking forward to gleaning more from seeing him at home. He lived in a brick-built town house whose plain exterior belied the splendid dimensions of the rooms inside. Duncan's flat was very pleasant, with a large front room full of exotic plants and Conran-style furnishings.

He put a sultry singer on the CD player and poured her a glass of brandy while he made coffee in his espresso machine. Shelley flicked through a book on Symbolist Art. Conveniently forgetting the disappointing aftermath of their previous love-making, she was beginning to fantasise that they might be starting a real relationship. She took the fact that he'd invited her back as a good sign. It would be even better if he let her stay the night.

Duncan didn't waste any time in idle chat. He came to sit by her on the leather settee and put his arm around her. 'You're a very attractive and sexy woman, Shelley,' he smiled, taking her hand. 'You should be with someone who appreciates you.'

She smiled, but said nothing. Somehow she didn't see Duncan as her father confessor. His hand moved to her blouse and began unfastening the buttons, making little shivers travel around her body and raising goose bumps on her arm. His touch was slow and deliberate as he moved in to caress the soft skin between her breasts. This time, she sensed, their love-making could be more like it had been in the hotel, not like the rushed episode in his office. She stretched languorously, catlike, throwing back her shoulders and pushing her breasts up in their shiny white satin bra.

Duncan began nibbling at her neck, intensifying the quivering in her stomach. When he reached her ear he whispered, 'Does it make you feel good then, Shelley, screwing your boss?'

She giggled. 'You know it does! I suppose it's every woman's fantasy to have some power over powerful men.'

'Ever wanted to be totally in control? In a sexual context, that is.'

She looked up at him, vaguely shocked. 'I don't know what you mean.'

'Oh, I think you do.' He stood up, holding out his hand to pull her to her feet. Mystified, Shelley followed him out into the hall and then into his bedroom. She could feel a visceral excitement beginning deep within, a forewarning of something new and strange. As she entered the darkened room she realised she was holding her breath.

Duncan switched on a subdued light. The bed was large,

covered by a navy duvet, with a brass rail at the head and foot. Shelley's eyes went straight to the headrail, where a pair of handcuffs was hanging as casually, and with as much dramatic effect, as a child's stocking at Christmas.

'Now do you understand?'

His voice was low, seductive, but it took some time for the truth to sink in. 'You like to be *handcuffed* while making love?' she said, incredulously.

He gave an ironic smile. 'I believe I'm not the only one in the world who does.'

'And you want me to do it, right?'

'Only if you're into it. If not, we could make love as we did before but I wouldn't enjoy it so much.'

'I see.' Shelley had heard of people who liked this kind of thing, of course, but she'd had no personal experience of it. Now that the shock was fading she thought she wouldn't mind. The business was beginning to intrigue her. 'What would I have to do, exactly?' she hesitantly asked.

He sat down on the bed, looking up at her. Something about his demeanour suggested helplessness, submission. Shelley was surprised to find herself responding to it with a sexual buzz. 'What I'd like,' he began in a soft, almost crooning voice, 'is for you to strip to your underwear and put on one or two extra things that I've got here. Then I want you to handcuff me to the rail and take off your panties. I'd like you to put my feet through the legs of your panties and tie them around my ankles. Then you can do what you like with me as long as you don't actually cause any injury.'

'What, you want me to hurt you?'

'Only if you want to. It's up to you, you see. It's entirely up to you. I'll be putting myself completely in your hands.'

Shelley resisted the urge to tell him how weird he was. Presumably he already knew that. But the idea of being in total control of the proceedings was proving very attractive. She could make him lick her for hours, presumably, use his dick to pleasure herself any way she wanted. He would be, almost literally, her sex toy.

'Okay, I'll give it a try.'

He smiled, a peculiarly secretive and exposed smile that made her feel awkward as long as she thought of him as her boss. Yet she was already moving away from her image of him as a powerful man, one who had control over her own destiny as well as that of others. It was like discovering that someone you thought was straight was actually gay. You couldn't help subtly reassessing them, reinterpreting their past behaviour.

Duncan walked over to the wardrobe and drew out a pair of stiletto-heeled black patent shoes. 'Do you think you could wear these? They're size six.'

'I'm normally a five, so they'll be a bit big.'

'It doesn't matter. You won't be walking far in them. And then there's this.'

He showed her a beautiful carnival mask, the sort Venetians wore. It was a pure, translucent white but decorated with green and turquoise sequins. In the corner of one eye a crystal simulated a tear. Shelley held it up to her face and regarded herself in the mirror of the wardrobe. She looked remote, exotic, inhuman.

Duncan stood by the bed. 'All right, you get yourself ready then. I'll lie down and wait for you to handcuff me. You can put the key into your bra.'

'Are you getting undressed?'

'No, I prefer to remain clothed but you may open my

196

clothes to gain access to my body. Oh, and please call me "George" throughout.'

'George?'

He nodded, curtly, and lay down on the bed with his arms above his head, waiting. Shelley felt a warm excitement curling up from her groin into her belly, filling her with the expectation of a dangerously novel kind of pleasure. She had never felt quite like this before. After taking off her skirt and petticoat she put on the shoes. They were a bit loose on her but not uncomfortably so. Then she pulled the mask over her face and tightened the buckle of the elastic that went behind her head. Glancing at Duncan through the almond-shaped eye holes she saw his face change too, becoming abjectly enamoured of her.

Shelley looked at herself in the wardrobe mirror for a second. Her auburn hair flowed freely around the mask, softening its severe lines. Her breasts stood out proud within their white satin cones, and her matching briefs showed beneath the frame of the suspenders that completed the lingerie set. Her stockings were charcoal grey, emphasising the length of her legs in the shiny black high-heeled shoes. She looked . . . magnificent.

Slowly Shelley walked towards the bed and took hold of the handcuffs. She examined them, turning them over in her hand, prolonging the suspense. Then she lifted both Duncan's arms and managed to get the cuffs first round one wrist then the other, snapping them shut. She fixed them to the rail so that he could move his arms a little without being able to escape. She smiled down at him, realising that all he could see was the fixed, impassive mouth of the mask.

Backing away from the bed so he could still see her she

unhooked her suspenders, watching his face all the while. His eyes were riveted to her with a fierce longing in them. She bent forward, knowing she was giving him a good view of her cleavage in the close-fitting bra, then began to roll down her panties between her loose, dangling suspenders. She saw his pupils dilate as her pubic hair was revealed, a reddish-blonde bush of soft curls, and realised that she was seeing herself through his eyes, narcissistically, appreciating her own sexiness. She re-fastened her suspenders to her stocking-tops then, reaching between her thighs, dabbled her forefinger in the liquid that was filling her secret crevices. Still with her eyes on Duncan, she put her finger in her mouth and sucked it.

He gave a groan, the first audible sign of his arousal, but it wasn't enough for Shelley. She needed to see his erection for herself. Stepping out of her panties, she did as he had asked and put his feet, still in their woollen socks, through the legholes. She managed to wind the satiny material tightly around his ankles, securing them. Her hand travelled up his trouser leg, feeling his shin, his knee, his thigh through the rough twill, all the time aware of him watching her intently, passively. She found the button at the waistband and then toyed with his zipper, inching it down by degrees, until the white bulge of his pants appeared. Duncan gasped as she pulled the elasticated top over his penis and then snapped it back down against his scrunched balls.

Freed from its constraints, his organ visibly expanded and rose up towards his stomach until it had reached its full proportions. Shelley squeezed it, pinched it, watched it swell and lift its head like some animal surveying its territory. She had never been so fascinated by the male member before. It lay there like a thing apart, her plaything, on Duncan's immobile body, challenging her to think of new ways of amusing herself with it.

First she wanted to see a bit more of Duncan's bare skin, so she undid his shirt buttons and exposed his pale, hairy chest with the purplish-brown nipples. She could see his eyes on her exposed bush and knew he could scent the muskiness of her quim. Standing about a foot away from him, she thrust her pelvis forward and parted her labia with her fingers to show him the dew-laden rose within. His eyes went dark with desire. She strutted near to him, teasingly cruel, probed herself, put her finger beneath his nose and traced a path across his lips. But then, when he opened them, she laughingly withdrew. She bent over and showed him her arse, pulling aside her cheeks to make sure he got a good view. Amazing herself, she indulged the exhibitionist streak that lay buried within her, the little girl show-off.

There was no knowing in which direction her imagination would take her next, and that was what made it so exciting. She was like an improvising jazz musician, picking up a melody and running with it. Her breasts wanted to be free so she took off her bra and the key to the handcuffs fell out. She giggled, dangling it in front of him and then, on a whim, tied her bra round his head like a blindfold. She laughed hilariously at the satin points sticking up where his eyes were. Now he couldn't see what she was going to do next. Bending to his still solid prick, she wiped her tongue over his glans in one long, lascivious lick and saw the muscles of his stomach clench with the sudden sensual impact.

Shelley looked around the room, seeking props. There was a hairbrush on top of a chest of drawers. She picked it up and tested the bristles against her palm. Beginning by brushing

Duncan's chest hair, she moved down the darkly hirsute line towards his genitals and, lifting his penis with one hand, proceeded to brush his pubic hair into a neat mound. Then she applied the soft bristles to his shaft, making him groan as they pricked the sensitive enveloping skin.

'I'm grooming you, George,' she told him, through the constricted mouth-hole of the mask. Her voice sounded muffled. 'Grooming you for Crufts. Obedience trials.'

His penis twitched as she giggled. Shelley could almost see the adrenaline flowing through his veins as he wondered what she was planning to do to him. It seemed a shame to waste such a fine erection, and she was feeling so randy that she wanted to use him for her pleasure.

Shelley got onto the bed and knelt astride him. Taking his shaft roughly in one hand, she parted her labia with the other and began to rub his glans against her swollen clitoris. She used him without mercy, like a dildo, sometimes probing just inside her entrance where she was drooling with juice, but mostly applying the necessary friction to take her where she wanted to go. The orgasm that swiftly followed was strong and satisfying, making her whole body convulse with paroxysms of bliss and leaving her dizzy and spent.

Letting his still strong penis flop back onto his belly, the glans now bathed with her juices as well as his, Shelley lay down on the bed with her head towards the foot and thrust her big toe into Duncan's mouth. 'Suck on that, George!' she commanded him. 'Give me a toe job! It's what all the best people are into.'

It felt like dipping a toe into some warm gloop. A feeling of deliciousness began travelling straight up her leg to her crotch, as if she were tasting her own flesh at the same time as being licked. She decided it would be nice to have his prick inside her while that was going on, so she got on top of him and managed to lower herself on to his erection, which was proving impressively durable.

Shelley gave a deep sigh of satisfaction as she inched her way down his shaft until he was fitting snugly inside her. She wiggled her toe in his mouth as a signal that she wanted him to continue and slowly raised herself up and down, bracing herself on her hands. With one leg immobilised she couldn't do anything else but, for a while, it was good enough, a little gentle – and genital – stimulation that was gradually taking her excitement up to a higher pitch. She knew it wasn't enough to take her all the way to an orgasm but it was very pleasant all the same.

After a while she changed toes, and when she'd tired of that she decided to make him use his mouth on her quim for a bit, just to get her more keyed up. She moved up his chest, straddling him, and thrust her mons in his face. 'Lick my pussy now, George,' she ordered.

While he performed the enthusiastic tongue-and-groove exercise, Shelley took hold of her own breasts and stroked them the way she liked best: first enclosing them in the open cradle of her fingers then stroking outwards, closing her fingers at the same time until she ended up tweaking her nipples with her bunched fingertips. She did this over and over, in a mesmerically slow rhythm, while she directed Duncan's tonguing more precisely at her clitoris by swivelling her hips and rotating her pelvis. Soon she felt the sudden carnal gear-change that indicated her climax was nigh but, instead of going for it, she withdrew from his willing mouth and slid back down his body until she could manoeuvre herself back onto his still turgid cock.

This time Shelley concentrated on bringing herself to

orgasm with swift efficiency. While she bounced rapidly up and down, her right hand was rubbing between her labia with just the right amount of pressure to bring her off quickly. Duncan's tool had become just that, an implement for the job in hand. In less than a minute she was thrashing around in wild ecstasy, abandoning herself to the powerful spasms that were delivering their payload of exquisite pleasure throughout all the nerve paths of her body.

She had completely ignored Duncan's pleasure, was oblivious of the fact that his penis was still hard after she had slid off it and lay beside him in exhaustion. Once her breathing and heartbeat had returned to normal, however, she couldn't help noticing that it was still in a very serviceable condition. Incredibly, her libido began to rise again as she put out a hand and enclosed the sticky shaft. She clambered back on, feeling her engorged tissues fit even more closely over the indefatigable organ.

For a while she took it very gently, finding the delicate stimulation of her vagina and labia most gratifying now that she was no longer in a hurry and could indulge herself on a purely sensual plane. Shelley even found time to caress Duncan's balls, reaching round behind her buttocks to where they lay, semi-trapped, beneath his closed thighs. She lifted them out of their crevice and heard his faint groan as her fingernails lightly scratched the taut, faintly oily surfaces. She temporarily stopped moving up and down and instead clenched her inner walls so that she could feel the sturdy dimensions of his shaft and wrap herself greedily around it, letting her slippery membranes embrace his and extracting every nuance of pleasure from the melding of soft wet flesh with hard.

Then, like a faint echo of her previous, more intense

orgasm, she sensed the approach of a second climax, this time stealing up on her far more slowly so that she had time to savour every second of her coming. The gradual build-up of bliss was one she wanted to prolong for as long as possible. She loved being held in that lazily erotic suspense. When the throbbing waves started they were so gentle that she sighed with sheer voluptuous pleasure. As their strength increased, she felt her whole being suffused with tender fire.

'Oh, that feels so good, so good!' she moaned as the subtle vibrations reached their quivering peak. She had almost forgotten about Duncan. He had become what he'd wanted to be: the mere instrument of her pleasure.

Feeling utterly disorientated, Shelley left the bed with Duncan still manacled to it, and went in search of the bathroom. She took a shower, taking her time, knowing that he would still be there for her when she went back. Presumably being left in suspense was all part of the fun for him. While the warm jets played over her relaxed body Shelley wondered what she should do to him next, but found she had run out of ideas. Now sexually sated, she no longer had the same enthusiasm for the game as before.

What was Duncan getting off on, she wondered as she lathered herself all over. Submitting himself to her will, presumably, having her control what happened to him. Well, maybe she could take charge of his orgasm, to have him hovering on the edge of coming, never knowing when she would administer the *coup de grâce* that would take him, mercifully, over the brink. Yes, that was the way. Thoughtfully she sluiced herself down then stepped into a fluffy white bath towel.

Back in the bedroom Duncan lay perfectly still. Shelley decided to remove his unorthodox blindfold. When she did he stared up at her with blank grey eyes, locked into some dream world of his own. She wiped the bra between her legs so that it was soaked with the juices that still streamed from her quim, scrunched it up and stuffed it in his mouth, like a gag. Then she took his penis in her hand. It had lost some of its stiffness while she was out of the room, but as she tugged softly at it she could feel the blood pumping back in, restoring its former vigour.

Bending until she could reach the swollen glans with her tongue, Shelley proceeded to give it a thorough licking. Duncan's restricted thighs were soon chafing restlessly together as his desire increased and he uttered a few small moans, only just audible behind the bra.

'Feels nice, does it George?' she enquired, in a mock solicitous tone. He nodded. When she returned to her task some bitter milk seeped out from the slit at the tip of his cock. She withdrew her mouth, afraid of him coming too soon, and instead began mouthing his balls in their soft, loose sac. Briefly she returned to lick the length of his shaft and suck momentarily at the bulbous head, then she changed to kissing his thighs.

Shelley could feel the strain building up in him, could sense the tensing of his body against the unexpected. He must be getting an adrenaline rush now, she guessed, wondering when she would return to stimulate his prick or, indeed, whether she would go back there at all. She had the impression that if she kept it up long enough she could make him climax by massaging his knees! His entire body might become one erogenous zone, if only she could keep it up long enough. But already she was flagging. Maybe there was another way. She got up and went back into the bathroom.

Looking in the cabinet over the hand basin, Shelley found

a box of elastic crepe bandage, the sort athletes use around their joints. She took some out and went back into the bedroom. Carefully she pulled a long sleeve of the stuff over his penis, doubled it then trebled it until it was binding his organ quite tightly. He winced a little when she adjusted it, so she knew she had it at the right strength. His purplish glans stuck out of the top and his pink balls stuck out the bottom. Shelley giggled. She grasped the reinforced shaft with her right hand and, squeezing it rhythmically, began to lick the exposed tip. His penis began to expand again but the tight constriction of the bandage must have made it uncomfortable, not to say painful. Shelley worked it harder and he began to breathe in short gasps, struggling against his various bindings. She could see the veins in his temples sticking out angrily, like a strong man in a weight-lifting contest, and his face was turning red.

Then, suddenly, everything seemed to explode at once. With a mighty effort Duncan expelled the bra from his mouth and a great roar came out. At the same time his penis shot its load of silvery juice right up onto his chest and beyond, so that some of it spattered his face. His ankles broke free of the satin panties and kicked them half across the room. His knees made a reflex jack-knife movement and hit Shelley in the back, half knocking her off the bed. She lost her balance and tumbled to the floor.

Shelley picked herself up and went to undo the handcuffs, to let him rest. His arms flopped down with obvious relief and he turned over with his face in the pillow, utterly drained. She lay beside him, exhausted too, and switched off the bedside lamp. What had happened between them already seemed like a strange dream, and soon Shelley was re-living it all in a real dream, flying around the room in an exhilarated state while she directed operations on an anonymous, inert body below.

The sound of a shrill alarm woke her abruptly at six. After she'd worked out where she was, Shelley was overcome by embarrassment. Duncan was stirring at her side, but she just didn't know how she was going to face him after what had occurred last night. She crept from the bed and into the bathroom, trying to collect her wits. By the time she emerged her boss was making coffee in the kitchen wearing a quilted dressing gown and whistling cheerfully.

'Coffee or tea?' he greeted her.

'Tea, please.'

'Earl Grey or Indian?'

'Indian, thanks. God, I feel shattered!'

'Have some orange juice.' He handed her a carton. It seemed surreal, all this polite talk, but Shelley hadn't the nerve to be the first to mention last night's fun and games.

While she was drinking her juice Duncan said, 'Look I have to dash off, obviously, but you can take your time. Have a shower, make yourself some toast. Or there's cereal in the cupboard. Then you can let yourself out when you feel up to facing the world again.'

Shelley was suddenly filled with resentment, knowing he'd laid her off until the following week. Her vague hopes of persuading him, through the politics of the casting couch, to let her keep her job were being fast eroded by his offhand manner. Perhaps it served her right. She'd had no idea, when she agreed to dine with him, what murky waters he'd be leading her into.

After he'd gone Shelley reflected on what had happened between them, fearing that it had hastened her demise, not prevented it. Would he really want her around, now she knew so much about his deviant desires? Maybe his plan had simply been to make use of her sexual services then eject her from the firm – and his life.

Yet she couldn't deny that she'd enjoyed having him at her command. It had been a kind of revenge trip, although she hadn't been capable of doing anything really nasty to him. And if it had backfired on her, then so be it. She would have to be looking for a new job sooner or later, so maybe Duncan had done her a favour. After all, the experience of controlling the man who once controlled her had already given her self-confidence a subtle boost.

Chapter Twelve

It was three in the afternoon and Ben was lying in bed, exhausted. This was not from his sexual exertions of the night before, however. Chance would be a fine thing, he thought ruefully. Since he'd started making tentative noises about more commitment, Sara had backed away. Now they only dated occasionally. He was sure she was seeing other men in between.

Meanwhile, it looked more and more as if he and Shelley were heading for divorce. She was still at her sister's, as far as he knew, but he hadn't heard from her in weeks. Was it depression that was bringing him down? He seemed to hit a low point every afternoon, once he'd spent half the morning working out. Was he overtraining, as Sara had hinted? Or maybe he was just bored.

The 'Ex-Exec' agency had come up with nothing, not so much as an interview, during the month he'd been on their books and Ben was getting fed up. Maybe he would go and get some menial job, just to fill in time before something more suitable came up. He might seem more employable if he already had some sort of work. Rousing himself from his torpor, he spruced himself up and went into town.

Much to his surprise, the woman in the Job Centre took

one look at him and said, 'I might have something for you.' She handed him a card: 'Door attendant at Bellamy's Nightclub'.

'Why me?' he asked, amused.

'Because you look the sort of chap who can take care of yourself. You're smart and well-groomed. I think you're definitely in with a chance there.'

Glad that he'd taken the trouble to make himself look presentable, Ben waited while she arranged an interview for later that day. Cooling his heels in a café until the appointed time, Ben mentally reviewed the pros and cons of such an occupation. He'd seen the club from the outside and it looked fairly respectable, but he wasn't sure what went on there. If there was any rough trade he could be risking some damage, but his new-found strength had given him confidence and he still knew a few useful self-defence moves, gleaned from his teenage years when he was a Bruce Lee fan. The late hours didn't bother him, since he often stayed up late on the Internet. Although the job wasn't well paid, there were hints that he could earn 'tips'.

Ben rang the doorbell of Bellamy's, feeling rather nervous, and a woman answered. After looking him up and down she said, 'Mr Derwent? I'm Kate Boniface, manager of Bellamy's. Come this way, please.'

She led him into an office and, although it was his first job interview in years, Ben started to feel more relaxed. It turned out that the club was basically a drinking venue but they did put on various forms of entertainment, including strip shows and discos.

'We like to deal with any troublemakers quickly and efficiently, so discretion is the name of the game,' Kate told him. 'If there is a spot of bother, the other punters usually aren't aware of it. But Wally will show you the ropes, he's in charge of the door and bar staff. Now tell me about your last job, and why you left it.'

The fact that he'd not done such work before was an obvious drawback, but he must have made a good impression because, after only a few minutes, she suddenly stood up and offered him her hand. 'The job's yours Ben, on a trial basis, if you want it,' she smiled. 'Shall we say one month? That should be long enough to see if you suit the job and the job suits you.'

He was introduced to Wally, a totally bald man of vast girth and amiable expression, and taken through into the club itself. The place was tastefully decorated, with chairs arranged around tables and a bar in one corner. There was a small stage too. They sat down at one of the tables and Wally began to explain the finer points of his profession.

'It's a lot to do with psyching people out,' he said. 'You can learn to spot potential troublemakers, even smell 'em. Then you keep an eye on 'em. First hint they're gettin' uppity and you make 'em aware of your presence, but in a non-threatenin' way, understand? Then, if they don't take the hint and start slanging off at someone, generally over some bird, you move in fast with a spot of the old verbal persuasion. If they're well past it you help 'em off the premises, with back-up if you need it. That means you've got to be ready to help your fellow bouncers, an' all. We work as a team, don't forget that.'

There were three others on door duty at any one time, Ben discovered, and either Wally or Kate would also be on the premises. He was issued with a club tie, dark blue with a 'B' monogram in red, and told to turn up at seven the following evening in a dark suit. When he enquired about 'tips' Wally gave a knowing smile.

'Sometimes you get the chance to do someone a special favour. But there are other perks of the job too. You'll find out.'

He wouldn't say more and Ben grew suspicious. Were they peddling drugs there? Pimping? It had to be something shady, but he had the feeling his involvement was optional.

Feeling elated at the thought of working again, Ben drove back home. He wanted to tell someone but he thought twice about letting Shelley know. She might assume that he had enough to live on, but the wage was small because he'd only be putting in thirty hours a week. If there was a divorce settlement in the offing, he would have to act canny about his finances. As for Sara, if he wanted to bed her there would only be his one night off or during the daytime. He wasn't that bothered, though. From the way Wally had been talking, he had the feeling that girls would probably come on to him in the club and he could more or less take his pick.

The reality proved to be even more interesting than Ben's fantasies. One thing that Kate and Wally had omitted to mention was that the club held various 'theme nights', with appropriate entertainment laid on. His first night on the job turned out to be 'Ladies Only', much to his delight. Apart from his assumption (wrong as it turned out) that the evening would be trouble-free, two of his colleagues were also women, and good-looking ones at that. Velma was a tall, willowy blonde while Jax was stockier, dark and somewhat butch but in a very laid-back style. They both wore navy trouser suits and white shirts but, instead of the tie, a small brooch in the shape of a B adorned their lapels. The other doorman was a middle-aged, well-built fellow called Cliff.

'I'm going to put you and Velma on the front door to start with,' Wally told Ben as they all met for a briefing in Kate's office. 'Later you can move inside, so you'll get some idea of the ropes. Look after him, guy and gals. If you don't watch his back, he won't watch yours!'

Velma, although she seemed pleasant enough, was not very talkative. Ben found her physically attractive, but he didn't get much of an idea about her personality and she didn't seem particularly interested in him. They stood just inside the entrance and, as the members began to arrive, checked their ID cards. At first there was just a trickle, and Ben had time to give each girl a good once-over. Some of them were dykey types, but not all. Then a bunch arrived all at once, apparently for a hen-party, and the atmosphere hotted up.

Soon there were around fifty people bouncing around inside to the beat of a juke-box or chatting at the tables and the stream of arrivals had thinned. Wally appeared and said he would take over on the door. Ben went into the dark interior and stood at the back, surveying the scene and trying to look as if he belonged there. Several of the women nearby were eyeing him up curiously, and he felt his libido rise a little. Some of them looked very sexy indeed, wearing fetish fashion such as shiny red or black rubber mini-dresses, studded leather and hot pants with thigh-high boots.

Then he caught the eye of a woman who completely took his breath away. He noticed her body first, as she was dancing very erotically and had a superb figure. She was dressed in cowgirl style, with a brown suede blouse and matching mini-skirt, both adorned with fringes. The blouse was half unbuttoned to display a formidable cleavage in a white lace uplift bra. The girl was black, with braided hair and finely-chiselled features, and at first she was gazing down through long, sweeping lashes. But when she raised her eyes towards his he gave a gasp. They were a brilliant pale blue, shining out like sapphires against her coffee-brown skin. She recognised his shock, must have seen the same reaction a million times, and gave him a brief, ironic smile before slowly revolving in her dance, showing him a delightfully pert and swaying butt. Ben just couldn't take his eyes off her.

Suddenly Cliff appeared at his side. 'Want to take a break? You'll find the girls in the rest room. Tell them to come back in. You're allowed twenty minutes, no longer.'

Ben made his way to the staff room in the cellar of the building. The lights were just as dim down there as in the club, but his eyes soon became accustomed to the darkness. In the corner, lying on the sofa next to the drinks machine, were Velma and Jax, kissing passionately. He could see Jax tweaking Velma's nipple through her cotton shirt and Velma's hand was under the other girl's jacket. No wonder neither had showed the slightest interest in him!

The two girls looked round as they heard him approach and, reluctantly, moved apart. He noticed that Jax's blouse was unbuttoned and her tits could be plainly seen beneath, small and pointed with pale nipples. She pulled it across her chest and began to fasten herself up. Velma regarded him with a petulant look and stood up.

'Our time's up then, is it?' she said, brusquely. She turned and looked down at Jax. 'Come on, sugar lips, the sooner we get our stint over with, the sooner we can get home.'

Jax smiled wryly, holding out her hand to be helped off the sofa. Ben tried to smile too, but both women ignored him and stalked out of the cellar, leaving him alone. He went to the machine and pressed for a black coffee. It was not yet midnight and the place didn't close till two, so he needed an alcohol-free stimulant.

As he sipped the acrid coffee, Ben thought about the gorgeous black girl who was presumably still shifting her arse around so delectably upstairs. He'd never made love to a non-white woman before, and the very idea filled him with lustful excitement. But how the heck could he chat her up when he was on duty? If he was caught he'd probably be fired on the spot and this job was too precious to him to be thrown away. There seemed no way he could get near her, but the tantalising effect that her dancing would have on him if it were a case of 'look but don't touch' seemed just too unbearable.

When he returned to the club the stage act had just started. It was a double strip-tease, two girls gyrating in their glamorous underwear to sleazy music. Velma and Jax must be loving this, he thought, looking across to where they were both standing. As his eyes returned to the stage the redhead unfastened the brunette's bra and removed it, waving it like a trophy before throwing it into the air. The brunette pretended to be shocked, covering as much of her ample breasts with her hands as she could. Then, while the other girl was bumping and grinding at the audience she sneaked behind her and removed *her* bra. It was obvious that the act was going to develop in this 'tit for tat' fashion until both women were naked.

Ben's eyes raked the crowd for the blue-eyed black girl. At first he was afraid she'd already left, but then she emerged from the loo and went over to the bar, where she ordered a drink and sat on an empty stool to watch the show. Ben had to get near her. Casually he sauntered through the engrossed crowd until he reached the end of the bar from where he had a good view of the girl's face and magnificent cleavage.

Her cocktail arrived, a poisonous-looking green concoction bristling with paper parasols and assorted fruit. She took one sip through a yellow straw then replaced the flimsy glass on the counter. The woman on the stool next to her was a short, butch-looking female in leathers.

When she waved to someone she knew on the other side of the room, she sent the black girl's drink flying all down the front of her brown suede outfit.

'You clumsy cow!' she cried.

Ben heard the irate words above the music and the buzz of the crowd. Several people turned round as the butch girl responded equally angrily. 'It was an accident, black bitch!' she hissed.

He moved in at once, sensing trouble. The black girl had stopped trying to mop up the drink from her clothes, and was glaring ferociously at the butch girl. She snapped, 'Don't you dare call me that, motherfucker!'

'Don't you dare call me motherfucker, black bitch!'

Ben couldn't see who slapped who first, it all happened so fast. By the time he got there, the butch girl had the black girl by her braids and had pulled her from her stool onto the floor, where they were biting and scratching like two alley cats. Ben grabbed hold of the black girl's shoulder and was aware of another bouncer dragging away her opponent. He knew this was his first real test, and it made it all the more difficult that he fancied the 'trouble-maker' something rotten!

'Now come on, darling, we can't have this,' he murmured, trying to pull her to her feet.

She wrenched her shoulder from his grasp and turned on

him, blue eyes blazing uncannily. 'Get your fucking hands off me!'

'Fine, but I must ask you to come quietly.'

'You expect me to leave in this state?'

Ben thought quickly. 'Come with me, I'll help you to get cleaned up.'

Still glowering at him, she offered no resistance as he clamped a hand on her shoulder and led her through the gawping crowd. On the way he passed Velma, who looked as if she'd like to take over.

'It's okay, I'll handle this,' he muttered. 'See if Cliff wants help with the other one.'

Ben took her downstairs where he knew there was a washbasin and some cleaning fluid that the staff could use if anything got spilt on their clothes. Kate liked them to look smart at all times. There was even a spare track suit down there in case of real emergencies. Evidently spilt drinks were an occupational hazard.

The black girl seemed to have calmed down by the time they reached the rest room. He handed her the spot remover then sat her down on the sofa and asked if she'd like a drink.

'Coffee, please. White with sugar.' She was rubbing away at the green-stained material to no effect. 'It's useless, I need a special suede cleaner for this. That bitch should be made to pay my dry cleaning bill.'

'I'm sorry if this has spoilt your evening. Do you want something to change into?'

'No, I guess I over-reacted a little. I've got my coat hanging in the cloakroom.' He handed her the coffee, which she sipped with obvious relish. 'Whew!' she laughed. 'I've been coming to this club for six months and nothing like that ever happened to me before.'

'Are you alone?'

'I came with my girlfriend, but she was chatting to someone she knew in the Ladies. I don't think she saw what happened.' She drained the cup and tossed it in the bin. 'Hey, I've had enough of this place. I want to go home. Will you call me a cab?'

'Of course. Stay here for a while and get your breath back. I'll see what's happening upstairs.'

Ben went up with his heart pounding loudly in his chest. Already he'd touched the girl, been near enough to smell her earthy perfume, seen the dusky bloom on her cheek, felt the musky aura that surrounded her and played havoc with his pulse rate. There must be some way he could keep in contact with her, if not this evening then another time.

It seemed his luck was in. When he went to phone for a cab, Wally intercepted him.

'I gather you had a bit of a punch-up to deal with.'

'Yes, I took one of the ladies downstairs. I hope you don't mind, but she needed to see to her clothes. I was just going to phone for a taxi for her.'

'The girl's name is Esther, she's one of our regulars.' Wally smiled. 'I should think she'd appreciate being run home in your own car, Ben. Cab drivers round here can be a bit ... well, racist, know what I mean?'

'But I'm still on duty here, aren't I?'

'Only if you want to be. I could get Cliff to take her, if you prefer.'

'Oh no, that's perfectly okay, I'll take her.'

Wally's smile widened. 'I somehow thought you would. See you tomorrow, then, same time. It's Singles Night on Thursdays.'

Ben went back down to the rest room and found Esther lying on the sofa with her eyes closed. He tapped her on the shoulder and her ice-blue eyes stared up from the spidery black lashes. 'I'll take you home myself now, if you like.'

'You will?' She beamed, suddenly, showing perfect milk-white teeth. 'That's very good of you, man. Some of those cabbies can be right bastards, y'know?'

'Okay. Put your shoes on then, and we'll get your coat.'

Ben felt himself trembling as he followed Esther's swaying behind up the narrow stairs. At the exit Wally grinned at Ben and gave him a wink, muttering, 'Here's something for your petrol.' He pressed a note into Ben's hand and disappeared. Somewhat embarrassed, Ben stuffed the money into his trouser pocket without looking at it.

While Esther collected her coat, Ben slipped into the gents and procured some condoms from the machine. Then they went out into the cool night air, with Ben leading the way to his car. As she got in beside him he got a glimpse of naked thigh almost up to panty level. He took a deep breath, telling himself not to get too excited as he had to drive.

'Where do you live?' he asked, as they swung out into the traffic.

'Oh, not far. Down here, first left. I'll tell you as we go. But tell me your name, man!'

'I'm Ben. And I know your name is Esther. Wally told me.'

'Ah, Wally!' She laughed, a rich dark sound. 'He lives up to his name, that one! Still, he picked a nice young man for me tonight. Thank you, Wally man!'

Ben couldn't help feeling he'd been somehow set up, but what the scam might be he hadn't a clue. Following Esther's directions he ended up parking in front of a pleasant block of flats, three storeys high.

Esther turned and faced him squarely in her seat. 'Well, you can drop me here like a good boy and go home, or you can come in and be a bad boy. Which is it to be, Benny?'

Ben couldn't believe his ears. If anyone had told him, when he first spotted the girl, that he'd end up at her place he would never have believed it, yet here she was offering him a frank invitation. He swallowed and said, 'I'd like to ... er, come in, if you don't mind.'

'All depends *where* you want to come in, bad boy!' she giggled. 'Okay, let's go.'

They walked towards the front door and Esther punched in the security code. The door swung open and they entered the lift. As soon as it began to rise she pinned him to the back wall and pressed her mouth to his, insinuating her tongue between his lips. It tasted hot and slippery, very lascivious, and Ben felt his already hard prick straining against his fly.

Inside her apartment, Esther led him straight into the bedroom. She tossed her bag onto a chair then turned and faced him with a defiant smile.

'My soiled clothes must be removed,' she told him. 'Will you take them off for me?'

He willingly complied. Soon he had unbuttoned her cow-girl blouse to the waist and was slipping her arms out of the sleeves, his eyes transfixed by her gleaming brown chest. 'God, Esther, you've got such a fabulous figure!'

'Tits and ass, my finest assets!' she laughed. 'I love to wiggle my tits and shake my ass.'

He scanned her face. 'You're so beautiful, too. I've never seen anyone remotely like you.'

She put her hands either side of his face, so he had to look her in the eye. 'Okay, let's get one thing straight. I'm not wearing those fake lenses that change your eye colour, okay? These are my true eyes, passed on in my genes from my maternal grandma, who was white. The rest of me I got from dear ol' Ma and Pa, though I don't know which bit came from who since my Dad disappeared long before the CIA, or the CSA, or whatever they call it came on the scene!'

She giggled, an infectious sound, and undid her waistband so that Ben could pull down her suede skirt. Underneath she wore only white lace panties, to match her bra, and sheer black tights. Ben longed to get his hands on all that lovely firm flesh but she ducked away from him and picked up her outfit. She folded it neatly and took it to the wardrobe, where she put it into a plastic bag with the name of a dry cleaners on it. Then she turned back with a smile.

'Now, Ben, I'm all yours. But I want you to do something more for me. Just a little bitty thing, and I'm sure you're going to enjoy it.' She reached inside the wardrobe and brought out a baseball glove. 'Will you take off your jacket and put this on your right hand, please?'

Completely baffled, Ben nevertheless did as she asked. The glove felt loose and awkward on his hand, but there was a button at the wrist which he fastened. Esther sidled towards him, her breasts rearing provocatively at him and his prick rearing as boldly, though less obviously, in his trousers. Still smiling, Esther walked to the end of the bed and, very deliberately, bent over so that her elbows were pressing into the duvet and her rear was sticking up. Ben looked at it, he couldn't help it. Through the transparent black tights he could see the flimsy thong of white lace that barely concealed the firm brown globes.

'Now give me a good whacking, there's a good boy. Makes the blood rush to my ass and gets me going.' She looked round at him cheekily. 'You'll be glad you did!' she added.

Ben didn't need any further urging. The sleek buttocks were crying out to be touched in one way or other, even if he was insulated from the smooth skin by the glove. He held up his hand and then brought it down hard on her backside. It felt tight as a drum. Esther gave a guttural gasp and began to rotate her hips, wiggling her bottom as an incitement to do it again. She began a low moaning, rubbing her mons against the hard frame of the bed as he whacked her again and again.

'Now roll down my tights and hit me with your other hand,' she invited him, after he'd given her a dozen or so spanks.

This is more like it, Ben thought, as he made contact with her naked flesh. At the end of each stroke he couldn't resist letting his hand linger there and caressing her a little as he removed it. She was wriggling hard now, gasping as if she was nearing a climax, and Ben was becoming extremely aroused. He began to think about taking her from behind, pulling down that thong and getting straight in between those wonderfully rotund cheeks.

Then, in a series of jerky spasms and with a great deal of noise, she came. Ben stopped slapping her and instead rubbed his palm all over her shaking behind until she flopped forward on the bed. She lay there inert and he thought he might as well get undressed, ready for what-ever was to follow. He was sure the action had only just begun.

After removing the baseball mitt and stripping quickly,

Ben knelt beside her on the bed. He unfastened her bra and began rubbing her back with long, slow movements. Her dark skin rippled under his touch and he slipped the waistband of her panties down so that hc had full access to her glorious behind. His prick was rearing like a beast now and he straddled her to let it lie along her crack, pushing up her buttocks to give it a fleshy massage. She groaned and flexed her strong gluteal muscles to aid the process.

When he could take no more, Ben covered his penis with the condom he'd secreted under the duvet, pushed her thighs apart and slipped into her silky pussy. She was like hot chocolate sauce in there, sweet and molten. Esther got up on all fours, pulling off her bra so that he could clasp her firm-fleshed breasts from behind. Ben had a sense of over-abundance, he hardly knew how to divide his attention between all the delectable portions of her anatomy. For a few seconds his hands held her heavy breasts, feeling the nipples become bullet-hard beneath his fingertips, but then he would feel her behind waggling against his stomach and his hands would seek those taut mounds, passing his palms over them again and again, pinching them, moving around to feel the coarse patch of her pubic hair at the front then up her round belly to play with her tits again. It was an endless circuit of delight.

It wasn't long before Esther was shaking her ass like fury at him, propelling herself towards another climax and, this time, taking Ben with her. The explosion forced him forward onto the flat plane of her back but he could still feel her buttocks shaking against his belly as the seed spewed out of him, accompanied by the kind of violent thrills and stomach-churning sensations normally associated with a roller-coaster ride. When it was over he gasped and slid out of her, then moved up the bed to tell her how fantastic it had been.

'I told you,' she grinned, her blue eyes regarding him with sultry intensity. 'If you're a tits and ass man, I'm your woman!'

'I guess that must be true. Except I bet you could convert any leg man, too!'

She laughed in a rich, raucous way that set the hairs on his neck tingling. He put out his hand and squeezed her left breast, making her purr quietly and stretch her long, slim legs in languid ease. After a while she murmured, 'If you carry on doing that you going to make me want you again. Are you ready for it?' She looked down the bed at his still-limp organ. 'Oh my, I think we're going to have to do something about that!' She reached down, took Ben's penis between her hands and gave it a preliminary jelly roll. It needed further encouragement, so she knelt down – offering Ben the opportunity to fondle her velvety bottom again – and took it to her lips. Ben felt his dick stir slightly as she gave it a first licking. He would have been ashamed of himself if it hadn't.

Despite the shattering orgasm he'd just enjoyed, Ben felt his desire slowly reviving and soon, thanks to the enthusiastic attention it was getting, his dick reached half mast. While Esther performed with tongue-twisting expertise upon both glans and shaft, Ben gave her hindquarters an equally thorough going-over, softly kissing or biting into her bum cheeks while his fingers explored her twin cracks, back and front. He was sure that any minute now his cock would be hard enough to follow where his fingers were leading the way, in through her puffed up pussy lips to the warmly cushioning tunnel beyond.

He reached down and tugged playfully on one of Esther's braids. 'I want to come inside you, *now*!' he asserted, hoarsely.

She laughed. 'You're not stiff enough yet, man. Let me lick you a little more.'

Ben was convinced he was well able to penetrate her, but he had no objection to letting her gorgeous lips work their magic for a bit longer. He reached down and felt her hard breasts, with their even harder nipples, and a surge of new strength went through him. 'God, I can't wait!' he moaned.

'Very well, you can try now.'

Esther turned around and lay beside him, unashamedly feeling her protruding clitoris and moving her thighs with restless longing. Hastily Ben got to his knees and prepared to enter her but the minute his penis was inserted into her swollen vulva he could feel it softening. He withdrew and gave it a tug, but it shrank even more.

'Blast!'

She giggled. 'I told you to wait a while, you're too impatient!'

Ben tried to revive his flagging erection, but it was no good. Esther sighed, rubbing her clitoris all the harder.

'Hey, can't I do that?' Ben said, feeling upstaged. 'Better still, I could lick you.'

'Go on then. Maybe that'll light your fire for you.'

He lay right down on his stomach, with his feet over the end of the bed, and parted her thick labia with his fingers. Her cunny was deep pink and purplish, extremely glossy with lubrication, and as he put out his tongue to lick her he could smell the mingling of their two scents, the male and female musk.

While Esther fingered her large, dark brown nipples, Ben

mouthed her pussy, licking right into her open quim. He let his finger probe her while he gave her distended clitoris some tongue-friction. It didn't take long before she was rolling around in the throes of another orgasm, but Ben was dismayed to find that his prick was still obstinately flaccid.

'Oh, Lord, that one was the best!' he heard Esther declare, still writhing around and pressing her thighs close together to prolong the tingling spasms.

He went to lie beside her, although he told himself he would have another go in a minute. His body was completely drained and, before he knew it, he was fast asleep.

Ben awoke feeling disoriented, and as the events of the previous night returned to him he looked around for Esther but she was nowhere to be seen. Puzzled he got up and explored the flat, but it was clear that she had left. Then he found a note by the kettle in the kitchen saying, '*Thanks for everything. Gone to work. See ya. Es.*'

He made himself some coffee, showered, then left the flat. Relieved to find his car was outside, he drove home through the mid-morning traffic in a daze. Being with Esther had been like entering another time zone and it would take him a while to readjust.

After driving for ten minutes Ben realised that he needed more petrol and pulled up at a service station. The attendant filled the car up and Ben was reminded of the 'petrol money' that Wally had thrust into his hand at the club. He drew it out from his trouser pocket and stared uncomprehendingly at the crumpled note. Smoothing out the creases he held it up to the light. It appeared to be genuine. But what the hell had he done to deserve *fifty* pounds?

There was obviously a great deal more going on at Bellamy's than met the eye and Ben wasn't sure he wanted to know about it. Still, he wasn't complaining. The job seemed to have the kind of perks that no red-blooded male would object to!

Chapter Thirteen

'The two-faced bastard!' Shelley scowled at her reflection in
the cloakroom mirror. She made a mock-sympathetic face and
repeated the words that she'd heard Duncan utter only
minutes before: 'Wish there was more I could do, Shelley, but
you know how it is. My hands are tied.' The worm had actually
dared to say that! He'd been as good as admitting that he was
getting rid of her because of their unorthodox session last
month. The worst of it was that, things being as they were at
Harcourt, she couldn't do a thing about it.

As Shelley searched her mind for ways she could have
avoided being sacked, she realised that Duncan had had her
over a barrel. If she'd refused to bed him, he would probably
have got rid of her anyway, out of pique.

She combed her hair, sprayed herself with cologne and left
the building without a backward glance. Her bitterness was
almost tangible, leaving a nasty taste in her mouth. She
hurried to the Tube station in a daze, just wanting to get away.
But instead of going straight to Evelyn's, she ended up on a
park bench, trying to think things through. One thing was
certain, she would have to enrol with at least one agency
straight away. The mortgage payments still had to be kept up,
even though both her job and her marriage were over. The
house was her only asset now and, although she intended to

put it on the market as soon as possible, it could be months before it sold. There was no way she could allow it to be repossessed before then.

And what of Ben? For a moment she felt guilty, but only for a moment. They'd both have to fend for themselves from now on. She couldn't afford to harbour any sentimental feelings. Briefly she recalled Steve's offer of alternative employment, but she shrank from becoming immersed in his dubious world. No, she would try the agencies first and see what came up.

At first her search was not promising. One agency advised her to retrain by taking a word-processing course, but she couldn't face that yet. Shelley was determined to give it two weeks. If, after that time, she couldn't get anything in her line of work then she would be prepared to take anything that came along, no matter how menial.

For ten days Shelley stayed on in Evelyn's flat, afraid to tell even her sister that she had lost her job. She would go out in the morning and mooch around the shopping mall or make fruitless visits to the three agencies she'd registered with. Then one morning, much to her surprise, Cathy at Job Vision told her she might have something for her.

'It's nothing like what you're used to,' she began apologetically. 'But it is in TV, and once you're in something else might come along. It's with a company called David McDale Enterprises and it's a producer's assistant job.'

Shelley inwardly groaned. It wasn't the company – McDale had a good reputation – but the position. She'd be nothing but a glorified dogsbody. It galled her to think that she would now be in the same position as the minions she used to boss around, but she metaphorically shrugged her shoulders and forced a smile. 'I'll go for it. How do I get an interview?'

They were able to fit her in that afternoon. It was ages since she'd had a job interview, having been at Harcourt for almost four years, and she felt very apprehensive as she approached the reception desk and was directed to a waiting room. Three other candidates sat there, each trying not to catch the others' eyes. Shelley resigned herself to the wait.

When her time came Shelley was pleased to see a good-looking young man behind the desk. He wore large, square-framed glasses behind which clear blue-grey eyes regarded her frankly, and his luxuriant black hair was swept back off his high forehead, giving him a marked resemblance to Clark Kent. Shelley suspected he cultivated the likeness.

'Do sit down, Ms Derwent. I'm Liam O'Brien. Now I gather you recently lost your director's job at Harcourt . . .'

The sticky bit of the interview was soon over. He seemed to accept her story that she was made redundant and offered his sympathies. 'Of course, this post is nothing like what you're used to. Bit of a come-down, I'd have thought. How do you feel about that?'

'I was hoping that if I got a foot in the door, so to speak, something might crop up later. It could work to your advantage too, of course. I mean, you'd get an idea of what I was like to work with, and then if my face fitted . . .'

He laughed. 'Thanks for being so candid with me, Ms Derwent, I appreciate that. We've nothing coming up in the immediate future, but if you think you could be happy biding your time in a more subordinate post . . . Of course, the work of the producer's assistant is vital, but I don't have to tell you that.'

As the interview proceeded Shelley found herself growing more optimistic. She could tell Liam liked her. The question was, did he think she was right for the job?

She was asked to wait with the others. When Liam finally emerged and called her in again from the waiting room she was overjoyed. He smilingly told her she had the post if she wanted it. 'It would be a great advantage to have someone who already knows the business!' he explained. 'We're under a lot of pressure here at the moment and training someone from scratch would be well nigh impossible.'

As she went back to Evelyn's flat, Shelley decided that she simply must look for a place of her own now, preferably one near the studios. She bought an evening paper and studied the classified ads, deciding to investigate one or two. Her sister seemed relieved when she heard about the new job. 'Now you'll be more settled and you can start again. Will you tell Ben?'

Shelley felt doubtful. 'I suppose so, eventually. To be honest, Evie, it's been nice not to have to think about him for a while, although I do miss him sometimes.'

'Of course you do.' Evelyn gave her a hug. 'You can't suddenly forget five years of being together, just like that.'

It was worse at night, when Shelley was in bed and images of the past returned to torment her with dreams of what might have been. Fortunately she had only to take a sleeping pill and she'd be out like a light, with nothing to remember when she awoke next morning. The only trouble was they left her feeling woozy for a good couple of hours after she'd woken up. Still, it would take her that long to get to McDale's from where she was at present.

Eventually Shelley found a small but pleasant flat, only half an hour on the Tube away from her new job. She soon settled into working again, although it was hard being at other people's beck and call. Her situation provoked her into thinking about the way people bossed others around, and made her ask searching questions about her own directorial style. Had she been the type to demand or to ask? Had she made people feel used or valued? Had she, in fact, got a kick out of ordering people around?

Inevitably her thoughts led on to what had happened with Duncan. With him she'd experienced both sides of the coin. As her boss, he'd had ultimate power over her, power which in the end he had used to devastating effect. But as her submissive sexual partner he had put himself in her power, let her take very intimate control over him. She still felt weird when she recalled how easily she'd slipped into the rôle of dominatrix. It had been an extremely satisfying experience.

Yet there was also a strange satisfaction to be gleaned out of being told what to do by others, have them take the responsibility and make all the decisions. Shelley began to understand how Duncan must have felt, handcuffed to the bedrail and dependent upon her every whim. He'd trusted her not to take things too far and then, within that framework, he'd been able to slip into an exciting state of mild fear and hopeful anticipation.

Which was, more or less, the state she found herself in these days, scurrying round trying to please her exasperatingly vague boss, Michael. How he had ever got to such a position of power she would never know. Half the time she was expected to read his mind and the rest of the time to guess what he wanted. Most of his communication seemed to consist of meaningful waggling of his eyebrows.

Still, there were other compensations in being at McDale's besides the regular pay packet. One of them was an attractive young researcher called Rob. Shelley had been liaising closely with him since Michael began planning a wildlife quiz show for a cable channel. It was Rob's task to dream up hundreds of questions about flora and fauna so he spent most of his day browsing through encyclopaedias and catalogues of natural history museums on the Internet. Shelley made it her job to provide him with a regular supply of caffeine.

'God, Shelley, if I have to look at another Latin name I'll go nuts!' Rob declared one day, seeing her enter with his third coffee that morning. He looked at his watch. 'Lunch time, Hallelujah! Will you join me somewhere other than the canteen? I must get out of this building to save my sanity.'

Shelley laughed. 'There's a pub that does decent food, the Crown. We could go there.'

'Is that where all the other McDale clones go?'

'Yup.'

'Then let's go somewhere else and make a solemn vow to talk about anything but work.'

Shelley laughed. 'You're on!'

She watched him take the jacket off the back of his chair and drape it around his shoulders. His light brown, curly hair just brushed the collar of his check shirt, and when he glanced at her his hazel eyes seemed to flash her a green light. Careful, she warned herself, this guy is at least five years younger than you!

Not that it seemed to matter. They had a lot in common, they discovered, as they ate pasta together in a quiet bistro a few streets away. They'd both been brought up in South London and had gone to rival schools. Rob reminded her of things she'd forgotten about her teenage years. They had a lot of laughs and the old sexual chemistry was beginning to spark up between them by the end of the meal.

'Hey, watch it!' Shelley told herself, as she freshened up in the loo. 'Not only is he younger than you, but he's a colleague too. Haven't you learnt your lesson?'

But that night, when Rob caught her on her way to the Underground and offered her a lift in his car, she just couldn't resist. Since she'd moved out of Evelyn's and away from the circle of friends that had centred on her and Ben as a couple, she'd been feeling quite lonely. So when he invited her for a drink at a pub near her flat, she accepted without a qualm. A drink wasn't a date, she told herself, resolutely. And she owed him one for the lift.

Yet one drink led to another, and by eight o'clock they were both feeling quite peckish again. Shelley produced a supermarket packet. 'I bought these two salmon steaks and they won't keep,' she said, the three gin and tonics she'd consumed making her reckless. 'Past their sell-by date. No rude comments, please!'

'None called for,' Rob grinned. 'Do I catch your drift? Are you inviting me to supper?'

'Only if you've nothing better to do.'

'I can think of nothing better. Beans on toast in your company would be a feast, Shelley!'

'You've not tasted my cooking yet. How does salmon in Drambuie strike you?'

'Very strangely, but I'm sure it's excellent. I'll try anything once.'

They walked the short distance to the Victorian terrace where Shelley had her basement flat. She felt happier than she'd been for ages, despite the niggling doubts that still plagued her. She opened the door and led Rob in, apologising for the state of the place.

'I've not lived here long, so I haven't had time to decorate or anything.'

'Maybe I could help you with that. I'm a dab hand with a paintbrush.'

He sees us as having a future she thought, amazed. For a few seconds she tried to convince herself that all he was interested in was friendship, but once they were in the sitting-room Rob suddenly put his arms around her and kissed her impulsively on the lips. She gasped and he released her, looking sheepish.

'Sorry, Shelley, I shouldn't have done that. It's just that I've been wanting to do it all day – well, for several days actually – and I couldn't help myself.'

'Oh, Rob!' Shelley sat down on the battered sofa she'd bought second hand. Slowly he sat down beside her, keeping his distance. 'It's not that I don't find you attractive. Believe me, I do. Very. But we work together and I don't want anything to spoil our working relationship.'

'I understand.' He sounded forlorn and she longed to embrace him, comfort him. Sitting stiffly apart from him was torture. Then he suddenly brightened. 'But my contract with McDale ends next month, and then maybe we could go out together. I'd really like to, Shelley. We seem to get on so well. I know you're a bit older than me, but frankly I find girls in their early twenties really boring. I've always gone for more mature types.'

Shelley got up with a determined air. 'Look, let's just be friends for now shall we? I'll go and get the dinner on. Choose some music, if you like.'

Alone in the kitchen, with strains of her old Motown favourites issuing from the next room (something else they had in common), Shelley tried to concentrate on the recipe in front of her but it was proving difficult. She hadn't made love in weeks and now her libido was rising with a vengeance, making her breasts ache to be touched, inducing tiny ripples of excitement in her empty vagina, filling her crotch with steamy musk. If he comes in right now and takes me in his arms I'm done for, she thought.

The meal only took about half an hour to prepare. Shelley served the fish with a bottle of New Zealand Sauvignon that she had in her modestly stocked wine rack, and Rob was most appreciative. His green eyes surveyed her thoughtfully, triggering the subtle circuit of arousal between the poles of her nipples and clitoris.

'I can't believe this, Wonderwoman is a cordon bleu cook, too! How come nobody's snapped you up before now, Shelley?'

She decided it was time to tell him. 'They did.'

'What, you mean you're with someone?' Rob couldn't help looking around the room, as if for clues. He sounded disappointed.

'Not exactly. I'm still officially married, but we're separated.'

'Oh, I see.' He might as well have added, 'That's all right then!' since the relief was so visible on his face. 'For how long?'

'What, married or separated?' She prepared to answer both questions. 'Married around five years, separated . . .' Shelley made a quick calculation. 'Around five weeks, I think.'

Rob's lean, chiselled face took on a sympathetic cast. 'I was engaged once, but she broke it off. I suppose that's nothing like what you're going through, but I can understand a little.'

Something vicious in her made her snap, 'I doubt it!'

Shelley started to clear away the things but he leapt to his feet. 'Let me do that.'

She went to sit moodily on the sofa while he took the plates through to the kitchen. Soon she heard the tap running, dishes clunking. He was actually doing the washing-up. Suddenly she came over very weary. She slipped off her shoes, rolled off her tights and put her feet up on the sofa, letting the warm tones of Aretha singing a familiar ballad wash over her. Before she knew it she was drifting off.

Dimly, as she returned to consciousness from her doze, Shelley was aware that her right foot was being massaged. One hand was cradling her heel while the thumb of the other hand rubbed the flesh with firm strokes. It felt immensely soothing. There was a hypnotic quality about the sensation which made her unwilling to open her eyes. So she lay there just wallowing in bliss while the sole of her foot, now wonderfully warm and relaxed, had all its bumps and creases smoothed over.

Then Rob's hands moved over to caress her left foot, stroking with equally firm but careful fingers. He worked all over the top with small circling motions of his fingertips and then began pressing harder into the fleshy pads beneath with his thumbs, easing away any latent tensions, aches and pains. She felt delightfully pampered, the sense of well-being not confined to her feet but filling her whole body.

Rob began fondling both her feet at the same time, making them feet feel vibrant and alive. Shelley wiggled her toes a little but kept her eyes closed, relishing the comforting warmth that was flooding through her veins. Her legs were tingling from the sensual contact and she could feel herself becoming quite aroused, the fleshy petals of her sex unfolding to let the bud of her clitoris swell and grow. Sighing, she shifted her position on the sofa to allow her hand to fall between her thighs, furtively pressing against her enlarged vulva with her thumb.

Then, incredibly, Shelley felt something wet and velvety enclose one of her big toes. The sensation was deliciously familiar. At once she remembered how she had made Duncan give her a toe job, and a thrill of enhanced desire flashed through her as she recalled the two exquisite orgasms that had ensued on that occasion. Shelley wiggled her toe inside the slippery hole that was Rob's mouth and pressed her thumb hard against the sensitive mound at the apex of her vulva. She knew it would be easy to make herself come again, but she was in no hurry. It was always better if you prolonged the build-up.

Rob's mouth moved to her other toe, licking it first with careful attention then letting it slip right in between his lips and move in and out, in a parody of intercourse. Shelley smiled to think of him giving her a blow job. His hands had begun stroking her calves in a languid rhythm. Was he aiming to seduce her entirely? If so, he was making a jolly good job of it. The throbbing in her love-bud was becoming more and more urgent, involving more of her body in the wild pulsations. She was convinced that, if he kept it up much longer, she would reach a climax.

Perhaps he sensed it, too, because his lips began to travel up from her feet, tracing a path up her shins, his tongue licking its way across her knees until his mouth met the ultra-sensitive flesh of her inner thigh. Shelley shuddered as his lips brushed lightly across the smooth surface of her skin, getting ever closer to the main source of her pleasure. Casually she removed her hand, offering a silent invitation to move right up into the area where her arousal was at its height and where he might successfully bring it to a conclusion.

His touch was infinitely gentle around her mons, delving softly beneath the loose leg of her French knickers, making her glad she'd not chosen to wear more tight-fitting underwear that day. His fingertips touched the crinkly hair within, tickling her as it pulled against the skin, making her long to take his fingers and plunge them right into her secret wetness. She was burning down there now, every nerve straining for release from the acute tension it was under. Yet something made her keep up the pretence that she was still half asleep and scarcely aware of what was happening to her.

Shelley felt her knickers being drawn down her thighs, exposing her bush and the moist crevice within. She sighed with relief as Rob's fingers finally found their way in and when his mouth followed, she knew that she wouldn't have to hold out for much longer. She was already on the brink of an earth-shattering orgasm and now his finger was insinuating itself well into her pussy, giving her what she'd been craving all evening. She wriggled to allow him easier access and, in the process, felt her clitoris reach that critical point of throbbing intensity from which there could be no going back. The fierce spasms shook her through and through as Rob penetrated her more deeply, filling her with gratifying sweetness, and the knowledge that he must be able to feel the rhythmic contractions of her vagina increased her satisfaction greatly.

'Oh!' she moaned, as the lovely strong waves of her climax reduced to mild ripples of delight. Opening her eyes, she saw Rob staring up at her with a smile. 'That was amazing!' she breathed.

He came up onto the sofa and kissed her, and she wriggled voluptuously against him. 'Mm, you really sneaked up on me there, didn't you? Naughty boy!'

'Did you enjoy pretending to be asleep?'

She giggled. 'Only half pretending. I did fall asleep at first, honest!'

They kissed again, but Shelley felt uneasy about continuing. She sat up and pulled her knickers back on. Rob looked at her questioningly and she held his face between her hands, looking into his candid green eyes. 'Look, I meant what I said earlier, Rob. What just happened was very nice, but I'm very tired and it you don't mind I want to go to bed now.'

'Do you really want me to leave?'

Shelley looked at the clock. It was gone midnight. 'No, it's probably best if you don't try and drive after all the alcohol you've had. You can stay here if you like, but on this sofa bed.'

He looked resigned, giving her a rueful grin. 'Okay, I suppose that'll have to do. Thanks, Shelley.'

'Don't worry, I'll give your shirt an iron if you like, to make you look respectable for work tomorrow.'

They kissed again, then Shelley went into the bathroom. When she came out Rob had set up the sofa bed and found the sleeping bag that she kept in its innards. She bade him a fond goodnight and went into her bedroom.

For a long while she lay awake, unable to get to sleep after her earlier nap. A part of her wished that she had been able to make love completely with her handsome young lover, yet there was an insuperable barrier within her and it wasn't just to do with Duncan. Somehow she felt guilty about the idea of hopping from bed to bed, as if her marriage to Ben really wasn't over. She hadn't been in touch with her husband for weeks, yet not a day had passed when she wasn't reminded of him in some way. She realised that, deep down, she'd been missing him horribly. Oh, when would she get the mess that was her emotional life sorted out?

Afraid that she would be too tired for work next day, Shelley broke one of her sleeping tablets in two and, instead of her usual dose, took one and a half. She had done that a few nights ago when she needed some extra help, and had dropped off to sleep almost immediately. This time it had the same effect, and she thankfully gave herself up to oblivion.

The morning felt strange when she awake, noisier and brighter than usual. And she'd woken without the alarm. Glancing at her bedside clock, Shelley was suddenly seized with panic. She'd thought it said half past nine. It *did* say half past nine!

'My God!' She leapt out of bed and ran into the bathroom, where she washed in frantic haste, her mind buzzing. She should be at McDale's by now. What the hell was she going to do? Then she remembered Rob. Still brushing her teeth she went into the dim sitting room and saw his figure hunched on the sofa. She went over and pushed his shoulder roughly. She shouted down at him, spraying white flecks of toothpaste all over the navy sleeping-bag.

'Rob! It's really late! We've got to get going!'

He grunted and stirred. She fled back into the bathroom, rinsed her mouth then hurried to her bedroom to get dressed. By nine-forty she was ready, and Rob was also up taking a leak.

'I slept right through the alarm,' she told him. Her head was still very fuzzy after the initial shock. 'Michael will be going crazy already. He depends on me when we're shooting and this is the first day. What the hell am I going to tell him?'

'Phone in sick.'

'I can't. You know how strict they are about doctor's notes.'

'Say it was a migraine. No one calls the doc for a headache.'

'I *can't*!' Shelley moaned. 'If they think I'm the sort who gets migraines on crucial days then it won't look good either. No I'll just have to go, and think up some excuse on the way.'

She left before Rob, but as she was getting into her car she realised she had the perfect alibi right there: a breakdown.

Hurrying to the nearest phone box she got through to reception and told them her car had packed up on her and she was coming in by public transport. A hold-up on the Underground would be enough to explain why she arrived an hour late. She couldn't afford to lose any more time, however. Getting back into her car she drove to Uxbridge, parked in a residential street and hurried to catch the Tube for the last few stations of her journey.

After her stuttering apologies Michael was tight-lipped, his eyebrows in menacing mode. 'Get yourself a more reliable vehicle,' he snapped, adding, 'You should have called a cab.'

It wasn't quite as bad as she'd feared, since the minibus carrying the contestants to the studio from their hotel had been held up in traffic and they were running a bit late. Even so, she was rushed off her feet for the rest of the day. When she went to look for Rob during her half-hour lunch break, she was told he hadn't come in. Shelley was surprised by her feeling of relief. She hadn't wanted to confront him with so many other things on her mind.

Once the hectic business of the day had evaporated, however, and Shelley found herself on a crowded train to Uxbridge, thoughts of the previous night returned. Something told her she shouldn't have let things go so far between her and Rob. She couldn't afford to have an affair with him. Neither, much to her surprise, did she really want to. He was very sweet, of course, and extremely attractive, but she couldn't cope with involvement right now. She sensed that what Rob needed was something far more meaningful than she could offer him. Well, if he began pestering her, she would have to be firm with him and not get herself into any more compromising situations. He'd have to get his own coffee from now on.

When she got home Shelley felt an urge to phone Ben. She

just wanted to hear his voice, so familiar to her for so long. But when she called there was no reply, not even his familiar recorded message, and she was disappointed. It would have been good to confide in him like she used to, except that she hardly knew what to say to him any more.

Once they would have faced everything together and Ben would have supported her through redundancy, if he'd still had his salary, not just financially but emotionally too. A guilty pang struck her. Had she been equally sympathetic when he'd lost his job? In her heart she knew she'd just regarded it as a nuisance and, as the weeks turned into months, began to resent the fact that she was the sole breadwinner. What a mess she'd made of everything!

At ten Shelley put the answerphone on, took a pill and went to bed, unable to face the rest of the evening. She awoke at dawn feeling really low, but didn't dare take another pill. She got up and saw a message waiting for her. Eagerly she played it back, hoping it was from Ben, but it was Rob saying how sorry he was that he'd made her late for work and asking her out to dinner to make up for it. She sighed. No way!

That weekend Shelley visited her sister, but Evelyn was caught up in a new romance and had little time for her troubles. Tired of hearing about Mr Bloody Wonderful, Shelley returned early on Sunday and rang Ben's number again. This time he answered.

'Shelley!' He sounded genuinely pleased to hear from her. 'I've been wondering about you. How are you?'

'You didn't try to ring me at Evelyn's.'

'I know, I'm sorry. I've been rather busy lately.'

'Busy? Doing what?'

Shelley knew she was sounding too suspicious, too ready to sneer. She told herself to relax, be more understanding.

But Ben suddenly went vague on her. 'Oh, like the song says. You know, "Busy doing nothing?" Anyway, how are things at Harcourt these days?'

'I wouldn't know. I quit. I'm working for another company now, David McDale.'

'What happened at Harcourt, then?'

'Nothing, I just decided it was time for a change. It's quite interesting at the new place. I'm working on a natural history quiz show right now.'

'Good.' There was a long silence. Shelley was disconcerted to find she didn't know what to say next. There was so much to say, or so little, depending on how you viewed the situation. It was confusing.

'Well, it's been nice talking to you . . .'

His absurd statement tailed off into the ether. Shelley pulled herself together. 'I suppose we should get together sometime soon.'

'Yes, I suppose we should.'

'I'll ring you when I've got a window in my diary.'

I don't believe I just said that, Shelley thought. Their conversation was sounding more and more like the screenplay of a movie.

After he'd rung off she sat holding the receiver for a few seconds, feeling numb. Calling her husband had made her feel worse rather than better. She wanted to see him quite badly, yet she couldn't bring herself to make a simple date with him. She hadn't even given him her new address and phone number. What was the matter with her?

Shelley felt utterly drained. She went to bed at nine, taking one and a half sleeping pills again to ensure that she slept right through. She reasoned that since she was going to bed that much earlier she should wake at the right time, but she didn't.

It was nine o'clock when she awoke and scrambled, panic-stricken out of bed.

'Late again, Shelley?' Michael frowned, as she grovelled her way into his office at ten-fifteen after a mad dash through the traffic. 'If it happens a third time . . .'

'It won't,' she assured him, firmly.

But the following Sunday she stayed up late to watch a film on TV and overslept once more. It was once too often. She found herself summoned to Liam's office as soon as she arrived.

Chapter Fourteen

After working out almost daily for months, Ben should have felt strong, but he didn't. He felt weak, very weak. Sometimes, at Bellamy's, he felt so bad he just wanted to put his head down and weep. And when he awoke, mid-morning, he felt so drained and depressed he had to drag himself off to the gym. In the mirror he looked great, his body sculpted into the shape he'd always wanted, but inside he felt a mess.

At first Ben put it down to late nights at the club, but he should have got used to the new routine after a couple of weeks. Then he wondered if he was suffering the effects of separation from Shelley. That phone call hadn't helped. They'd talked like total strangers. He wanted to see her but, somehow, he couldn't bring himself to ring Evelyn's number.

Then, one afternoon at the gym, Ben was going through his shock-set programme when he suddenly collapsed. He tried to get up off the mat but his muscles refused to work and his body lay there inert, like a lead weight. Someone ran for help and Ben was dimly aware of people fussing round him, his pulse being taken, instructions yelled to phone for an ambulance.

Ben knew he was still breathing and his heart was thumping

strongly, but it was as if every muscle in his body had seized up and refused to work. He could hear Sara's voice in his ear telling him not to panic. 'You're going to be all right, Ben. You've been overdoing it, that's all. Try to relax and take deep breaths. We'll get you to hospital so they can check you over.'

The ambulance men rolled him onto a stretcher. Ben felt weird, as if he were some kind of fraud. He knew he wasn't sick, not enough to be taken to hospital at any rate, and yet he felt kind of paralysed. He couldn't even manage to speak.

Whether they gave him a shot of something on the way he never found out, but the next thing he knew he was waking in a hospital bed with Sara sitting beside him. He gave a faint smile and she squeezed his hand. 'Thank God! You're going to be okay, Ben.'

He tried to speak but his mouth was dry. He gestured towards the carafe of water by the bed and she poured him a glass. He gulped it down thirstily.

'What happened? I just remember collapsing in the gym, then everything went blank.'

'You were overtraining, just as I thought. But that wasn't the only cause of your collapse. You should have told me you were taking steroids, Ben. I could have told you about the dangers you were running.'

He gave a rueful grin. 'You did tell me, I seem to remember.'

'Yes, but only in a general way. I had no idea you were taking them yourself. The doctor here would like to know the brand names, so he can work out what damage you've been doing to yourself. Do you remember them?'

Ben reeled off the names and Sara wrote them down. Then she shook her head. 'You know, you've been really stupid.

God knows what you've done to your system with this mix. Where on earth did you get them? No one at the gym, I hope.'

'No. I ordered them through the Internet.'

'Idiot! Well I'd better tell the medics you're back in the land of the living.' She kissed him on the forehead. 'Goodbye, Ben. I'll drop in again tomorrow, if you're still here.'

By the evening Ben was fit enough to phone Bellamy's and say he was off sick. Next morning the doctor gave him a thorough examination, lectured him on the dangers of indiscriminate steroid use, and said he could go home provided he rested for three days then went to his GP for a final check-up.

Above all, Ben felt foolish. He'd been warned, but believed he knew best and had come a cropper through his own stupid fault. Sara visited him early on Saturday night and cooked him a meal. He was very grateful to her, but it was clear that she disapproved of his behaviour and she left the house promptly at nine-thirty. He had the impression that she had another date, but he couldn't blame her. Why would she want to spend any more time with a loser like him?

By the following Thursday Ben was back to normal. He rang Wally at Bellamy's and told him he'd be back that night, but he sounded none too pleased. Ben had the impression that he was no longer trusted. Maybe they thought he might collapse on the job. Still, at least he hadn't been given the sack – yet. He did a few press-ups just to get himself back into the old routine, but somehow his heart was no longer in it. He suspected it would take him a while to get back into physical exertion on the scale that he'd become used to. Perhaps he never would.

Morale-wise, Ben was at an all-time low. Was he going to remain a nightclub bouncer for the rest of his life? He'd had plenty of time to review his situation while he was lying in that hospital bed, and the one person he'd wanted near him was Shelley. But she was the very person he didn't want to worry. It was all very complicated.

While Ben was browsing through the Internet the phone rang. He was surprised to hear a girl say she was ringing from the Ex-Exec agency.

'We'd like you to call in later today, if possible,' she told him. 'Something's come up that we think you might be interested in, but we'd like to discuss it with you first.'

Ben was instantly cheered. After the trauma of the past few days he needed something to give him hope, in one area of his life at least. He showered and changed into his suit, doing his best to present a positive image. Don't get your hopes up too high, he warned himself, as he set out for the agency. He knew that even if he liked the idea of the job, when it came to the crunch he might not get it.

But Joanne, the agency boss, was enthusiastic. 'It seems right up your street, Ben,' she smiled, handing him the job description. He glanced through it. The computer firm was new and small, but according to the hype had great export potential since they were specialising in a field where there was as yet little competition: medical diagnostic programs for the Third World. The skills required were exactly those which Ben already had, but there would be provision for re-training if he needed to be brought up to date.

'Shall I ring them and make an appointment?' Joanne asked.

It was strange having everything done for him through the agency, since he'd always applied for jobs himself before. An interview was fixed for the following afternoon and Joanne wished him luck as she shook his hand.

Ben drove to the address full of trepidation but was soon put at ease by the two young, friendly guys who interviewed him. They seemed impressed with his track record, despite the fact that he'd been so long out of work in his own field.

'Someone with your expertise should have been re-employed by now,' Don declared, and his partner took up the theme.

'Unfortunately the home market has remained stagnant for too long. That's why we're looking to the Third World. The countries that are investing in new technology are keen to do so in socially beneficial areas like medicine, as well as more commercial fields. The governments of countries like Zimbabwe are using technological reform to maintain the loyalty of their electorate. That gives companies like us a head start.'

Ben didn't need much convincing. It sounded just the sort of firm he'd like to work for, but would they want him? At the end of the half-hour interview he had the feeling that he was definitely in with a chance, and he left the office in a buoyant mood. If only he could get this job then everything else in his life might start to fall back into place. He thought of Shelley. How would she react to the news if he got into full-time employment again? He hoped she would at least be pleased for him.

That night, as Ben put on a crisp new shirt over his smoothly defined chest, he felt *good*. He hadn't felt this good in ages, probably because those steroids had been depressing him. The doctor had explained all the side-effects, and they were horrific. But now he was in the clear and there was the prospect of a real job at last, a job where he could use his brain, not just his brawn. When Ben walked into Bellamy's in his Armani suit, smelling of Antaeus and feeling a million dollars, he just knew he had to get laid. It was almost a superstitious thing. If he could pull some gorgeous female

251

then he knew he could pull the job. Kind of sympathetic magic.

It wasn't long before he'd chosen his woman. It was Thursday again, Singles Night, so he knew she was available. Somehow he had to have her, and there would be as much pleasure in the chase as there would be in her final surrender. She was dancing with a female friend, but her eyes – sultry brown ones, gleaming coquettishly beneath long lashes – were swivelling everywhere, checking out the talent. Her hair was long and blonde, falling in waves to just below her shoulders, and she wore a skimpy black and silver top that fully emphasised her wonderfully globular breasts. Her movements were slow and very sexy, slim hips swivelling in a figure of eight and her mons shifting back and forth, round and round, sending out erotic signals. Her bottom, in the skin-tight pink satin jeans, was tight and perfectly divided into two rotund hemispheres. As he watched her sensual display, resembling the mating dance of some exotic bird of paradise, Ben felt his erection grow to vast proportions. He had to have her!

It was difficult deciding just how and when to make his move. Should he approach her while on duty, or during his twenty-minute break? He felt disinclined to wait. She was so obviously gorgeous that some other punter was sure to move in soon. Ben racked his brains. How could he think of an excuse to break into her rhythmic reverie and get her to focus on him?

Then it came to him: one way to use his position of power in the club to get acquainted with the girl. He sidled over to where she was dancing and murmured in her ear, 'Excuse me, Miss, but would you mind coming outside for a few moments.'

She stopped dancing and stared at him. 'Who the heck are you?'

'I'm employed by the management to keep order here, Miss.'

Her manner grew truculent. 'Are you saying *I'm* out of order?'

'Not at all. But I would be very grateful if you would just step outside the room for a few moments. I'd appreciate it if you didn't make a fuss. We have to be very careful here.'

She stared at him sullenly, her lovely lips in a petulant pout, then decided to go along with the strange request. Excusing herself from her girlfriend, she followed Ben through the dancing crowd and out into the corridor. He looked round to make sure no one was spying on them, then invited her to follow him downstairs to the staff rest room. She hovered uneasily.

'It's all right,' he assured her. 'You've done nothing wrong, Miss. I just wanted a brief word. Shan't keep you long.'

Obviously mystified she followed him down to the dark cellar, where he switched on a lamp and invited her to join him on the beat-up sofa. She looked nervous and slightly annoyed, but the flush that coloured her plump cheeks and the slight sweat that gleamed on her impressive cleavage only served to accentuate her extreme desirability. Ben's pulse was thudding away alarmingly and he made a conscious effort to relax. He couldn't afford another breakdown, not when such a prize was within his grasp.

'I'm sorry to drag you away like this, but we are very concerned about drugs being pushed on the premises and we think you may be able to help us.'

She looked affronted. 'What are you saying, for heaven's sake? You want to strip search me, or what?'

Ben couldn't resist a smile. 'It's an attractive proposition, Miss.' He glanced down at her pert bosom, now heaving with pent-up anxiety. 'But that wasn't what I had in mind. No, I merely wanted to ask you to report to me if anyone should offer to sell you any form of controlled substance during the course of the evening. You'll appreciate that we are concerned for the reputation of Bellamy's, and this sort of thing is very difficult to control without the co-operation of members such as yourself.'

'Are you asking other people to report pushers as well?'

'Of course,' Ben lied smoothly. He was in up to his neck now. May as well be hung for a sheep as a lamb.

'I suppose that's all right, then.'

'So you will report back to me at the end of the evening? You might witness a deal, see something suspicious. Any information would be useful to us, however insignificant it may seem. We have to stamp out this evil traffic at source, you see.'

'Okay. Should I tell my friend, Linda? The one I came here with?'

'Er . . . no, I think not. We must be discreet, you see. I have to have people posted all over the room and you and your friend will probably stick together, so only one of you needs to know about this.'

'I see. So what shall I tell her? About what you wanted.'

'Um . . . tell her I thought I recognised you, thought we were at school together, or something.'

'Okay.' She suddenly brightened. 'Wow, this is a bit like being in a James Bond movie, isn't it? Do I refer to you by number, or what?'

He laughed, relieved that she was taking it so well. 'I do have a name. It's Ben.'

She held out her hand. The long slender fingers were covered with rings. Her eyes gleamed cheekily at him as she said, 'Well, I'm Sandra. Do we rendezvous here at midnight, or what?'

'Good idea. Look, why don't you go back now by yourself, to avoid suspicion? Don't want you blowing your cover now, do we?'

Ben practically had hysterics as he watched her gloriously swaying butt climb back upstairs and disappear into the darkness. The daft cow had swallowed his story wholesale and, if his luck lasted, he would be inside her knickers before the night was out.

He'd never played such a game before, and the effect was exhilarating. Ben got himself a coffee from the machine and sat there savouring his triumph for a while. That girl would be playing the rôle of undercover agent for the rest of the evening and he would milk it for all it was worth. What a hoax! He longed to share his glee with someone, but he didn't dare. If he were to succeed he must keep it all to himself and snare that gorgeously gullible creature in his net. Roll on midnight!

While he was on duty upstairs Ben amused himself by sending out occasional signals to the vigilant Sandra: a nod, a wink, a secret smile. She was clearly enjoying the situation immensely – not least, he suspected, because her girlfriend knew nothing about it. Even when the two women went over to sit with a couple of guys who bought them drinks, Ben didn't fret. He knew that Sandra would be keeping her midnight tryst with him and that any liaison she might form before then would prove to be strictly temporary once she had succumbed to his charms. Tonight, Ben told himself confidently, everything would be going his way.

As midnight approached Ben's excitement grew, and he was feeling extremely randy. The club was winding up, since they were only allowed to go on until twelve on weekdays, and by half-past the place would be deserted. If he could only manage to keep his quarry in sight till then he would be home and dry.

Ben went down into the rest room and was relieved to find it empty. He waited in fidgety suspense until he heard a pair of heels clattering down the stairs and knew it would be her. She looked at him as she entered the room and giggled. He put his finger to his lips.

'Ssh! Take those shoes off, please Sandra. We don't want anyone to hear us down here.' She took off her high-heeled shoes and closed the door quietly behind her. 'Well, anything to report?'

'I'm not sure. You did say to mention everything . . .'

'That's right, anything at all.'

'Well, I saw this guy with red hair whisper something to this woman and they went outside. They came back ten minutes later and she was acting really weird, as if she were high or something.'

'What did she look like?'

'She had a green dress on, very short. And black curly hair, quite short too. Oh, and she smokes. So does he.'

'Good. Excellent. Anything else?'

'Yes. I saw someone slip something into someone's pocket.'

'You did?'

'Mm. A small packet of something. It was a woman with jeans and a red top. Lots of eye make-up. She had brown hair, a bit frizzy. The man was short and fat, black hair but a bit bald on top. He wore jeans and a denim jacket.'

'Thank you, Sandra, you've been most helpful.' Ben lowered his voice to a murmur. 'Look, darling, would you mind staying down here while I investigate? I don't want anyone to see us together. You'll be quite safe down here for a few minutes. I'll get you a Coke, if you like. You can sit behind that old screen over there, but I don't suppose anyone will come down.'

She was obviously enjoying every minute of the intrigue. He had the feeling that it was getting her going sexually, too. Her brown eyes were gleaming at him excitedly, and when he went over to the drinks machine she put her hand on his arm, standing very close, and their fingers touched as he handed her the paper cup.

'You'll be okay down here by yourself? Just for a few moments?'

'Of course I will. Just make sure you come back and get me soon.'

'Would I abandon a lovely girl like you? Of course I'll be back, just as soon as I can.'

He took a risk and gave her a light kiss on the cheek. She seemed to like it. 'I'm in!' he thought, the words echoing with thundering volume inside his head.

Upstairs the crowd had thinned but Linda was still waiting for her friend, looking bemused. He went straight over to her. 'Excuse me, are you Linda?' She nodded. 'I've a message from Sandra. She says she got a lift home and you're not to worry about her.'

'Who's she with?' Linda asked, suspiciously.

Ben shrugged. 'I dunno, I'm just the messenger. She looked pretty happy as she went out the door with this guy, though.'

'The bitch!'

Linda stormed off, and Ben saw Wally eyeing him from the other side of the room. He sauntered over to him. 'Hi, Wal. Pretty quiet night, wasn't it?'

'It's not over yet!' Wally snapped. 'Get out on the front door, Ben. Do your job.'

As he went into the corridor Ben saw that Cliff was already at the door. He decided to take a risk and go back downstairs. When he entered the rest room he found that Sandra had dragged the sofa behind the screen and was lying on it, sipping her Coke. She looked up and smiled as he moved the tattered screen back.

'Hi! Did you see those people I told you about? Is the coast clear now?'

'I reported your findings to the boss. He seemed to know who they were, and we'll be keeping an eye on them in future. It will be a long undercover operation, but if we can catch those scoundrels in the end it'll be worth it.'

She sat up, looking at him provocatively over the rim of her cup. 'So everyone's gone home, have they? Did you see my friend Linda?'

'She's gone home too. But you don't have to worry, I can give you a lift.'

'You already have.' She raised the cup to him. 'With this Coke, I mean. It always gives you a lift, doesn't it? They say they used to put real cocaine in it. I wonder what they use now. It's a secret recipe, handed down through generations of the Coke family.'

She giggled. Ben sat down beside her, hardly able to contain himself. She smelt of cheap scent and hairspray, crude but arousing. He forced himself to say, 'Ready to go, then?'

'It's quite comfy here,' she smiled, settling back against the mildewed arm of the sofa. 'If I go home before Linda goes to bed, she'll only ask questions.'

'Oh, you share a flat with her, do you?'

Sandra grimaced. 'Yes, worse luck! When I moved out from my boyfriend's I had nowhere else to go. Say, we won't get locked in if we stay here for a while, will we?'

'No chance. I have a key to the back door. But are you sure you don't mind . . . ?'

'Not if you don't.' She put one hand on his shoulder, smiling up at him. Ben felt his prick leap in his pants. 'I thought it might be rather nice, down here.'

She shifted her thighs apart, stretched and thrust her breasts out, then put her legs across his lap. She wore floppy pink socks. Slowly Ben rolled them off her feet and she wiggled her toes at him. He began to caress her small, naked feet and she sighed, leaning back and closing her eyes. 'Mm, this is nice. I just love having my feet massaged.'

Upstairs it had gone very quiet. No music, no voices, no more footsteps, bangs or thuds. Ben began to relax, and his hands travelled up to her tiny waist where they undid her belt buckle, then her zipper, and slowly began to remove her satin jeans. They were very tight-fitting, the bulge of her crotch showing clearly, and she helped to push them down over her thighs until they loosened. She had slim thighs, as satiny to the touch as the material they'd been encased in. Ben first stroked and then kissed them, making her moan softly.

Sandra wore a pair of close-fitting silky black panties. The black and silver blouse just skimmed the waistband, exposing maybe half an inch of lightly-tanned torso. Ben's fingers crept under the edge of her top and felt the velvety curve of her stomach. Her moans grew louder, signalling that she was becoming really aroused. His dick surged impatiently beneath the weight of her thighs. If he didn't screw her soon he would come in his Calvin Kleins.

Up and up his fingers travelled until they found the undersides of her bra cups, filled to bursting with solid flesh. She gasped as he blindly explored the maze of underwiring, padding and lace, finally finding his way to the erect buttons of her nipples. Greedily he pushed up her top and exposed them. They reared above the lacy half-moons of her bra, red and swollen with desire, sitting on top of the plump golden breasts that had been pushed up from their confining bra and were now struggling to free themselves. As he gazed at the delightful sight, Sandra arched her back and reached behind herself to release the fastening, flopping back with a sigh of relief as her breasts were finally allowed to do their own thing.

'Wonderful tits!' Ben murmured, lifting the scraps of cotton and lace out of the way so that he could see them better. His mouth fastened greedily on one rosy nipple while he gathered up the other breast with his hand. It was decidedly more than a handful.

Sandra was pressing herself against him now, from the waist down, and Ben sensed that she needed some stimulation there. One hand slipped down the front of her pants to feel the damp, curly hair, moving on down until it found a deep reservoir of slippery wetness. His fingers continued to travel on, like intrepid explorers of exotic regions, until he found the gaping chasm that was her quim and disappeared into the damp interior.

'Oh yes, finger me, fill me up!' she encouraged him.

Ben kissed her mouth, their tongues immediately meeting in a sensual caress. He thought of penetrating her elsewhere with his tongue, and the straining sensation in his groin intensified. Now he felt afraid that he couldn't hold out long enough to give her what she so obviously craved, a good shafting. Maybe he should get in there quick, make sure of it. With his free hand he struggled to undo his fly.

To Ben's relief, help was at hand. Deftly she unbuttoned and unzipped him, felt for his aching tool and brought it out from his overstretched underpants, making his erection all the more impressive as she pulled and fondled.

'There's a condom in my bag,' she whispered. 'Quick, do it to me now! I want you inside me now, while I'm good and ready for you.'

Her words excited him enormously. He withdrew his hand from her pussy and fumbled for the packet of rubbers. Frantically he kicked off his trousers and pants but didn't bother with his shirt, just loosened his tie. Unused to such hurried sex, he nevertheless found it extremely exciting.

Sandra lay brazenly open to him, her clothes in complete disarray and her body in utter voluptuous abandonment. Ben hadn't been this aroused for ages. He knelt between her naked thighs and looked down at the glistening pink folds of her sex and his prick sprang up fiercely. Taking the condom between his fingers, he rolled the end over the glans and began to ease it down his shaft but his penis was so ultra-sensitive that he felt a hot rush beginning in his groin. He tried to stop the premature flood, aiming to thrust his organ into her at once, but there was to be no stemming the tide. With a groan he felt the pent-up fountain gush out of him into the rubber teat, and although he did his best to push in through her engorged lips into her expectant cunny he knew he was racing against time.

Two thrusts and his erection began to weaken. At first Sandra seemed unaware that anything was wrong, but as he felt his penis sagging Ben knew that he couldn't possibly last long enough to give her satisfaction.

'I'm sorry,' he muttered, as his tool slipped ignominiously out of her. 'I seem to have come too soon.'

Her pretty face contorted into an ugly frown. 'Blast! And I was really ready for it! Can't you at least suck me off, or something?'

'I'll try.'

Although he felt shattered, Ben sat on the floor beside the sofa and did his level best to perform cunnilingus on her. She made a lot of noise, thrashing around and moaning. So much so that he didn't hear the footsteps wending their way down the uncarpeted stairs, or the creak of the wooden screen as it was pulled back. Only when a voice boomed out behind him did Ben realise that they were not alone.

'What the fuck's going on 'ere, then?'

Ben knew it was Wally. Hastily he scrambled to his feet, then realised that he was showing the man his bare arse. Not that it mattered. It was quite obvious what he was up to.

'Mr Derwent, may I speak to you in private?'

Wally's tone was stiffly disapproving. He turned to Sandra in disdain. 'Miss, I advise you to make yourself decent straight away. I shall ring for a taxi to take you home.'

Upstairs in Kate's office, Wally told Ben exactly what he thought about employees who brought Bellamy's into disrepute. He said he'd had his suspicions about Ben's suitability for the post from the start but had been prepared to give him the benefit of the doubt. He also cast aspersions on his having been 'off sick'. Ben said nothing, since there would have been no point. He was not surprised when Wally said he'd be recommending to Kate that she fire him straight away.

On his way home Ben reflected that he had now burned his boats. If he didn't get the job he'd been interviewed for that afternoon he would be unemployed again, and probably unemployable too. Yet he couldn't help smiling when he thought of how he'd seduced the lovely Sandra into playing Pussy Galore to his James Bond. If he'd only been able to give that sex-bomb the rogering that she deserved, it would almost have been worth losing his job for.

For a couple of days Ben stayed at home, unsure about his future. One thing was certain, he wouldn't be working at Bellamy's again. Kate rang to tell him, with more stuff about how he'd let the side down. It didn't make him feel good about himself. Already Ben was in danger of sliding back into apathy. He'd stopped going to the gym and spent most of his time on the Internet again, reading the nerdy fantasies of those who, like himself, had nothing better to do.

And his thoughts were all of Shelley, especially when he went to bed. The full impact of her absence from his life was hitting him, and he was filled with regret. He even rang her sister's number once, but when Evelyn answered he put the phone down, not being able to face the humiliation of having her make some excuse on Shelley's behalf. He reasoned that if his wife really wanted to get in touch with him she knew where he was, but she obviously didn't care. He tried to write a long letter, pouring out his feelings, but after throwing four efforts into the bin he gave up.

Then came the call from the Ex-Exec agency. Joanne sounded bright on the phone, and his heart lifted for the first time in days. 'Have I got the job?' he asked, eagerly.

'Yes. Congratulations!'

Ben tightened his fist around the receiver and thrust it high into the air in a gesture of victory. 'Yes!'

When he put it to his ear again Joanne was already explaining, '. . . but we would like you to call in later today, if that's possible. We'd like to go through the terms of the contract with you, to make sure you understand them.'

It was amazing how his mood could swing from despair to exultation in just a few seconds. Ben began to wonder if he was a manic-depressive type, until he remembered that he actually had good cause for his mood-swing. That phone call had literally changed his life, so of course he felt good. Maybe things would start to go right for him from now on. One thing he was sure of, he wasn't going to do anything stupid and waste this precious chance of a job.

The interview with Joanne was lively and upbeat, since she seemed almost as pleased as he was. He reckoned she'd really earned her ten per cent of his first year's salary. When they'd gone through all the technicalities and drafted a letter of acceptance, he walked out of her office feeling on top of the world.

Until he saw who was sitting in the waiting-room. Suddenly all his new-found confidence evaporated and the old, dull ache returned. Because there, looking ill at ease beside a middle-aged man who was browsing the *Financial Times*, was Shelley.

Chapter Fifteen

Shelley looked up and gasped with shocked recognition. It was definitely Ben, but he looked so amazing in that suit, so incredibly ... well, dishy! His brown eyes were sad as he smiled at her. The icy lump of despair and resentment that she'd been carrying around inside her began to melt slightly. She managed a wan smile in return.

'Hullo, Ben.'

'Shelley! What are you doing here?'

'Same as you, I imagine.'

'Not looking for a job?'

'That's why people generally come to these places, isn't it?' Her tone was sharper than she'd intended. But curiosity overcame her pride, prompting her to ask if he'd had any luck himself.

'Yes, as a matter of fact,' he replied. 'I've just landed a new job. But I don't understand why you're here. Aren't you still with that company making quiz shows?'

'No.' She hesitated, not wanting to discuss it with that stranger's ears flapping next to her.

Then the door to the inner room opened and a woman appeared. 'Miss Morris?' she called.

Shelley could see how put out Ben was that she'd gone back to using her maiden name. She gave a wry grin. 'Look, we can't talk now. Can you hang on here till I've had my interview? Maybe we could have dinner together.'

'I'd like that.'

He sounded as if he really would, too. Shelley couldn't believe how good it felt, seeing him again, reminding her of how much she had missed him. But there was something subtly different about her husband, a new attitude and style that impressed her. Reluctantly she followed the agency boss into her office, hoping Ben wouldn't change his mind and leave her in the lurch.

It was hard to concentrate as Joanne keyed her details into the computer. Shelley's memory kept regenerating an image of the new Ben, so suavely handsome in that dark suit with the mildly flamboyant tie. His face had been transformed by an expression of self-confidence and even his body seemed surer of itself, filling the small room with his presence.

Shelley was intrigued, but she was aware that there were other, darker emotions lurking beneath the surface. Envy and resentment figured largely, much to her disgust. She recognised the unpleasant fact that having him out of work and downtrodden had suited her. It made her feel superior. Now the shoe was on the other foot and those ugly emotions had surfaced, making her feel ashamed.

Joanne seemed confident that she could find Shelley more work in the television industry, on a temporary basis, at least. It seemed she would probably have to resign herself to being on short contracts from now on. When she came out after the interview she was relieved to see that Ben was still there, smiling at her. He stood up and she caught a whiff of pungently sharp spice – his Polo aftershave. He used to wear that when she first knew him, and a wave of nostalgia overtook her.

'We could go to La Grotta if you like,' he smiled.

Shelley almost said no. It was where they used to dine in the early, besotted days of their relationship and she didn't know if she could stand the poignant reminders. What was he trying to do to her? She threw him a quizzical look. 'Is that a good idea?' she said at last.

He shrugged, still smiling. 'We know the food's good, and it's a nice place for a quiet chat.'

'That's not what I meant,' she sighed. 'Oh, okay. I suppose it'll do no harm to remind ourselves of the good old days.'

'Since we have to pass the house on the way, why don't we leave one of our cars there? No point in taking both.'

Of course it made sense. Shelley agreed, but she still felt uneasy. That meant she would go back to the house after the meal, and she wasn't sure she would want to. Still, she didn't have to go indoors. Why am I so afraid to go back, she wondered. For weeks she'd been trying not to face it, living with the few things she'd taken with her, but she knew that one day she would have to return and sort everything out. One day, but not yet.

As they left the building, Ben took hold of her elbow, a casual gesture that she would have thought nothing of in the old days but which now filled her with an electric charge. They travelled to the restaurant in Ben's car. As their thighs brushed, Shelley was aware of the solidity of his flesh, the muscle he'd built up in the gym. Her heart flipped a little.

Being in the passenger seat reminded her of the early days of their marriage, before she'd bought a car of her own, when she used to travel to work by Tube. After Ben lost his job she'd wanted him to get rid of his beloved Golf for economic reasons, but he'd flatly refused and she'd realised that to insist would have been to emasculate him psychologically. But now she was the one who felt disempowered, the one without a job, the failure, and having Ben in the driving seat just rubbed it in.

The restaurant was just as Shelley remembered it: a little piece of Italy in a London suburb. They'd gone to Sorrento for their honeymoon, so the place had come to have a special attraction for them. Strangely, she didn't feel sad as she walked through the door, only glad that they'd once shared such happiness. She stared across the table at him, over her menu. 'I can't believe the change in you, Ben. You look fantastic. Tell me about the new job.'

Shelley was impressed with the ethos of the company. It sounded really good. Why the hell hadn't a job like that come up for him sooner? Sadly she reflected that they might still be together if only he hadn't drifted into the long-term unemployed category. Was she about to go the same dismal route?

Almost reading her mind Ben asked, 'What happened at Harcourt? I thought you were really settled there.'

Shelley had an urge to tell him the absolute truth. 'I screwed up. Literally.'

'What, Duncan?' She nodded. His face broke into a grin. 'Daft cow!'

'I should have known better.'

'I just lost a job for the same reason. Let my prick turn me into a dick-head. Good thing this other opportunity came off, or I'd be kicking myself by now.'

They both laughed. Shelley found it incredible that they could both take things so lightly. She knocked back her martini and laughed again, louder. It was good to be with her husband, despite everything. There was no one else who could share her dreams and disappointments, who would accept her just as she was, warts and all.

'Are you ready to order, Sir?'

The sober tones of the waiter brought them back to studying the menu. Shelley had her favourite dishes, aubergine with tomatoes followed by grilled swordfish. Ben asked her about her second job, and she gave a sardonic laugh.

'I suppose you could say sex screwed me up there, too. I took this toy boy home with me then I overslept and was late for work.'

'Shelley!' Ben gave her a look of mock disapproval. She could tell he was enjoying her confessions. If this was to be their last meal together at least they could make it one to remember. 'You're not safe to be let loose in public, are you?' he teased her. 'Except perhaps on a long leash.'

'Really?' She looked straight into his brown, laughing eyes and a flash of real desire went through her such as she hadn't experienced in ages. 'That's how you'd like me, is it, on a leash?'

He eyed her thoughtfully. 'It's a nice idea.'

'Got any other ideas like that?'

'I might have.'

The wine she was knocking back with her starter was making her reckless, but what the heck? She had nothing more to lose. Suddenly Ben was like a seductive stranger to her, someone she could play dangerous games with. She'd never seen him in this light before but it was extremely interesting.

Ben made a polite enquiry about Evelyn, and Shelley gave a censored account of their Greek holiday, but it was clear that they were only making small-talk to pass the time during the meal. He had taken off his shoe and soon his foot was in her lap under the table, his toes wiggling in her crotch, making her aware that there was some other unfinished business that needed seeing to, something far more important and fundamental, that couldn't possibly be carried out in a public place. She caught his eye and it was filled with some dark inscrutable appetite that made her half afraid.

They drove back to the house with Shelley's head resting on her husband's shoulder, the way they used to come home after a night out together. She felt as if a great weight were being lifted from her. The alcohol she'd consumed was making her feel giddy and randy, but that wasn't the only cause. Somehow she was intoxicated with Ben, with his new-found confidence and irresistible sex appeal. She was reminded of the man she'd fallen in love with, the man she thought she'd lost forever, and it was hitting her right in the groin. By now she knew him well enough to know that he wanted her as urgently as she wanted him.

They got out into the balmy night air, and Ben put his arm around her waist as they walked to the door. The contact was comfortingly familiar, as well as arousing. 'Do you remember when we first came to view this house?' Shelley asked him. 'And what we did the day we moved in?'

'How could I forget?' He grinned down at her, his teeth bright in the moonlight.

'I feel as if I'm entering the house for the first time.'

'Really?' He unlocked the door and then, before she could begin to protest, swept her up into his arms. He was strong now, his muscles scarcely aware of her weight, and when he walked it was with smooth, self-assured strides. 'Over the threshold with you, then!'

'Daft bugger!'

He set her down in the dark hall. The house was quiet, expectant. Shelley knew that she could still turn back, seek out the safety of her own car and disappear into the night. But she didn't want to. The place seemed full of tantalising mystery – or was it just that Ben had become exciting to her? On the surface the idea was ludicrous, since they'd lived together for five years. Yet this was no longer boring old Ben, poor downtrodden Ben, the Ben who had been unfaithful to her more by default than intent. She'd been glad of the excuse to leave him but, by some perverse trick of fate, he had ended up being more desirable to her than ever.

They went through to the front room without switching on any lights and the atmosphere was ghostly, magical, with only the silvery moon peering through the front window. Ben still didn't put on the light. He pulled Shelley into his arms and began to kiss her with an eager mouth, overcoming her slight resistance with the sheer force of his desire, making her want him to overpower her and take her by force, right there on the carpet.

Ben drew back from her for a few seconds, reading her face. His eyes were hard and glittery in the semi-darkness, making him appear formidable. He put his hands on her shoulders and forced her down to her knees before him. She could only look up at him in abject silence, not knowing quite what he wanted from her.

'Do it!' he commanded her in a hoarse whisper, his hand moving to undo his fly.

Shelley stared in wonder as the pale phallus appeared in all its erect glory, challenging her to take it in her mouth. Slowly she bent her head to taste the delicate flavour of the glans, only slightly musky as yet and still faintly scented with the shower gel he'd used earlier in the day. She licked all around the ridge of skin and into the small slit at the top, making the penis quiver with delicious anticipation. Then she was aware of a corresponding shiver within herself, a similar moistening in her secret crevices and a sharp quickening of her desire. Right now her sensual appreciation was confined to her mouth, but other parts of her were subtly awakening to the possibilities of titillation and ultimate fulfilment. It was like taking the first mouthful of a gourmet meal in which there would be several courses, each more delectable than the last.

'Take all of me into your mouth,' she heard Ben command her, and she willingly obeyed. The thick length of him filled her, almost choked her, but she managed to accommodate almost all. Even when he began his gentle thrusts Shelley kept from gagging and was soon employing her tongue to good effect, licking all round his shaft while he moved slowly in and out, reaching up to fondle his loose balls while her mouth filled with the taste of his musk.

'That's enough. Now take off your tights.' Shelley looked up at him, questioningly. His handsome face was shadowed, distant. 'Take them off!' he repeated, harshly, already lowering his trousers.

His taking command of her was new and surprising. She was in unfamiliar, even scary, territory but instead of making her feel affronted she was fascinated, and couldn't deny that she was aroused by the novelty of the situation. Her breasts were straining inside her bra, nipples itching to be touched, and the familiar tingling inside her pants was resulting in an uncomfortably wet gusset. Briefly she thought of Duncan, and how she'd wondered what he had felt when they'd played the same game in reverse. Perhaps she was about to find out.

As soon as Shelley had stripped off her tights, Ben pushed the sofa right back against the wall. He made her kneel on the cushions, facing the wall with her hands behind her back, and quickly secured her wrists with the tights. Shelley rested her head on the top of the upholstery, her breasts and stomach pushed against the back of the sofa. She felt Ben lift up her skirt, then her slip, and tuck them over her arms out of the way. He stroked her buttocks through the silky knickers, making her thighs tremble. It was becoming an ordeal to remain upright.

There was something wickedly erotic about having only her bottom exposed, while the rest of her was clothed. Slowly Ben pulled down her knickers and caressed the smooth globes of her behind. Then, with sudden force, he gave each buttock a hard slap. She felt them sting, wobble, grow hot and tingling. He pushed them apart and Shelley felt a slick finger explore her crack, delving in a little way and waggling round, making her whole lower area feel wet and open, back and front.

Ben removed her panties and knelt just behind her, his weight sinking into the cushions. Then he pushed her thighs apart. His penis nosed between her labia from behind and, once the glans had located her open entrance, he pushed straight in, without preliminaries. She was tight and snug in there, only half-ready for him, but as he began to thrust she became more lubricated. Soon he was slipping and sliding in and out of her with ease, ramming her hard against the sofa back as he raced blindly towards his climax.

Unable to cling onto anything with her hands, Shelley was buffeted against the padded upholstery, abandoning herself to the relentless force of his desire. Suddenly Ben seized her roughly and pulled her back against him, his hands clamping onto her breasts over her blouse. His mouth sought the smooth skin at the back of her neck and he bit gently into its peachy softness, making her squirm with a tickling sensation. She pushed her buttocks against his heaving groin, working herself up while he fiddled frustratingly with her nipples through two layers of clothing. She heard him grunting in time with the rhythm of his fucking and knew that he was near his end. Her clitoris ached to be stimulated more directly but she was at his mercy, unable to do anything herself.

'I shall turn the tables on him,' Shellcy promised herself, a surge of excitement flowing through her veins. She knew, now, that she could subject a man to her will, that this charade she was going through with Ben could easily flip into her taking charge of the proceedings. She was content to bide her time, to enjoy the feeling of being subjugated, because she knew that when his will was sated she would have the upper hand.

With a final series of rapid shoves that banged her feverish mons hard against the back of the sofa, Ben reached his goal. Shelley could feel his prick shuddering deep inside her, pulsing out the liquid accompaniment to his orgasm. When he let her go she collapsed, with her head right down on the seat. He quickly released her bonds so that she could stretch out and relax fully. She lay beside him on the sofa in utter exhaustion, her vulva and vagina still hotly vibrating, and closed her eyes. She was amazed to find that she was feeling triumphant, not cowed. Her husband had thought he'd subjected her to his desire but he didn't know what kind of woman she'd become, a sexual chameleon, able to play many different rôles.

Lying there inert, Shelley wondered what Ben would do next. It occurred to her that he had been too predictable for too long. She had come to despise his compliance. As long as she'd been earning the money she'd been calling the tune, making him do what she wanted, reducing him to the status of a dependant. This new assertion of his rights made a welcome change. More to the point, it was now possible for them to relate as sexual partners again, each equally capable of taking authority over the other. If he had changed, really changed, perhaps there was a chance that they might make a go of their marriage after all.

Suddenly Shelley had an urge to pee. She straddled Ben's bum, leaving a sticky mark, then got up off the sofa. He said nothing as she padded from the room and went upstairs. In the bathroom she took the rest of her clothes off and stared at herself in the mirror. Her face was flushed, her nipples hard and ripe with arousal at the tips of her firm breasts. She turned round and caressed her buttocks, still faintly pink from the friction. Her vulva was throbbing with unsatisfied lust and the thought of submitting herself again to Ben's selfish use of her as a sex object was unappealing. She needed to come, with an urgency that could not be denied. Although the temptation was strong to finish the job herself – which wouldn't take her fingers long to accomplish – Shelley resisted the urge and went downstairs.

Ben was still stretched out on the sofa but on his back this time and, to her utter amazement, he was wearing her panties! She approached slowly, savouring the sight of his tackle encased in an inadequate triangle of black silk and lace. The pink tip of his penis was rearing cheekily over the top and his balls were bulging out of the legs. His eyes were closed and there was a serenely innocent expression on his face.

'Take them off!' she told him.

His eyes flicked open, staring up at her impassively, and he made no move. 'You look ridiculous. Take them off!' she repeated.

His expression grew defiant, challenging. Shelley was aware that he'd consented to them entering a new phase of the game. A warm thrill went through her as she surveyed the infinite possibilities. She lifted her foot and placed her toes over the provocative bundle at the base of his stomach, squidging the soft flesh. His erection grew instantly, more of his penis peeking over the lacy trim. She rolled her foot over his shaft, enjoying the feel of silky material and rapidly hardening flesh against her sole.

Carefully Shelley inserted a toe under the lacy waistband and rolled it down over his genitalia. His penis sprang up from its confines as she hooked the pants up and over, then on down his thighs. She left them there halfway down, pinning his legs and squashing his balls together. He did look ridiculous! She straddled him and sat on his chest, placing a pillow behind his head to get him at the right angle and thrusting her pubic mound in his face. 'Lick me!' she commanded.

He obliged at once. The fresh sensations began to flow through her like balm, easing the pain of longing. She lifted his hands to her breasts and he stroked her hungry nipples, intensifying her excitement. To aid her progress towards ultimate gratification, Shelley clenched and relaxed her buttocks rhythmically, feeling his coarse chest hairs tickle her sensitive parts. It was good to feel this in control again, to know that he would do as she asked. Knowing that they could switch rôles at whim was even better.

To test his compliance, Shelley suddenly pulled off him when she was edging near the point of no return and told him to get up. Ben did so unquestioningly. She lay down in his place with her legs spread apart. 'Now screw me!' she ordered.

Once again he was spearing into her but this time it was what she had demanded of him. It was the same driving action, but Shelley marvelled at how very different it felt. Instead of being the passive recipient of his lustful desires, she was making him satisfy hers, turning him into a power tool for her own pleasure. For the first time she realised how large a part the mind played in making subtle distinctions between pleasure and pain, give and take, dominance and submission. Yet even those lines of demarcation were blurred between them. At any moment he might take command again, and she would have to choose whether or not to surrender. The unpredictability was what made it so exciting.

Ben was gasping now, nearing his second climax, but Shelley didn't want their mutual bliss to end. She put her hands on his shoulders to stop his thrusting. Then she made him get out of her and go back to licking her pussy. His tongue on her overheated labia was blissfully cool and sensual. She gave a sigh and relaxed into the luxuriously indulgent feelings that were spreading through her entire body, filling her veins with sweetness. It didn't take long before she was being swept into a gentle orgasm that filled her with unexpectedly tender emotions. She caressed Ben's thick hair as the delicious throes held her, suspended in bliss, before she began her slow descent into languor again.

They cuddled up together after that, and Ben's erection subsided of its own accord. For a long while they just lay in each other's arms saying nothing. But that didn't mean that nothing was being communicated. Shelley had the extra-ordinary feeling that she knew exactly what was going through her husband's mind because his thoughts mirrored her own. She was thinking that they had just discovered each other for the first time, that everything before had been a charade, a pretence, and now that they had laid their souls bare for each other there could be no going back.

Soon they both fell into a doze, the kind of comforting snooze they used to share in the early days after making love for hours on end. Suddenly Ben woke with a violent start, rousing Shelley in the process.

'Oh God!' he moaned, his face distraught. 'I was dreaming that I'd blown everything, Shelley. My job, my health, my marriage...'

'Don't worry, love,' she smiled, kissing him tenderly. 'Everything's under control.'

A Message from the Publisher

Headline Liaison is a new concept in erotic fiction: a list of books designed for the reading pleasure of both men and women, to be read alone – or together with your lover. As such, we would be most interested to hear from our readers.

Did you read the book with your partner? Did it fire your imagination? Did it turn you on – or off? Did you like the story, the characters, the setting? What did you think of the cover presentation? In short, what's your opinion? If you care to offer it, please write to:

> The Editor
> Headline Liaison
> 338 Euston Road
> London NW1 3BH

Or maybe you think you could do better if you wrote an erotic novel yourself. We are always on the look-out for new authors. If you'd like to try your hand at writing a book for possible inclusion in the Liaison list, here are our basic guidelines: We are looking for novels of approximately 80,000 words in which the erotic content should aim to please both men and women and should not describe illegal sexual activity (pedophilia, for example). The novel should contain sympathetic and interesting characters, pace, atmosphere and an intriguing plotline.

If you'd like to have a go, please submit to the Editor a sample of at least 10,000 words, clearly typed on one side of the paper only, together with a short resumé of the storyline. Should you wish your material returned to you please include a stamped addressed envelope. If we like it sufficiently, we will offer you a contract for publication.

Adult Fiction for Lovers from Headline LIAISON